Erik's Clan

Erik's Clan

Book 6 in the New World Series

By

Griff Hosker

Erik's Clan

Published by Sword Books Ltd 2022

SWORD
BOOKS

Copyright ©Griff Hosker First Edition 2022

The author has asserted their moral right under the Copyright, Designs and Patents Act, 1988, to be identified as the author of this work.
All Rights reserved. No part of this publication may be reproduced, copied, stored in a retrieval system, or transmitted, in any form or by any means, without the prior written consent of the copyright holder, nor be otherwise circulated in any form of binding or cover other than that in which it is published and without a similar condition being imposed on the subsequent purchaser.

A CIP catalogue record for this title is available from the British Library.
Cover by Design for Writers

Contents

Erik's Clan i
Prologue 2
Chapter 1 3
Chapter 2 11
Chapter 3 20
Chapter 4 31
Chapter 5 39
Chapter 6 49
Chapter 7 57
Chapter 8 67
Chapter 9 73
Chapter 10 85
Chapter 11 95
Chapter 12 102
Chapter 13 112
Chapter 14 128
Chapter 15 135
Chapter 16 144
Chapter 17 152
Chapter 18 161
Chapter 19 170
Epilogue 179
Glossary 182
Historical references 183
Other books by Griff Hosker 185

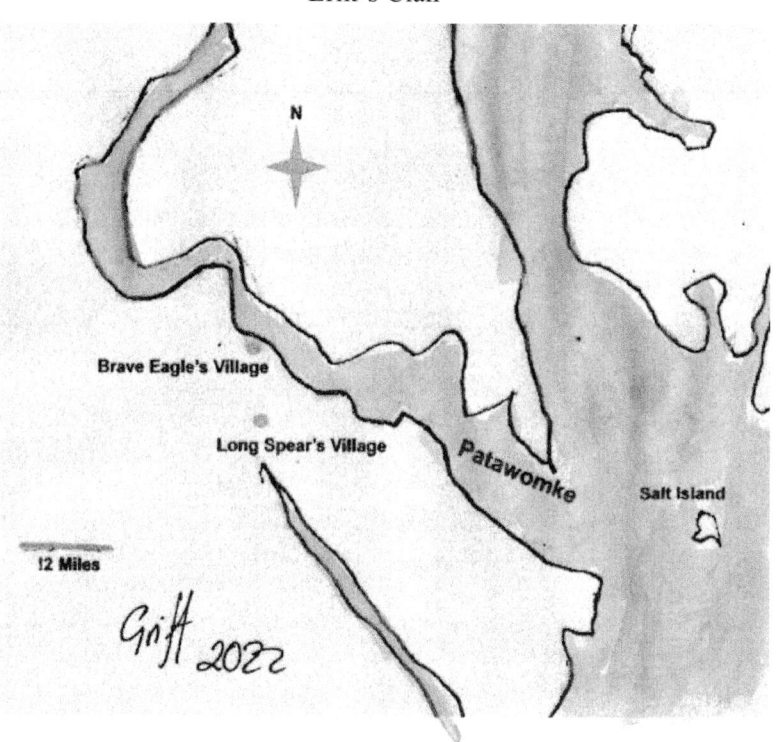

Erik's Clan

Prologue

I am Erik, called the Navigator by my first family, but I am not the boy who grew up on the islands of Orkneyjar, close to the land of Hibernia. I am not even close to the young man who led his clan across waters never before sailed to reach the land of Ice and Fire. I have changed and I have become part Viking and part something else; a traveller of the New World. When my clan left this new world, I found myself alone, save for the young woman from the Mi'kmaq tribe, who would become my wife. When I look in the waters of the beck where we moor our snekke, **'*Gytha*'**, and I look into it to see my reflection I see a face that looks nothing like the other members of the tribe. I have a beard and my hair is not dark. My skin, though burned by the sun, is still paler than the Powhatans amongst whom I live. My children are also paler. Flecks of grey in my hair and beard now show the passage of time. The tribe no longer stare at me for I have lived amongst them for some time but when visitors come and come they do, then I find them staring at me. They wish to touch me to see if I am real. Many, especially warriors, wish to touch my iron weapons, the helmet, sword, seax and hatchet. To people who make weapons from bone and stone, they are magical objects and add to the aura of Erik, Shaman of the Bear. I have my wife, my children and my friends and I am happy but I know that these visits by strangers who have sometimes travelled hundreds of miles do not bode well for it means my name and my weapons are now known to many. When I left the summer camp of Wandering Moos it had been to save that tribe from the Penobscot who had a grudge against me. I thought I had disappeared but as the raid on my new home showed it was an illusion. The new home was a happy place but it was not safe and in my heart, I knew that one day I would have to leave to find a haven where I could raise my family in peace. My life was ruled by the Norns. The three sisters wove their spells and toyed with my life. I now knew that no matter what I did danger would come. I had to accept it. I had accepted the challenge but it angered me for it meant I was endangering my wife and my children not to mention the tribe who had taken us in. My life was not my own and I could do nothing about it.

Erik's Clan

Chapter 1

The Patawomke River

The children borne to us grew well and only Golden Bear could still be considered a child. He was too small to hunt and to go to sea in the snekke. While the elder boys joined me to fish, Little White Dove was learning to be a woman and helping Laughing Deer to make the food, plant the crops and make clothes. My other two sons, Moos Blood and Brave Cub, had become accomplished sailors. They could sail the snekke almost as well as me. Indeed, in the waters of the Powhatan land in which we lived, they were my equal. On the seas, to the east, it would be a different matter but I knew I would never sail to see my brother Fótr and the rest of the clan. They were still in my heart, my head and my dreams but I would never see them in the flesh. The Norns had seen to that. Here I was the Shaman of the Bear and the snekke, *'Gytha'* was considered a magical beast that could fly across the water without the need for paddles. Many men were envious of her and what they saw as my power.

There was a pattern to our life in Brave Eagle's village. The clan with whom we lived, Brave Eagle's clan, suffered as we had done at the hands of the Penobscot. Our vengeance raid to rescue the captives from the Penobscot, up the Muhheakantuck River, had ended that threat but his clan was one of the smaller clans in the Powhatan tribe. They hunted the lands and they raised crops but it was my sons and me who sailed to harvest the rivers and when the weather was benign, the sea. We brought in far more than we would ever need and so the clan prospered for there was always food. We were skilled at what we did. We used nets and spears to hunt for fish. The spears were for the larger fish, the hunters of the sea. I was not a fool and I hunted nothing that was close to the length of the snekke. When we brought back such bounty we were hailed as heroes. The birch bark boats of the clan could sail the seas but the risks were too high for them to do so and to fish. Most of the time our fishing expeditions were restricted to the Rappahannock River and the Patawomke. Even Long Spear's clan, the largest in the tribe, sometimes went hungry in harsh winters but not Brave Eagle's.

By reckoning, counting back the summers since they had been born, Moos Blood had seen more than fifteen and Brave Cub eleven or twelve. They were now warriors and Moos Blood would be like his father and have a beard. Their hair was a mixture of their mother's and mine while their skin showed that they were Norse. Like me, their little sister, Little White Dove and their younger brother, Golden Bear, it marked us as different but they were accepted in the clan and that was because of my reputation and what I had done. I now had the luxury of watching my two sons as they steered and took in the sail or let it out. They were both competent helmsmen. I was almost a man of leisure. The time had gone when I watched them nervously, for a mistake. The three of us were also dressed in the same way. Our paler skin meant that we wore tunics made of hide as well as hide leggings. Sadly my sealskin boots were long gone and I now wore, as did my sons, mockasins, but they were not as useful as seal skin boots. I had made other changes too from the Viking warrior who had led his people west. I had finally melted down the mail byrnie. It had become old and I had doubted that it would stand up to a fight. I melted it down and used the metal to make arrowheads. They were a prized possession of my sons. When I gave gifts to my brother warriors it was a couple of arrowheads. They were considered more valuable than a golden horde to the warriors. When they were used for hunting they struck deeper than the stone or flint ones. We always recovered them. I had left my helmet in case I needed it for war. I kept it in a bag of sand to stop it from rusting. That and my bearskin, won when I had slain the bear on Bear Island, I had kept. They had helped us to rescue the captives taken by the Clan of the Hawk. The skin was showing its age but it marked me as what my new clan called the Bear Shaman.

That day, as we sculled around the river, had been a good one. We knew where the fish would bite and we had a net to catch them. With the wind behind us we had sailed well upstream, and we were almost ready to turn around for the well of the snekke was full of fish when the Norns spun. We were some miles from our home but the voyage back would be easier for we would have the current with us. I was amazed at the size of this river for in places it appeared as wide as a sea. Now, as the tide turned, we would be able to use the power of the river to head south and our home. The rest of Brave Eagle's clan marvelled that we could do so. They could have paddled as far upstream as us and they could have fished but they would have been exhausted had they done so. For the three of us, it was almost leisurely. The hardest effort was in getting the catch aboard. Had we been on a birch bark boat we might have overturned it.

"That is enough bounty, Moos Blood, turn us around and head back. Brave Cub, reef the sail."

Although we all spoke the language of the Powahatans my children and I, along with my wife, also spoke my language, the language of my birth. It was not pride that made us do so but practicality. There were words we used, for the snekke and suchlike, which did not exist in Powhatan. On the snekke, we spoke Norse.

As we sailed south, we did so whilst watching the riverbanks. We were no longer in the land controlled by Long Spear and sometimes bands of young warriors would use the river to make war on other tribes. War was a way of life and young warriors would often travel for a hundred or more miles to make war on another tribe and kill their first enemy. I suppose it was no different to the raids by the Norse except in the case of the Norse there was normally treasure associated with a blooding raid. It had not happened for some time but that did not make us complacent. As Moos Blood steered the snekke, Brave Cub watched the bank to larboard and I watched the one to steerboard. We had seen no boats on our way north and so we expected to see none on our return but we looked for warriors who came to the riverbank. My eyes were still sharp and I was the one who saw the arm draped around the log close to the bank of the river. I strung my bow and said, "Brave Cub, arm yourself. Moos Blood, take us into the shore but do so carefully." I pointed, "I see an arm around a log. It may be a trick to lure us inshore or it may be that the Norns have been spinning."

We always brought our bows and arrows with us. I left the metal headed arrow in the case and nocked a stone-tipped one. The metal arrows were too valuable to risk losing in the water. Brave Cub did not come next to me but shuffled to the prow. The snekke was a well-balanced boat and we had a heavy catch but it did not do to risk unbalancing her. I had my back to the mast and I peered at the arm. I could not tell if there was a body attached but I had to assume that there was. I risked standing as Moos Blood skilfully aimed us at the bank. It effectively slowed us down and afforded me the opportunity to look for danger. The log appeared to have jammed against an underwater obstruction and I saw rocks beneath the overhanging trees. I spied no human danger but the rocks could rip the bottom from the snekke.

"Edge closer. Brave Cub, you keep watch and I will try to see if the arm is alive or dead." Laying down my bow I squatted as Moos Blood took us closer to the log. The hand was wrapped tightly around the log and I knew that if it was a corpse, I might have to leave it there. Prising a dead arm from a log would not be easy. As I neared it, I saw that the arm was attached to a body and I saw the head of a young man. As we reached the log and bumped next to it, I grabbed the arm and felt warmth. He was alive.

"Brave Cub, come and help." The longer we rubbed next to the log the more damage we would inflict upon the boat.

Erik's Clan

As I pulled on the arm the log rolled, turning and bringing the boy toward us. That made it easier for us to pull the boy aboard but he must have been injured for he moaned as we hauled him to land on the catch. I waved my arm for Moos Blood to continue south and I took my seal skin cape to lay over him. I did not recognise him. He was not of our tribe. I examined his body as I covered him and found a wound in his side. It had been made by a stone-tipped weapon. I had come to recognise the wounds. I used a cloth to clean it and then wrapped another piece around it. The wound was not bleeding and I took that to be a good sign. I took the skin with the ale in it and put it to his mouth. I forced some liquid into him and he did not bring it back up although he remained unconscious.

"There is a tale here, father."

I nodded, "Aye, Brave Cub and the Norns have been spinning. He has come downstream and I see no tribal markings that I recognise but he looks to be Powhatan." I had learned to look for the clues that indicated a man's tribe. Back in the world of the Vikings, the world I had left, we would look for the signs on the shields but here we looked for the way they dressed and the things they wore. As we sailed south, now with more urgency, I looked at the boy who looked to be of a similar age to Moos Blood. How had he been wounded and by whom? There were more questions than answers. Brave Eagle would know better than I. I was still, after all these years in this new world, learning. Brave Eagle's wife, Running Antelope, was a healer. She would care for the boy. I could not help the feeling of disquiet as we headed up the beck that led to our mooring. The Norns had sent the boy to us and that never boded well.

While Moos Blood and I tied up the snekke, Brave Cub ran for help. By the time my younger son returned we had lifted the boy from the snekke. Brave Eagle and his son, White Fox, along with two other warriors were there. Brave Eagle nodded, "We will take him to my wife." He smiled, "Once again one who has never heard of you will be grateful that you came to this land. You seem to harvest people from the sea as much as you do fish!"

We had woven baskets ready to take the fish and after filling them we slipped them on our backs. We had a good catch and they were heavy. We trudged along the path back to our camp. The number of yehakin had grown over the years. Some of those we had rescued from the Clan of the Hawk had grown into adults and married. We were becoming a sizeable clan. While many of the clan raced to see the boy carried by Brave Eagle and his son, others ran to us. The bounty from the river was for the clan. Some would be cooked immediately while

Erik's Clan

some would be salted and preserved and others smoked. We did not fish every day but we did it enough times to ensure a bounty of food. Laughing Deer and Little White Dove came from our yehakin. My wife held Golden Bear by the hand. The rest of the women who came to claim the fish would allow my family to choose what they wanted first.

They did not take too many and as we headed back to our yehakin and our fire my wife asked, "You found a boy?"

I nodded, "It was luck more than anything. I spied an arm on a log. He was wounded."

She looked up and I saw the understanding tinged with fear in her eyes. She was a clever woman. A wound meant it was no accident and any such wounding had implications for us. We lived in a world where raids and the taking of slaves were both commonplace. I saw her eyes go to Little White Dove. When we had rescued the captives from the Clan of the Hawk my wife had heard of the abuse they had endured at the hands of the Penobscot. She too had been a prisoner of the Penobscot and her mother had been killed by them. My wife had a knife in her belt that ensured she would not go quietly into captivity a second time.

While the boy was not of our clan he was not an enemy and Running Antelope attended to him.

The boys were full of the rescue as was Little White Dove. It was a bone of contention with my daughter that I had not taken her as a member of my crew. Both she and Golden Bear badgered me constantly to teach them how to sail. I had plans to do so but I had been putting it off.

"Father."

"Yes, Moos Blood."

"How was it that you saw the arm draped over the log and I did not? I thought I was being a good helmsman and watching for danger ahead and to the side."

"You were being attentive but you saw what you expected to see. You saw the log." He nodded. "This land is all new to me, Moos Blood. The rivers I sailed when I was your age were tiny becks and streams. I always observe closely to see what I have not seen before."

"Ah." He seemed relieved that he was not at fault.

What I did not mention was that I was convinced that the Norns had directed my gaze. I had found Brave Eagle on the seas close to Bear Island and since then I was doubly vigilant.

It was evening before Brave Eagle came over to speak to us.

"The clan thanks you, Erik." Brave Eagle had learned to address me as Erik and it made us close. The clan gave me the title Erik, Shaman of the Bear. He was a link to my time with the Mi'kmaq and had endured the long and dangerous voyage to this, his home. "The fish you brought will fill many bellies. There will be no hunger so long as you fish."

I nodded, "You have given us a home and we will repay that gift so long as the Allfather permits it." I might have mentioned the Norns but it did not do to invoke their name however kindly meant.

Laughing Deer ventured, "And the boy?"

Like the rest of the clan, we were all curious about him. Few survived on the river without a boat and a wound from a spear caused much speculation. I gestured for Brave Eagle to sit. When we had cleared some trees from the entrance to the beck I used, we had felled an enormous tree. I had used some of the logs to fashion round seats.

He sat and spoke, "His name is Fears Water." My eyes widened and he nodded, "Aye, it is strange is it not that one who fears water should have been plucked to safety from it? He and his tribe live in the foothills close to where the river he calls the Shenandoah joins the Patawomke and their village was on the bluffs above the Patawomke. From his language, they are Powhatan for we can understand each other. His clan was a small one and some days ago they were attacked by a tribe from the north and west of them." For the first time, he frowned, "The boy said they were Moneton." He shrugged, "I have never heard of them and the boy says that they are fierce warriors. They came quickly into their village when they were asleep and slaughtered the men who were in Fears Water's family. When he was speared his mother told him to run and he did. He did not mean to go into the river for, as his name suggests, he feared it but he tripped when the warriors were almost on him. The tree root saved his life for he fell over the bluff and landed in the water. When he awoke it was daylight and his arm was wrapped around a log. I think it must be the one you saw. He was terrified to let go." Brave Eagle smiled, "Having been saved in such a way myself I can understand that. He thought he had died for he dreamed his death dream and then awoke here in our village."

Laughing Deer had been listening and she stood to fetch some ale, "Then he has no one."

"So it would seem."

I had often thought of exploring the enormous river that brought us our bounty. I had wondered if Brave Eagle wished me to return the boy to his home. Now it seemed unlikely that there would be an opportunity. I was disappointed.

"I do not think we are in any danger from this tribe but I will send scouts to the borders of our hunting grounds to look for signs that there are others who seek slaves."

Erik's Clan

When Brave Eagle had been speaking, I had been filling in the gaps in his words. Men were killed but women and children were enslaved. They would become workers for the tribe that captured them. Some, especially young boys brought up by the aggressor, might become part of that tribe and increase the force of warriors that would be available to fight. The captured women and girls would be used to breed more warriors. I knew from speaking with the elders of Brave Eagle's tribe, when we visited the chief of the tribe at special events, that while the Powhatan were now peaceful it had not always been so and they had gained this land through force of arms.

Brave Eagle stood, "I thought I would come and thank you for your catch was a mighty one."

I stood, "And I have given thought to how we can increase that bounty." I saw Moos Blood and Brave Cub prick up their ears. They had been party to my plans for we had spoken of them on the river. "Moos Blood is now a good sailor and we can double the size of our catch if we build another snekke."

Brave Eagle smiled, "And we would have two powerful boats should danger come." When we had rescued the captives from the Penobscot the crossing of the river had almost cost us people as the birch-bark boats of the Lenni Lenape could not carry as many passengers as our snekke. We had spoken of it on the way back. "You can build another boat?"

"It takes time and when it is built, we shall need a young warrior for me to train to help me to sail it." I pointed to the sea, many miles to the south and east, "I am still the only one who can sail to the sea to fetch the huge fish and I cannot do it alone." When we had the new snekke I might fulfil Little White Dove's dreams and take her and her little brother to the Patawomke River so that they could sail my snekke but I would not risk either of them on the ocean. The voyage south from Bear Island had shown me the dangers to my family. That we had survived had much to do with luck and I would not try to live on luck. I would be more cautious from now on.

"There are many who would learn from you, Erik. They see your skill as magical. I know from speaking with you that it is not magic but, even so, I know that you are unique. How else could you sail from another world and live in ours? If you need any to help you to build it then ask."

"We will begin on the morrow. I know the tree I wish to use. First, we will need to clear another part of the riverbank to make the slipway where we can work."

Erik's Clan

That night, as I lay in bed with Laughing Deer nestled in my arms, my restless mind would not let me simply drift off into oblivion. Since the rescue, I had sought some other task to occupy me. The spirits still visited me and told me that I still had a quest. I had brought my clan further west than any other Viking and since they had returned home, I had come further south. I was meant to keep sailing. I had thought to head south, towards the warmth, but since we had arrived here in the land of the Powhatan the mountains to the west had intrigued me. There was also a line of blue hills not far away; they marked the boundary of Powhatan land. The tales of rivers that headed far inland were a lure. I was a fisherman and knew the danger of lures. Many of the fish I caught were attracted by the shiny lures I used on my bone hooks. My mind wrestled for the lure could be a trap set by the Norns. Exhausted, I finally fell asleep.

Chapter 2

The first thing we had to do was clear the saplings, bushes and shrubs from the land close to where we moored *'Gytha'*. We would need to double, at least, the size of the landing. We would have to make the bank solid and line it with wood. At least three of the trees could be used for masts and spares while one was straight enough and long enough to be used for the keel. The bushes we removed were fruit-bearing and would mean we had to go further afield to find them. There was always a price to pay. We used my wood axe to hew down the trees. Both Moos Blood and Brave Cub asked for the chance to wield the iron blade. I knew we could not replace it and my heart was in my mouth as I watched them use it. I was relieved when they did not damage it. Golden Bear could only look on as his brothers used iron while he hacked at the branches with a stone axe.

"Now, Brave Cub, sharpen the axe while we take the branches from the tree." I knew that my father, long dead and watching me from Valhalla, would be unhappy with what I did next. I used my sword to hack through the branches while Moos Blood used my hatchet. The sharpened blade made short work of them. In a perfect world, I would have had more iron tools but I did not. I had a small bag with some shipbuilding tools but the sword was the most effective way to take off even thick branches. The timber was sorted into piles. We would burn some on the fires but the usable wood was put to one side. We then had the task of removing the roots. That was hard work but I knew it was necessary. Three of the trees were pine trees and their roots would give us pine tar. I knew of another stand of pine trees but it was upstream. By the end of the day, we had an area the size of two snekke and we were exhausted. The skin on our hands was broken and wounds would need to be healed, but Laughing Deer had made a fine fish stew and we ate well that night. She was a good cook and our diet was the most varied in the village. She had brought recipes from her home in the north and was not too proud to incorporate them into the Powhatan ones.

As we sat before the fire Moos Blood asked me again for the story of how I had helped my father to build *'Ada'*, the first snekke. I did not mind. I knew that one day I would die and these stories would be passed from father to son. The story of the building of the boat would help my descendants to build such boats through the retelling of the story. It meant the story of my father would never die and that gave me comfort.

Erik's Clan

It was not a saga but I used a singsong voice to tell it. I saw some of the Powhatan looking at us strangely for the tale was told in Norse and all that they heard was the music in the words. The telling of the story also helped as it prepared my sons when it came to the building.

The first part of the building was the most crucial. We had a good piece of timber for the keel and while it was long enough and had the slightest of curves, we would need to accentuate the curve. Little White Dove was able to help us as we stripped the bark from the tree. Even Golden Bear, the youngest of my sons, helped for flint scrapers were the best tool to do so. The bark was laid aside to be dried and used for kindling. That done I trimmed the trunk to the right length. There was still excess that I would trim when the boat was done. I then took the adze from my precious bag of tools. It was sharp and I began to take long slivers from what would be the top of the keel. I needed it to be flattened. The bottom would also have wood taken from it but not yet. I let my four children watch me but did not let them near the tool. One mistake at this stage could ruin the wood and, even worse, damage the adze. It was irreplaceable. By late afternoon I was satisfied and we took the timber to a shallow part of the beck. We entered the water and dug a channel in the mud and silt. When that was done, we laid the timber in the water and then began the laborious task of piling stones on the middle section. We buried it beneath enough rocks to crush a man and then I attached lianas and vines to what would be the bow and then the stern and tied them to the overhanging branches of an ancient tree. The boughs were thick and they did not bend. It took my sons and me a good hour to gradually pull the lianas until the two tips of the keel emerged from the water. It would give the wood the shape we wanted. A good shipwright would be able to make a perfect shape. I was not that good but the river and the trees would have a part in the growing of the snekke and that was no bad thing.

"There, now we wait. It will take some time for the keel to bend but the tree was young and supple. It will become the snekke. Tomorrow, we seek the ribs and the day after we fish. You have done well, my family."

That evening my sons asked me about the ribs. I nodded as I ate the fish stew that had been enriched with venison hunted by Brave Eagle. "We let nature do our work for us. We seek young trees that naturally fork. In a perfect world, we would find at least twelve." I stood and put my arms out, above my head and to the side. "We are looking for trees like this and the branches will be the thickness of my arms. We cut them and bring them back here to shape so that they are identical. They will be attached to the keel when that is finished."

Erik's Clan

"How?" Little White Dove was also curious.

"If I was back in Orkneyjar then I would go to the blacksmith and buy some nails. We have no blacksmith."

"Buy?"

Again I smiled for Brave Cub's question was a good one. There were no coins in this land. Items were bartered. Each time we met new people I sought out rocks that could be melted to make iron but thus far there appeared to be none. Perhaps the Allfather had given this land so much bounty in terms of food that he had neglected to give them iron and gold. I took out the purse that contained the coins I had accumulated in my lifetime. I had been forced to make a new bag when the old one had split at Wandering Moos' camp and I had lost four of them. Since then I had kept them although I knew not why. I showed them the coins. They had all been minted far from here. I knew which kings' faces were supposed to be on them but the years had rubbed them almost smooth. "In my homeland, we exchange these for goods or services." I saw the incredulous looks on their faces. "I do not lie. They are metal and, as such, are considered valuable. We will melt these down and some of the rings left over from my byrnie and we will make nails." The puzzled looks on their faces made me elaborate. "Very thin and long pieces of metal that can be driven through wood to join them. We will also make wooden nails but it is these metal nails that will give strength to our snekke."

It took all day to find six trees that fitted my requirements and we cut the ribs from them. We left the trees which would regrow but the branches we took, apart from the ones for the ribs, would be used to make the wooden nails. We left the ribs, once we had stripped the bark from them to season for a few days. We put shipbuilding to one side the next day when we went fishing and this time we headed downstream, towards the sea. Sometimes bigger fish came from the sea. They did not come too far upstream but where the water was still salty enough they came to hunt the river fish. We took advantage of the bounty. I took Golden Bear with us that day. He had shown when we had worked on the boat, that he was growing and no longer a child. I had him sit close to the mast. We had fire-hardened spears as well as stone clubs, my hatcher, seax and sword. These fish fought to the death when they were dragged aboard but the red flesh was greatly prized by the clan. We were lucky and managed to spear four of them. Even Golden Bear was able to use a stone club to subdue the fish. Along with the netted river fish, we had a good haul and when we wearily carried them into the village we were cheered. The bones from the larger fish were much prized as they could be more easily carved and shaped than animal bones. Golden Bear looked so proud as he carried a fish almost as big as he was. Little White Dove would not be happy that her little brother had done that which she had wanted.

It was that day, as the clan were given their bounty, that Brave Eagle brought Fears Water to speak with me. I saw a mixture of fear and wonder on the boy's face when he saw me. I was well aware of how different I looked from every other warrior in the clan.

"This, Erik, is Fears Water and he wishes to thank you for saving his life." He smiled, "Speak slowly for while I can understand all your words his language is slightly different to ours."

"Thank you, Shaman of the Bear."

I smiled for Running Antelope had first seen me dressed in my bearskin and always called me Shaman of the Bear, "You are welcome, Fears Water. I am pleased to see you are becoming well." I deliberately chose the shorter words so that he might understand me.

He nodded, "I should like to go with you on the river when I am healed. I hear that it is the wind that makes her sail."

I nodded, "And you will be more than welcome."

We went to the snekke so that he could see her. The boys had cleaned her up but she still smelled of fish. "Aieee, it is wondrous and what is that at the front? A fearsome beast?"

Although we did not have a dragon prow as such, I had carved a mixture of a sea serpent and a woman, meant to represent Gytha, the volva whose spirit still came to me. "It is just a carving to protect us when we sail."

"Ah."

"And your name, Fears Water, how were you named?"

"When I was a baby I fell into the river and bawled so much I was named."

"Yet you survived in the river. Strange is it not?"

He nodded, "And when I awoke I found that I did not fear water. When Running Antelope told me how I was found I was determined to travel on the water."

"When we have time, then, Fears Water, we will take you."

We returned to our shipbuilding the next day and after tramping for four or five miles found a stand of almost perfect trees. We harvested more branches for the ribs and even had one as a spare in case we damaged one. After stripping the bark and roughly shaping them we left them to season while we worked on the spare masts. The more ribs a snekke had, the stronger would be the vessel. Moos Blood was tireless and was the last to cease work each night. He knew that the new snekke would be his and he wanted as much of his sweat in it as he could. The days passed and my children and I worked happily. It was not hard work with the four of us working and they enjoyed the transformation from something that was of nature to something that was man-made. Before we began to make the strakes, which would involve the splitting of a tree and be time consuming, I decided to make the nails. I had already made charcoal. I had done so in the anticipation of melting metal. We needed a fire hotter than one that might cook food. I dug a pit close to our yehakin and placed some of the dried bark and kindling we had collected. I placed plenty of dried wood on the top and then the charcoal. I lit the fire. I had asked Brave Eagle for the lungs of some of the deer he had killed. He was curious how I would use something that even the resourceful Powhatans discarded and, combined with some bladders, I fashioned bellows. While the fire reached its temperature, I carved the moulds for the nails. I made more than I needed for the wood could always be used later. The pot I used was a stone I had found in the river. The motion of the water, sand and time had eroded a natural bowl in it. By using two sturdy pieces of wood I would be able to lift the stone off the fire to pour it. Of course, I did not know the nature of the stone and so I invoked the help of the gods by making a blót before I started. I did not want the stone to crack and lose the irreplaceable metal. At the back of my mind was the thought that in the hull of ***'Gytha'*** lay a stone from the land of Ice and Fire. When we next emptied the hull I would search for the rock that would bear the heat of a melting fire.

With the coins in the hollow, I set the boys to pumping the bellows we had made. We drew quite a crowd as we always did when I made metal. I saw the clan hold tightly to their totems for protection from this strange magic. Surprisingly, it did not take as long for the metal to melt as I had expected and, even more miraculously the rock did not break. It told me that the coins were not as pure as they might have been. I used two sticks to carefully lift the stone and then, using the lip I had carved in the stone, I carefully poured the molten metal into the moulds. As I had expected I had spare moulds but I had not wasted a single drop of metal. Until I found some iron stones, I would not need to do this again. As I placed the red-hot stone on the grass, where it hissed, I could not help but look to the north, to the distant mountains. Would I find iron there? Perhaps there might be some even closer, in the blue hills.

The clan continued to watch for a while as though expecting more magic and when it was clear there would be none they drifted off. I sat with my sons, while Little White Dove helped her mother prepare the fish for our meal and we carefully fashioned wooden trenails from the small branches we had left. Some required little work and those put a smile on our faces while others had to be worked until they were the same size. I had a bone drill and it would make a tapered hole into which the wooden trenail could be driven. Nothing was wasted. The shavings were placed in an old pot and kept for kindling.

The next day saw the backbreaking work of making the strakes for the side of the snekke. We had already taken off the bark and I used the stone chisel to make a line along the tree. The boys placed specially angled pieces of stone in the line I had made and then I used a stone club to split the wood. It was time-consuming and sometimes the planks did not break off smoothly. We discarded nothing for smaller ones were always useful. As with the trenails we made more than we needed and it took three days for us to have our supply ready. The last job we had to do was to make a bed for the keel and we used wooden spades and shovels to make one. With the nails removed from the moulds, we were ready and we went, nervously, to the keel. It was a chilly morning when we removed the stones that had kept it below water and took the keel from the water. It was heavy and my sons struggled to lift their end. I did not ask for help. I knew from the making of *'Ada'* that if just the family worked on the boat then we would be rewarded. Our first snekke had been a sound and faithful servant for us. Once the keel was in place, we stood back to admire it. The soaking had worked and there was just the right curve. I knew that compared with the work of a skilled shipwright ours would be crude but that could not be helped.

We began to mark out where the ribs would go. Once marked I allowed my sons to help me carefully, using stone chisels, cut out the wood in the keel where they would fit. Each rib was individually made but all were the same size so that when we hammered the strakes onto them it would be a good fit. After a week the ribs were placed in the notches we had made and then left there to continue to dry out. We had made some glue from animal hooves and used that to secure them. They would need trenails but the glue would help. That done we went fishing again so that the glue had time to dry.

The drilling with the augur took time. It was not hard work but it took time to bite through the ribs and into the keel. There were two trenails for each rib. I was not sure that was the right number but it was the number we had made on *'Gytha'* and she had sailed well. That first day we drilled and hammered in the trenails on four ribs and I was well satisfied. By the end of a week, with another day off for fishing, we had finished the nailing of the ribs. They were comfortingly close together and would give a sound structure. She would be able to endue the seas of the ocean. If the boys thought we were done then they were in for a shock. We had to cut the braces for each of the ribs. These planks were crucial and were made slightly bigger than the gap so that we had to hammer them in. It created tension and made for a better boat. Once done we drilled them and hammered in the trenails. The snekke was taking shape.

It was seven days later when we had the accident. It upset Laughing Deer and pleased me causing a rare argument between us. It was Moos Blood's fault. He had become overconfident when using the stone chisel to prepare the keel for the steerboard. It slipped and gashed his hand. Blood flowed and went into the keel. We hurried him back to the village where his hand was tended to. It was his left hand and I knew he would heal. When Laughing Deer saw me smiling, as was Moos Blood, she erupted like the freshly fanned embers of a dying fire.

"You laugh at our son's pain! What kind of father are you?"

Her words slapped the smile from my face and I held her, "I do not laugh at his pain. He will learn, the next time, to be more careful, but the cut has given the keel a bath of blood. Such a birth for a snekke is propitious. It means that part of our son is now in the snekke and there is a bond. I spilt blood in *'Gytha'* and she has never let us down, has she?"

Slightly mollified she said, "I would rather he had a small nick and did not need the wound to be sewn together."

I shrugged, "Such things are out of our hands."

After that, we were all more careful and the work progressed well. Four moons after we had begun the construction, the hull was coated in pine tar and left to dry for a week. All that remained to do was to launch her, fit her mast and sail and then after I had carved the prow, name her. Our preparations, were, however, put to one side when Chief Long Spear summoned Brave Eagle, Fears Water, and me to go to his camp. Of course, I took the boys and as we marched through the forest the next day, they asked me why the summons had been issued.

I did not know although I suspected that it was something to do with the boy we had found. Brave Eagle heard the question and my response, "Long Spear allows us all to do much as we wish but any contact with those who are not of the Powhatan tribe is of concern to him. He will want to question the boy, that is all."

They had been young the last time we had visited and now, as they entered the largest settlement in this part of the world, I saw their eyes widen. Compared with the towns I had seen in my homeland, it was a tiny village but to them it was huge. I was accosted, as I entered, by the warriors who had come with me to rescue the captives. The ones who had survived were good warriors. Their motives might have been suspect, they had wanted to be blooded but unlike their wilder companions, they had satiated their blood lust and would now be the reasoned veterans Long Spear would need. I also saw the warriors who, the last time we had been here, had been the youths on the cusp of manhood. There were many of them and they, too, crowded around to try to see the magic sword they had heard about. The veterans shooed them away.

We would not be returning home that night and a yehakin had been prepared for us. Water and food were provided to refresh us and a messenger said that the chief would speak with us after we had eaten. When we were alone, I said to my sons, "Listen and speak only to answer. I have brought you here as a courtesy. We are of Brave Eagle's clan now and that is where our first loyalty lies."

They nodded and I could see that they were overawed. There had to have been sixty or seventy warriors in the settlement. Brave Eagle had less than twenty. They understood.

Long Spear had aged since our last visit and looked old. With that age came wisdom but I knew from Brave Eagle that there was more. He had a great deal of power. The tribe was enormous and spread all over this part of the land. He could summon a thousand warriors if there was a threat to him. He managed to hold on to such power by using people and cunning. He was not a man to be underestimated. I did not equate him to King Sweyn Forkbeard for unlike the Danish King who had driven us from our homes, Long Spear was not ambitious but I knew that if he had to be he could be ruthless.

The food was, as one would expect, excellent and was not spoiled by anything other than comments on the flavour and the taste. When it was finished and the pipe passed around then was the time for talking. The men remained and Fears Water was asked to stand and to tell his tale. He was questioned closely, especially by Eagle Claws, one of Long Spear's sons. When their curiosity had been satiated, he sat and Brave Eagle took up the tale. The accounts having been given then men put their heads together to discuss the matter. I saw that Long Spear and his sons kept glancing over at me as they spoke and it did not bode well.

"Brave Eagle, I cannot understand what the fuss is about. Fears Water has lost his family and he will, I presume, stay with us."

Fears Water nodded, "I have nothing to go back to. The Moneton will have taken my mother and sisters as slaves. I might not be happy about that, Brave Eagle, but I am not a fool and I know I can do nothing about it except join my father and brothers and die."

Brave Eagle smiled, "And you can stay with us as long as you like. Long Spear is just interested in the matter, that is all."

I was not so sure.

Erik's Clan

Eagle Claws was obviously Long Spear's nominated successor for it was he who stood and silence fell, "My father will speak and all will hear his words."

To me, that sounded ominous.

Long Spear's voice was still loud enough for all to hear but it cracked at times and showed his age, "The words of Fears Water and Brave Eagle have given us much to think about. Fears Water's clan are part of my tribe. We had rarely seen them but that is because they lived at the borders of our land. This tribe who do not speak our language, the Moneton, are new and that disturbs us. Do they wish to make war against us? My sons will send messengers out to the outlying clans and ask for news of these new warriors." He looked directly at Brave Eagle, "We will send to you, Brave Eagle, when we have need of you, your warriors and the Shaman of the Bear and his magical boat. You are now part of this tribe and, as such, your magical boat will be used to aid us."

My heart sank. I knew that there had to be a purpose to my inclusion and I was less than happy. I wanted to get on with my life. Was this my fate so long as I lived amongst the Powhatan warriors?

Chapter 3

As we made our way back to the village, I wondered what the words of Long Spear meant. Fears Water was also worried. "Brave Eagle, I am happy living with the clan and I do not wish to leave. I will work as hard as any for my place there. I feel safe with your people."

"And we are happy with you. Fear not, Long Spear just worries about that which we do not know. Until now the only danger to our people came from the Penobscot and now that the danger from there is gone, he looks for other dangers. That is what a good chief does." Brave Eagle's words sounded reasonable and yet I could not help but worry.

"If you would allow me, Erik, Shaman of the Bear, I would help you and your sons to work on your new boat."

"Of course, Fears Water."

Back at the new boat, I threw myself and my sons into its completion. Fears Water also seemed happy to help and his strength made the difference. We made much better progress. Within ten days we had launched her, fitted the mast and steering board and I had carved a small figurehead. We just needed to name her.

"So, Moos Blood, your blood is in the keel of this vessel and you can name her."

Fears Water asked, "Her?"

I nodded, "Yes, Fears Water, all boats are named after women. It is the tradition of my people."

I saw Moos Blood thinking long and hard about the decision and he saw his mother approaching, "The wound to my hand caused my mother so much hurt that I would name her 'Laughing Deer'.

I nodded, "And yet I am not sure your mother would like that. How about a compromise, *'Doe'* is a female deer and we would know it was named after your mother?"

It suited us all and my wife frowned as she approached, "What is causing you all so much mirth?"

"We have named the new snekke. She is *'Doe'*." I looked to see if she was offended but she seemed happy. "And would you like to sail on her first outing?"

Shaking her head she said, "You and Moos Blood can sail her. I will risk but one of my children."

Moos Blood laughed, "Fears Water, how about you?"

He gave a shy smile, "I died in the river and was reborn. Let us see if the rebirth has completely rid me of my fear and besides, I should like to see how this magic boat sails."

Fears Water was a novice and once Moos Blood had boarded and was seated at the bow, we placed Fears Water with his back to the mast. "Now sit there and try not to move. Moos Blood needs to get to know our new vessel. I will steer first, Moos Blood, and when I am happy, we will exchange places."

Brave Cub was unhappy at being left but he untied us from the bank and I loosed the sail. Golden Bear had stormed off when his mother had said only Moos Blood would sail. There was little breeze in the beck but the current was strong enough to take us towards the river. Moos Blood had the oar we used to fend us off from the bank but we did not need it and as soon as we emerged onto the river, I put the steering board over to head downstream. I would not risk the sea yet but I wanted the wide river to play with the new boat. I was able to watch Fears Water as his eyes widened. *'Doe'* flew. We had been lucky with the ribs and the snekke had sleek lines. The extra ribs ensured that there was little flexing in the hull and she was as straight as a well-flighted arrow. Moos Blood turned and elation was etched all over his face. This would be his snekke and he was happy, "She is fast, father. Perhaps we should have named her hawk for she is as fast as a diving hawk."

I shook my head, "No, my son, for that would be bad luck. *'Doe'* is a good name and does are fast too. They can outrun most animals. All is well." I allowed the sail to billow full and bye. We had placed ballast in the hold and I was pleased that I appeared to have chosen the right amount. She was well balanced. She seemed to skim over the river. The wind was with us and when we were a few miles from our home I turned her and with a full sail we virtually stopped.

Moos Blood knew what I had done. He would be able to sail back but he would have to tack and turn against the current and the wind. He shook his head, "You are like Loki, father."

I shrugged, "Let us see how she does when the wind is not with her. Let us change places."

I used the steerboard side and Moos Blood, the larboard. That way the snekke remained balanced. The current was still drifting us towards the sea but the flattened sail acted as an anchor. I had also wanted to watch Moos Blood and see how he coped. He did everything that I would have wished. He checked the steering board and withy. He looked at the fore and aft stays and only when he was happy did he turn and begin to tack up the river. He needed all his concentration to do so and I was happy that, as we edged back to our home, he did not make a mistake. He and the snekke were as one. I had been like that with *'Ada'* and it boded well.

The one who was most excited, after we had landed, was Fears Water. He had loved every moment of the short voyage down the river. "I would like to sail again."

"As far as I am concerned then you are welcome but you will have to work." He nodded. "Moos Blood, could you sail with Brave Cub as your crew?"

"Of course."

"Then tomorrow we will use both snekke. I have an idea to increase our haul of fish but we will need some others to help us."

Moos Blood was intrigued but I did not enlighten him. Instead, I went when we had finished with the new snekke, to speak with Brave Eagle. When I outlined my plan, he was delighted. Soon the days would begin to shorten and the clan would need all the food we could collect.

When I mentioned what we were going to do Golden Bear became agitated. "You will take Fears Water but not one of your sons. That is not right."

"You are right but you have to do all that I say when we sail."

"I promise I shall."

I gathered my sons and Fears Water to explain what I intended, "It will involve us working together. The two snekke will need to be as one."

My sons were eager while Fears Water was just excited to be part of something.

The plan was simple enough. We did not sail far into the river and with our anchors out and sails reefed Moos Blood and I strung a net between the two snekke. Brave Eagle and the other warriors waited downstream of us in three boats. When we had filled the net with fish, and it did not take long, we lifted it, a birchbark boat would paddle up and we deposited the catch in the bottom of their boat. By noon we had more fish than we had ever caught and returned to the village. I was pleased as we had all worked together and yet the hardest work had been done by the river itself. It would not do for us to repeat too often but we had enough food for at least a month or more already. We would preserve it.

It was as we watched the women preparing the fish that Brave Eagle said, "We need to find more salt." That was not as easy as it sounded. "It means a voyage to the shore and we need to find a piece of beach that is not used by another clan."

"You are wrong, Brave Eagle. That is easy. When we sailed here, we found many unoccupied islands at the mouth of the estuary. We sail there, set up a camp and while some boil seawater to make salt the rest can fish. The problem is that we would need to use both snekke as well as four birchbark boats and their crews."

"You are thinking the village would be left unguarded?"

"If Long Spear's fears are true then the ones who destroyed Fears Water's village may come further downstream."

Shaking his head, Brave Eagle said, "There are many clans between our village and the Shenandoah. We will risk it."

When I told my wife about the trip, she asked why we needed the snekke at all. "That is simple. The snekke both have holds. We take pots and we can carry far more back in our two snekke than in the birch bark boats. I fear that the birchbark boats may be in more danger than we are for they are not made for the open sea."

I had already decided where we would land. When we had sailed here, I had kept a map for the simple reason that I was not sure if we would be welcomed and I wanted to know how to return north, if we had to. At the mouth of the Patawomke, where I normally fished, there was a string of islands. Some were little, no bigger than a spit of sand sticking out of the sea but there were some that were as big as Bear Island. None had water on them and so were uninhabited. I had stayed overnight on one of them on more than one occasion. I would use that one for although it had no water there were some trees and it seemed to attract driftwood. The beach I had in mind faced west and the tribes on the mainland would not even know we were there. Most importantly I knew that the water there was salty and that was what we wanted. We would be away for seven days or more and so we took water skins. We could fish and would not need much food for we could eat freshly caught fish. We would tow the birchbark boats and that was the one part of the plan that had me worried. Would Moos Blood cope?

The clan came to see us off. Brave Eagle's sons would stay in the village with older warriors. The younger ones, while they knew they would not be blooded, were keen for the adventure. Emerging from our basin was harder than normal as the two snekke had pots for the salt in the centre and they were a distraction to the eye. Once we were on the river then the birchbark boats were attached in a line and we hoisted the sail. I knew that it would be harder when we returned but setting sail south was easier than we might have thought. The current helped and the warriors in the boats added their efforts to the paddles to get us going.

For almost everyone else, apart from my sons and I, this would be a new experience as the river widened closer to its mouth, so that the two shores were hard to see and it felt as though we were on an ocean. I kept one eye on Moos Blood who sailed next to me. His new boat was faster than mine. That was to be expected for it had a clean hull. I had to order him to reef his sail so that we could sail together. I had Golden Bear with me and he was as good as his word and obeyed every instruction instantly. The current and the wind enabled us to reach our destination in one long day.

As we neared the island I had chosen we saw pinpricks of fires on the far shores where fishermen had fished during the day and were now preparing their catches. They would not see us but, the next day, the smoke from our fires would tell them that intruders were at the mouth of the river in what they would regard as their waters. We would have to be wary.

Although it was dark as we approached the sandy shore of the place I named Salt Island, the moonlight helped to illuminate the sand. I had chosen the island and the beach because I knew that it was rock-free and safe. We cast off the birch bark boats fifty paces from the beach and that allowed the two snekke to concentrate on our landing. I smiled as Fears Water staggered when he stepped upon the sand. We had sailed for a whole day and his legs would not obey him. We pulled our boats up above the high-water mark. Here, closer to the ocean, there was the chance of sudden storms that could wreck us and that was the last thing we needed. With no trees on the island to repair damaged vessels we would be stuck there.

We lit our first fire. It would be for the cooking of food rather than the making of salt but it would be the source of fire we used while we stayed on the island. We had brought kindling and faggots from home but we would need to forage when daylight came. My sons and I had brought sealskin capes and we rigged those up as shelters. Brave Eagle and the others had not had the foresight to do so and I saw envy on their faces when, after eating, my sons and I, along with Fears Water were able to roll in our furs, away from the sand whipped by the breezes from the sea.

I planned on fishing as well as collecting salt but the first morning was all about gathering seawater and making salt as quickly as we could. We had brought four large cooking pots to harvest the sea and they were placed on four fires. While my sons and Fears Water scavenged driftwood and shellfish from the shore, we began to fill the four pots that would bubble away all day. It took longer than I had expected and I did not manage to fish. We ate the shellfish that was collected. The boys had done well and we had a good supply of wood. Brave Eagle organised his warriors to watch and feed the fires. By the end of the first day, one of the pots was full of the precious salt and we lifted the pot from the fire and then scraped out, using the shells of the crabs we had eaten, the salt into the clay pots. The cooking pot was refilled with seawater.

Brave Eagle looked at the ten clay pots we had brought for the salt. We were being ambitious for ten pots would last us almost half a year. "This will take time, Erik."

I nodded, "I know and the longer we are here then the more curious will be the locals."

He knew what I meant. The mainland to the east of us was not Powhatan. We had encountered, on our voyage south, warriors who objected to our presence. When I fished in the sea, I was not there long enough for them to be able to investigate.

"We will be ready for danger. You will fish tomorrow?"

"I will take Brave Cub, Golden Bear and *'Gytha'*."

"We will continue to watch and to forage." He smiled at some of the younger warriors who were already looking miserable at an adventure that seemed to consist of hard labour. "The young warriors will learn what it is to be a warrior."

By the time we left, the next morning, one of the clay pots had been completely filled and another was half full. It was progress. I headed towards the open sea. There would be less chance of meeting other fishermen there and we might only need to catch a couple of the large fish that had the fins sticking up from their backs. We did not know their names. We had not caught any close to Bear Island and so we called them the fierce finny fish for it seemed to suit them. Good to eat, they fought to the end when we caught them and there were two stone clubs in the bottom of the snekke to despatch them.

We saw a shoal of them feasting on the shiny silvery fish. I allowed Brave Cub to steer, commanding him to keep a straight line and go with the wind no matter what happened. I prepared the spears. Golden Bear was given a club in case any fish needed to be stunned. They had bone heads and I had carved them myself. They were barbed and would hold on to flesh. The spears were attached to the snekke by rope so that when I threw the spear, I could retrieve it. The carved head had taken me a moon and was not to be lost lightly. The shoal of shiny silvery fish was a large one and the fierce finny fish were gorging themselves.

"Brave Cub, no matter what happens hold a course that is true. This will be a veritable maelstrom of fish through which we sail."

"Aye, father." I sensed the nerves beneath the words.

"Golden Bear all that I wish you to do is be ready to strike at the head of any fish that fights."

"Aye, father."

Erik's Clan

We were lucky in that the shoal of fish were going with the wind and the two shoals were so large that I had plenty of targets. I hurled one spear at a fish that was just a boat's length from me and it died quickly. The body would act as an anchor and I had to throw the other two quickly. One struck a finny fish that had come almost next to the snekke while the third was a good hit on a fish four paces from us. The fish were fierce fighters and they fought death. They dived and swam with every piece of life that was left to them. They began to pull the snekke off course and we were in danger of broaching.

"Father, I cannot hold her!"

I heard the fear in Brave Cub's voice and I went to the steering board. Golden Bear clung to the mast as we began to heel over. By throwing my weight on the steering board I forced us back on course and the three fish, two dead and one dying, were dragged around to the stern. They would slow us up but Brave Cub would be able to steer.

I smiled and ruffled his hair, "You did well, now hold this course while I drag the fish aboard."

The fishes were dead weight and it was not easy to get them all aboard. The two shoals of fish began to draw away from us. Golden Bear needed no club and I threw the dead fish to the bottom of the boat and after checking that the barbs were still whole returned to the prow. The pickings were leaner for we were no longer in the middle of the feeding frenzy. I had to choose my targets carefully. I saw a huge specimen ahead of me but it was a throw of fifteen paces. I would not have risked it but he looked worth it. I threw and hit him. Before I could send another after him, he had dived and I knew that he might be strong enough to make the bows of the snekke dip beneath the water. I hurried to the stern and was just in time. My extra weight made all the difference and the bow stopped just short of the water. I held the steering board with Brave Cub.

"We let this one tire himself out."

It took, by my reckoning, almost an hour for the fish to die. By then the shoals had disappeared and we were far out to sea. The land was a smudge on the horizon. We turned the snekke and then Golden Bear and I hauled the fish to the surface. It was so large that it took both of us and Brave Cub to land him. Exhausted I took the steering board and headed west. The sun gave us our direction and while I had to tack for a while the weather was still benign and the two of us were elated with our success. The smoke from the fires gave us a direction and we landed just as the sun was about to dip beneath the horizon.

Brave Eagle looked concerned as I jumped into the sea to haul the snekke onto the sand, "We feared you had been lost." He looked into the snekke and his eyes widened when he saw the last fish we had caught, "You fought a monster."

"We will not need to fish again."

It took us all to land the fish and begin to prepare them. The bones, along with the remains of the shellfish would make a good soup while the flesh would be cooked on the open fire. I knew that it was so fresh that it could be eaten raw but the smoke from the fires seemed to impart a better flavour.

"We have done well, Erik. Already we have filled another two pots."

That night as we sat around the fire, Fears Water asked us about the voyage we had made from Bear Island. Moos Blood had told him some of it but I had been the navigator and it was my tale. The young warriors from the clan gathered to listen. I did not exaggerate anything but each time I told the story it seemed more fantastic than the last time and, not for the first time, I realised that the Three Sisters had much to do with our survival.

The next day with two more pairs of hands to help we managed to fill all but four of the salt pots. However, one of the vessels we used to heat the saltwater looked in danger of cracking. With no clay on the island to repair it we knew that our stay might need to be extended.

Fears Water repaid our kindness in rescuing him the next day for he was on watch and his sharp eyes spied the birchbark boats heading from the mainland to the east. While their arrival might be peaceful our experience with those tribes made us wary and prepared for war. Leaving the four boys to watch and feed the fires the rest of us armed ourselves. I strapped on my sword and I strung my bow. I had made some good flint arrows. I had found the flint half a year earlier and through trial and error, I had learned to make flint arrowheads. They were far sharper than the stone ones and I had twelve such arrows with me. I had more back in the village and, as we spied eight boats, each containing five warriors, I regretted not bringing more. There were just seventeen of us.

As they neared the shore Brave Eagle said, "These are not Lenni Lenape and they have marks on their faces. They come for war." He turned to the young warriors. "Those with bows stand behind us, the rest of you flank Erik and me. Today you will learn to fight and see a real warrior. Whoever these people are they are in for a shock when they come up against the magic of the Shaman of the Bear."

Although I did not like the praise, I knew why Brave Eagle said what he said. He was bolstering the confidence of these warriors who had yet to be blooded. Brave Eagle had a seax I had given him and would give a good account of himself. He had a bow that was equal to mine and the two of us would be more likely to hurt the enemy than the others.

I said, "Moos Blood, you, Brave Cub, Fears Water and Golden Bear are to guard the snekke with your sling shots."

"Aye, father."

He turned to me, "We hit them first. They will be vulnerable when they beach their boats."

"You are right. You take the ones to the left and I will take those to the right." There was little point in giving specific commands to the young warriors. A man's first fight was always a blur of decisions made too quickly allied to a sort of panic.

I nocked an arrow. I had made all my own arrows and I chose a good one. As the boats bobbed up and down on the surf I pulled back. The warriors were less than forty paces from us and we had the higher ground. As one warrior leapt from the boat to help drag it ashore, I loosed an arrow that slammed into his back. Even if it was not a mortal strike the man would be incapacitated and his hands fell from the prow and he sank into the surf. Brave Eagle's arrow was an even better one and smacked into the chest of another. I nocked another as the younger warriors sent their first missiles. Only one struck anything but the flurry of feathers had an effect and the warriors coming to rid their land of us had to raise their hide shields for protection. It delayed their landing and in that time two more of my arrows found flesh as did Brave Eagle's. He shouted, "Loose an arrow only when you are sure that you can hit. Do not waste arrows."

Although there were seven warriors dead or wounded, we were still outnumbered and now with their boats beached they hurled themselves at us like berserkers. We had hurt them and they wanted vengeance. I managed to hit two more of them before I discarded my bow and drew my hatchet and sword. Once again, the sight of the two weapons drawn against an eastern sky made the sunlight flash and reflect off them, making the warriors recoil a little. When we had attacked the Penobscot, it had been the flash of light from my sword that had allowed Brave Eagle to close with and rescue the captives. Now it made the enemy pause and, in that delay, the young warriors managed to hit another four of them. One of those racing to close the gap between us had a clutch of feathers in his hair and he shouted something and ran at me; I deduced that he was a chief of some kind. I think that Brave Eagle knew that would happen and that was why he had placed himself close to me. He guarded my left.

The chief had a shield and a sharpened antler club. Although the club was a terrible weapon, I had a sword. As he swung the longer antler club at me, I blocked it with my sword and my sharp blade cut into it. At the same time, I swung my hatchet at his shield. The hide shield would have stopped a stone weapon but the metal head hacked through it and I saw the chief's eyes widen as the hatchet bit into his arm. He pulled back his antler club to bring it down to my head but I forestalled the blow by punching up with the hatchet head. It slowed down the antler club and allowed me a free swing with my sword. His wounded arm meant he could not raise his damaged shield and my sword hacked into his neck. There is a vein there and I sliced into it. The blood sprayed both the enemy warriors and the ones who, ironically, had yet to be blooded. As he fell, Brave Eagle rammed his seax into the gut of a second warrior. It was too much for the enemy and they turned and ran to their boats. Barely twenty managed to make it and they left the other boats beached.

The young warriors cheered and screamed insults as the warriors left. We had survived with just a couple of slight wounds to Stone Calf and Tree Climber. Brave Eagle and I knew that we had been lucky. He turned to me, "We leave with whatever salt we have. They will be back."

I nodded, "But not until tomorrow. We leave after dark and that will give us more time to harvest the sea. We can load the snekke in daylight."

He gave me a dubious look, "You can sail at night?"

I smiled, "We did when we came from Bear Island and besides, towing birchbark boats upstream means that we will not move quickly."

The four boys had left the fires and come to join us. Their eyes widened when they saw the bodies. I turned, "Did I say to leave the snekke? Go now do as I command, feed the fires."

Brave Eagle said to the young warriors, "You are now blooded. Bring the boats that the enemy left around to the other side of the island. We will take them home with us."

I said, "That will slow us even more."

He smiled, "And I do not wish to give them the chance to pursue us. We leave their dead so that they can be buried and if you are right then, by the time they arrive, we shall be gone and the river will hide us."

In the end, we lost little of the salt. We had one empty jar but when we emptied the four pots we had been heating we found that they each contained salt. We placed them in the four birchbark boats we had captured and, as the sun set, headed north to sail home. This time I strung two ropes between the two snekke. It made for a cumbersome voyage but I wanted my sons safe while we sailed in the dark. By dawn,

Erik's Clan

we were far enough upstream for me to let Moos Blood loose. With an empty estuary behind us, we were safe from pursuit.

Chapter 4

Our safe return with not only the salt but also the fierce finny fish and blooded warriors was a cause of great celebration. This was harvest time and we normally celebrated the gathering of the crops but this year it was an even greater feast for we had much to eat. The finny fish needed to be eaten quickly and they, along with some of the new crops and a young deer that had been hunted were the central features of a feast that saw all of us eating together.

Fears Water had long ago left Brave Eagle's hut and after a short time with the young unmarried warriors, he had joined my family. It was crowded and so I decided that when the feast was over, we would build a second yehakin. I would use my shipbuilding skills to improve the design. After the feast, while the rest of the village, my wife and daughter included, preserved food for the winter, my sons, Golden Bear included, and Fears Water began to build a larger yehakin. There was more than enough land and I knew how to make a yehakin that would be sound. I also decided to incorporate sod for the roof. I knew from Bear Island that the turf would keep the dwelling warmer in winter and cooler in summer as well as affording protection for the winds that the elders had told me sometimes whipped through the settlement, tearing the yehakin to shreds. We finished the new yehakin in a day. It helped to have so many hands as well as the tools and the supplies we needed to make it. Even Golden Bear, young though he was, contributed. He had been to sea and was now becoming aware that he could contribute to the family. He was so small and light that it was he who was able to place the sods on the roof and when he descended, covered in soil, he had a smile as wide as a sunset.

The new yehakin was for the boys. My wife and daughter would continue to live with me in the original yehakin. As the days grew shorter and the air became colder we settled into a routine. We fished once every three days and gathered berries for the others. Golden Bear, emboldened by his success during the salt hunt begged to come sailing and I took him with Fears Water and myself on **'Gytha'**. As I knew he would, he loved it. Fears Water took the steering board a few times. He could steer the snekke but unlike Moos Blood and Brave Cub, I knew that he would never be able to captain the boat. He knew it too but he was happy just to steer now and then.

Winter came early that year, before the shortest day of the year and we had snow. We had already lifted the snekke from the water, removed their masts and laid them upside down. They soon disappeared under the coat of snow. The elders had experienced snow but not often. While the children found it to be an entertaining novelty, I knew the real misery of snow having lived in the land of Ice and Fire. I sat in the new cosy yehakin and taught my sons how to make flint arrows. The time huddled away from the snow was not wasted. Even when the snow melted the winter was cold and my decision to turf the new yehakin made that the warmest home in the village. The boys offered to share it with Laughing Deer, Little White Dove and me but we were warm enough, cuddling beneath our furs.

As I had experienced living close to Bear Island, winter brought death to the village. The old died. It was a reminder to us all of our mortality. Even though we were not close to any of those who died it brought my family closer together. As spring came, I saw a change in both Fears Water and Moos Blood. They were no longer boys but young men and I caught both of them looking at the young women in the village not as playmates but as mates. Little White Dove was also approaching womanhood. That was one major difference between growing up here, in Brave Eagle's village, and back in the land of my birth, Denmark or Norway. There, young men had a way of satisfying their urges. They could raid. My brothers and cousins and I had not done that but I knew that many drekar had left their homes to seek not only plunder but also women. Brave Eagle had told me that some tribes did the same here. The Powhatans were not such a tribe.

Laughing Deer noticed their looks and spoke to me, "You need to speak to the boys, husband. I would not have them violate a maiden. They need to understand how such matters are decided."

I scoffed, "They are both good boys and they will respect women."

She shook her head, "I would rather it was made clear." She looked suddenly sad, "When I was taken by the Penobscot then my life changed. Had you not come into my life…" She shook her head as though to clear the memory, "I was lucky. Let us not rely on luck for the girls in this village. Speak to them."

I nodded. My wife rarely spoke to me like that and I was wise enough to heed the words. As luck would have it, I was about to attend to the snekke in any case. I took my three sons and Fears Water with me. It would do no harm to have Golden Bear and Brave Cub hear them too and I could deliver the speech while they worked.

We first cleared all the winter detritus from them and then I set them to cleaning the hulls properly. I had learned how to make the concoction to deter both weed and worm while on Bear Island. The stinking liquid was bubbling away and we had raccoon tails to apply it. I waited until the four of them were painting the hulls before I took a deep breath and began.

"Moos Blood and Fears Water, you are about to become men. With that change in your life comes great responsibility. You will have to train with the other young men to become warriors who will defend our people." I saw all four of them nod and smile. "When the snekke are back in the water we will make weapons for you." Their smiles grew. "However, as well as becoming warriors you will find that you will experience urges." I saw both the elder boys start. "They will have begun now. As part of the process of being a man, you need to control them. There are many lovely young women in our village. They should be treated as you would wish Little White Dove to be treated. Do you understand me?"

They looked at each other and nodded. Moos Blood said, "But, father, some of the others have already taken some of the young women off into the forest."

I nodded, for I had seen them too, "That does not make it right. You four share a roof that I built and you know that I do not issue commands lightly." Even Golden Bear nodded, "Then obey me and all shall be well." I smiled, "If you find a young woman you wish to be your wife then tell me. I will help you to win them but do it the right way, the warrior's way. We are not Penobscot who just take."

Fears Water looked sad, "Nor the Moneton. They are animals."

I like to think that it was my speech that helped the boys to see the way ahead but, in truth, I know that it was Fears Water's words that did it. I knew that the boys, in their own yehakin, spoke long into the night and it would be the graphic description of the attack on his home that would have shown them the right way to behave.

I was as good as my word and I helped them to make weapons. The first weapon was easy, a spear. My skills with the napping of flint had improved and I was able to make two spear heads for them. We made practice spears and used stones for the heads. It would not do to use the flint spears until they were necessary. Then I turned my attention to shields. I no longer used a shield. Hatchet and sword were my offence and defence but I knew that the boys would need a shield. Hide shields were all very well but I preferred wooden ones and while they were heavier could also be used offensively. We made two wooden shields and the boys painted them with designs. They were then able to join the other young men who practised with Brave Eagle once a week. Once a month every warrior, I was the exception, would join the young men and the whole clan would be taught tactics to fight as one.

Erik's Clan

Life was falling into a familiar pattern. Each day was marked by particular activities. Fears Water and Moos Blood both found young girls and there was mutual attraction. While some of the other boys were beaten for infractions my stepson and son did their courting the right way and there was a promise of marriage when the fathers of the girls deemed it right. Little White Dove bloomed and I knew that within a year or two she would be courted. The talk with her would be the remit of my wife.

All seemed well and then the Norns spun. A messenger arrived from Long Spear's village. Fears Water, Brave Eagle and I were summoned to meet with Eagle Claws and my heart sank. This time I did not take my sons. I left them to continue to fish the river and just three of us headed through the forest to the village of Long Spear. We marched in silence for none of us were happy about the meeting. We had thought, as so much time had elapsed, that Long Spear had forgotten about us but he had not and the fact that it was his son who had demanded that we attend did not bode well.

As soon as we arrived in the village, we could see a difference. It had a belligerent air about it. The young men were all practising for war. The village had always seemed to me to be a haven of peace but now it was not. The women and the children all toiled in the fields but the men, young and old were arrayed for war. I glanced at Brave Eagle who shook his head. He was not happy either but we needed to be silent.

Eagle Claws came to greet us and I saw that he wore the regalia of a chief. Was Long Spear dead? I remained silent for there was a protocol to such matters and Brave Eagle was the chief of our clan.

"It is good to see you, Eagle Claws. Where is your father?"

With an impassive and emotionless face, the warrior said, "My father is ill. His face fell to one side and he cannot talk. Until he recovers, if he recovers, I have taken on the duties of the chief."

"I would like to speak with Long Spear."

"That is impossible, Brave Eagle. Sit." I did not like that. Why was the simple courtesy of a chief speaking with the high chief denied?

The three of us obeyed.

"As you can see my warriors prepare for war. News has come from the outlying villages that the Moneton tribe was not just satisfied with destroying Fears Water's village. They have attacked others. I intend to make war on them."

Brave Eagle and I said nothing but we feared the worst.

"As my warriors are now preparing for war your village, which is close to us, must provide us with our fish and meat. Your warriors will hunt for our tribe and when we go to war, they will fight alongside us."

Brave Eagle shook his head, "That we cannot do. We have barely enough to feed our clan."

"Then you will go hungry. I have made my decision and you will feed the tribe."

"And if we refuse?"

For the first time he smiled, "Then my warriors would not have to practise war, they could make war on your clan and we would win for we outnumber you by ten warriors to one."

"This is not your father's way."

"And as my father has been struck down, perhaps the spirits think it is time for a change." I knew that there was more to come. Fears Water and I had been invited too. If this was just a demand for food then Eagle Claws would have just sent for Brave Eagle. "You, Shaman of the Bear, have a magic boat. You will take three of my warriors and Fears Water. I would have you return to Fears Water's village. My warriors will scout out the enemy and find their numbers. You will take them and bring them back."

I knew that Fears Water would be terrified of such a trip and I was far from happy. It would be a long voyage and for what? Just so that Eagle Claws could make war. This was even worse than the rule of Sweyn Forkbeard. That had led us to flee west. Was it now time for me to move west again?

Brave Eagle said, "That is not right, Eagle Claws. Are you punishing our clan?"

He gave a thin smile, "Let us just say that from now on there will be more order to the tribe and my wishes will be obeyed."

"And the council?"

"Will do as I say." He gestured to three warriors who were standing behind him. "Snake's Bite will go with you and his brothers. You, Shaman of the Bear, will obey his every command."

I looked at the three brothers. They were powerfully built warriors and they had shaved their heads to give themselves a crest that they had stiffened and painted. They had feathers hanging from it. It looked as though they had deliberately scarred their own faces and bodies. Unlike the other warriors, we saw these were bare-chested and they were festooned with weapons. I had seen many Skraelings who adopted the same pose. All had been the warriors who were the toughest and all had a reckless view of life. They hurled themselves into battle without any fear whatsoever. I had heard of such warriors amongst the Danes and if these three were anything like the Danes, then there was a strong chance we would not return from our voyage.

Snake's Bite gestured to us, "Come, we will spend the night in your village." The imperious tone of the shaven-headed warrior left us in no doubt that we had to obey. Their presence also meant that we could not speak on the way back. I knew Brave Eagle well enough to know that he seethed with anger. I would not put it past him to refuse the request and risk a war. It would be a mistake. I was more pragmatic. I knew that we could catch more fish. Eagle Claws might expect meat but he had not specified quantities and I knew we could feed the tribe and the clan. The problem would be the wear and tear on the snekke. The more immediate problem was the voyage to Fears Water's camp.

When we reached our village, it was dark and people were eating. Cupping his hands Brave Eagle summoned the clan to gather. It was an unusual request and, seeing the three large shaven-headed warriors, I saw his sons and some others take their weapons. I waved Fears Water to our yehakin.

"I have news that you all need to hear."

Snake's Bite snapped, "You have no time for this."

Brave Eagle lived up to his name and he faced them, "This is still my clan and I am still chief. You are here as guests, unwanted guests but guests nonetheless. If you wish to start a war then draw your weapons."

The warriors who had weapons now aimed them at the three warriors. I had my seax and hatchet close to hand but the three warriors backed down. "Speak but when we return to Eagle Claws, we will tell him what you did."

"Good." The warriors lowered their weapons but did not drop them. "Chief Long Spear is ill and his son, Eagle Claws, has taken on the mantle of the chief. He takes the tribe to war against the Moneton and also demands that we give his village half of the food that we produce." There was an outburst of angry voices and Brave Eagle held his arms up to calm the voices. "If we do not agree then he will make war on us." Brave Eagle stared at the three shaven-headed warriors who were looking increasingly uncomfortable. "Although it is likely we would lose I believe that Eagle Claws would lose far more men than we. He did not come to rescue our captives." That had been a bone of contention when we had returned. The ones sent by Long Spear had all been very inexperienced men. Eagle Claws and his brothers had stayed at home. "There is more. He has commanded the Shaman of the Bear and Fears Water to take these…" he did not add any more and the insult was clear, "to Fears Water's old camp."

There was an even greater outburst of noise. Hides Alone raised his good arm and said, "No. Let us kill these three and fight this Eagle Claws."

The three shaven-headed warriors looked nervous and fingered their weapons. Had they touched them then they would have been slain. I wondered how events would have turned out had that happened. I held up my hand and such was my reputation that silence fell. "Hear my words. Like you, I do not like this thing but I do not wish my sons to be slaughtered because a warrior has ambition. He is not worth it." Three pairs of angry eyes noted the insult. I was already planning how we might defeat Eagle Claws but first, we needed to feign obeisance. "Fears Water and I will take these three," I paused for effect. Having insulted them once I felt emboldened to do it again, "pretty boys, where they want to go and I will catch the fish that I hope will choke them."

The whole village laughed and Snake's Bite hissed, "You go too far."

I laughed, "I have sailed from one world to this one so do not tell me about travel. I have seen more of the world than you can dream." I patted my hatchet. "Believe me this weapon is not even my best one so while you are with me mind your manners. You can only get to this village if I take you. Remember that." I knew I had made a serious enemy and once we returned, he would happily crush my skull with his stone club.

Brave Eagle said, "Are you sure?"

"I know what I am doing. The sisters have spun."

Brave Eagle nodded, "Then the tribe will see you off. Let us eat."

I headed for my family. Snake's Bite said, somewhat lamely, "What of us? What do we eat and where do we sleep?"

It was Brave Eagle's turn for a cruel smile, "There is a forest and a river full of food. Find it. As for sleep? Sleep if you must but I would sleep with one eye open. I will not soil my seax with your blood but there are others…" He left his words hanging.

Had I been the three then a return to Eagle Claws would have been my chosen course of action but these three, as I came to discover, were keen to impress the new chief. They sat close to the fire with weapons in their hands. I do not think that they enjoyed a full night of sleep.

"You cannot go." Laughing Deer was terrified. I could see it on her face and in her words. "Fears Water is fearful to return and I would not lose you."

I nodded for I saw the fear on Fears Water's face "Fears Water, trust me, we have to do this but I believe we can return but if we do not then Eagle Claws cannot make war."

Erik's Clan

"I trust you but Laughing Deer is right, I am frightened and if that makes me less of a man then so be it. I would marry and have a family and not have my head stuck on a Moneton spear."

I nodded, "Moos Blood, until I return then you will be the man. Continue to fish but take no risks. You must all practise war for no matter what happens to me war is coming and it cannot be avoided."

That night as we lay together Laughing Deer wept salt tears and bemoaned our fate. I kissed her, "We are in the hands of the Norns, my love, and I do not believe that I am destined to die just yet but this is a more parlous predicament than any we have faced. Perhaps we should have stayed with Wandering Moos but then again that might have brought the Penobscot. No, my sweet, we live as best we can and do all to survive. I have plans." I tapped my head in the dark, "They are here in my mind. The three warriors who come with us are mindless killers and I have outwitted their kind before. It will be hard for you but this is a test for our family. Can you survive and prosper? I believe you can."

Chapter 5

I was up before dawn and woke Fears Water and my sons. I needed to speak to them before Eagle Claws warriors joined us. The three were still huddled close to the fire. They had to have fed it during the night for it still flamed. One was awake but his back was to us and we slipped to the snekke. The boats were moored far enough from the camp to enable us to speak if we did so quietly. We spoke as we loaded the boat with the supplies we would need.

"Fears Water, I do not want you in any danger on this trip but I know that is a vain hope. I want you to watch out for yourself. If the opportunity arises, I intend to abandon the three warriors and head back here."

Moos Blood voiced his opinion, "Is that not dangerous, father? It might bring the wrath of Eagle Claws upon us."

"Perhaps but that will be my decision. I am leaving my sword, helmet and hatchet here."

"Why?"

I looked at Brave Cub and smiled. Just touching the sword brought a smile to his face. "The three warriors may choose to take them from me and I will not give them that opportunity. I will take my bow, my new flint hatchet and I will secrete my seax in my boot." We had almost finished loading the snekke and I turned to face my three sons. "War is coming in one shape or form and I need you three to hone your skills. Even you, Golden Bear, can practise with your sling. Gather river stones to throw. You older boys should use your bows every day. You need your arms to burn before you stop. Make arrows for we will need plenty and fish every day." I nodded to Golden Bear. "You need to take your brother with you. The whole family must work together."

Moos Blood stood a little taller, "I promise that although I am just a shadow of you, father, I shall be a shadow that will do you proud."

"I know. One more thing, Fears Water, you can speak some of our language for I have used it to teach you to sail. I will continue to use it as we head upstream and we will use my language to hide our words and intent from our three passengers."

He beamed, "I will be steering?"

"You are one of the family now, of course you shall and one day, when we have three snekke, who knows?" The look on his face was one of pure joy. Speaking Norse might be the one thing we could use to our advantage.

Erik's Clan

We managed to sneak back into camp without being observed and we made it look as though we had just emerged from our yehakin. We lit a fire to cook breakfast. Seeing us the shaven-headed sentry roused the others who came over to us. Snake's Bite nodded, "It is good that you rise early. I would leave this village as soon as I can. When we return, I will have much to tell Chief Eagle Claws." His tone left us in no doubt that he would attempt to bring the wrath of the new war chief down on us.

My sons and Fears Water heard the threat in the words. The insults the three men had suffered would, if they survived the journey, come back to haunt us.

Laughing Deer and Little White Dove came to help us prepare the food and soon the whole village was awake. Brave Eagle and his sons and grandson, Black Feather, came over to speak to us. "You are all ready, Erik?"

"I am and I have left instructions for my sons. Speak with Moos Blood when we have gone. He will let you know all." Moos Blood had heard Snake's Bite's words and he would let our chief know of the danger.

We were rushed, unceremoniously, to the snekke as soon as the three warriors had eaten. If they thought they were in charge then they were in for a rude shock. As they neared the boat I said, "You will sit where I say and you will not move around. Fears Water and I can sail this snekke and you cannot."

Snake's Bite said, in a surly manner, "I command."

Shaking my head I said, "On *'Gytha'* I command. Once we land you may give your orders but until then you heed my commands. If I tell you to move then you do. Your Eagle Claws wishes to use my magic boat to get you far upriver. If you wish you can take birchbark boats and paddle. Then you will command. You do not know how to sail this snekke." I almost spat the unfamiliar word at him. "It is not a birchbark boat and I will not have some clumsy oaf like you capsize the boat and cost us our lives. Eagle Claws wants us to get to this village alive and then to return."

His eyes narrowed and he nodded, "Until we reach our destination then you command but I will not forget these insults."

I smiled, "Good, then they are not wasted." I took my hide bag and placed in it treasures that we might need. I had my flint, spare arrowheads, as well as dried food and my bjorr skin hat. I also had a small pot of salve and one of honey as well as hide strips. If we had damage to the steering board, I needed to be able to repair it. Attached to my bag was my ale skin. The bag and the skin would stay around my body until we returned home.

After I had placed them exactly where I wished them to sit, in a line from the mast to the prow, we set off and the clan cheered. Laughing Deer was tearful and I knew that she thought she might never see me again. I had not been visited by the spirit of Gytha for some time and I determined that when we returned, if we returned, from this quest, then I would visit the steam hut, smoke the pipe and dream. I needed her advice.

As we headed north, I asked, "Fears Water, do you know how to get to your home?" I spoke in the Powhatan language for I wanted our passengers to hear my words.

He shook his head, "I ran away from the enemy though I was wounded and I headed for this river. I decided to hide close to the water and hope that they missed me but they were close and when I hid behind the log it moved and I was so scared I clung on for dear life until you found me. When we are close to the place I entered the river then I might recognise it but I cannot promise."

I nodded. It was as I had thought, "Then we will sail north until we find somewhere that you recognise." I raised my voice, "I do not think this will be as easy as Eagle Claws expects."

I saw the three warriors look at each other. Their confidence was already oozing away.

The first twenty or so miles were familiar to me. I had often sailed upstream. After twelve miles we had to turn to larboard and sail due east. I smiled when we put the steering board over and the snekke lurched alarmingly. The three warriors gripped the gunwale for fear of their lives. When, ten miles later, I turned to steerboard and headed north once more they were gripped with fear. Had I had any consideration for them I might have given them a warning but I enjoyed their reaction. Our progress north was far faster than it would have been in a birchbark boat but we were sailing against the current and the winds were not always in our favour. Even so, we managed to make, by my estimate, forty miles, before I decided to land. I saw a suitable landing site on the northern bank of the river. There were some steep bluffs and they would afford some protection from both the weather and, should there be hostile warriors, from them too.

Fears Water and I had conversed in my language all the way north. He knew most of the nautical terms but he was still learning the other words. I told him to leap over and drag us ashore when we were close. I would have asked our passengers but I did not want them to learn skills that would help them to sail the snekke. I wanted them to feel helpless and totally dependent upon Fears Water and myself. I still worried that they might try to get rid of us once we had got them where they needed to be. I took great pleasure in their unsteady steps as they tried to get ashore. They were each like a baby taking his first steps and they did not like it. We lowered and secured the sail. While I dropped an anchor over the steering board, Fears Water tied us fore and aft to two trees. We two had our own food and drink. The three warriors had also taken food from the camp but ours was better. None of us even suggested a fire, despite the biting insects. Fears Water and I ate and then climbed aboard the snekke to sleep.

"Why do you sleep there and not on the shore with us? Do you mean to leave us here?"

I laughed, "Snake's Bite we are close enough to Eagle Claws' village for you to reach it in two or three days of walking. I have said I will take you to Fears Water's village and I am a man of my word. We sleep in the snekke so that I can feel any danger from the river. If there is then I can rouse you and we will save the snekke. This is our lifeline now."

Perhaps my words had the right degree of sincerity for he nodded. Fears Water and I had a more comfortable night. The gentle rocking motion of the river sent us to sleep and the seal skin capes ensured that we were kept insect free. We were awake first. Had I wished we could have slit their throats and abandoned their bodies to the river but I had given my word and I kept it. A man cannot change his nature no matter how much he wishes to.

All of us were alert as we headed up the river. This was totally unknown territory for all of us as we were not yet close to the land that Fears Water might recognise. We even spied birchbark boats on the river but the warriors in them were Powhatan and while they were wary of us, they must have feared our snekke. The sail, the length and the prow made her look like some fantastical water beast. The speed with which she almost flew across the water also appeared nothing short of miraculous. Word would spread that we were heading north. If the Moneton heard the rumours then there might be armed warriors to greet us. I found myself clutching my hammer of Thor and invoking the protection of the Allfather.

The change in the wind meant that we made slower progress and by the end of the day Fears Water had still to see a familiar landmark. When we did stop it was because there was an island in the middle of the river and it would be a safe place to land. This time our passengers managed to step ashore without looking like a deer taking its first steps.

As we ate, I said, "Does nothing seem familiar?"

"I remember that the river ran north to south and the river called the Shenandoah joined this mightier one. When we see where the rivers meet that will be close to my home."

I shook my head, "We will have to land before we reach that point. Such river junctions are difficult to navigate. There are currents and eddies that can swamp even this boat."

It was the next day that, while the three shaven-headed warriors scanned the two shorelines for danger, Fears Water said, "Up ahead I see the place I joined the water. I remember that stand of trees."

"Then we will camp there and you can say that this might be the place but you are not certain."

He asked, "Why do we not tell them the truth?"

"Because if you are certain then we are no longer useful to them. I have watched the three of them. Often, they have watched us working the boat, especially when we change direction. They are learning how to sail the snekke and that means that we may no longer be needed. Keep your weapons to hand from now on. I suspect that Eagle Claws wishes this snekke and my death as much, if not more, than the knowledge about the Moneton."

We landed on the west bank of the river beneath the bluffs. One more I forbade a fire and it was good that I did for when the wind changed direction, in the middle of the night, then we smelled woodsmoke. It might have meant nothing but as Fears Water thought that we were somewhere close to his village then I believed we had found what Eagle Claws wished us to find. I did not tell the three warriors until morning. I was interested in what they would do.

Fears Water and I were up first, before dawn, and I roused the three warriors. "Fears Water thinks that his village might be close to us."

Snake's Bite's eyes narrowed and he glared at a terrified Fears Water, "Then why did he not say so last night?"

Fears Water was patently too terrified to speak and I answered for him, "It was dark when we arrived and now that he can see the other bank and smell the land then it is familiar to him. Over there, Fears Water?" I pointed.

He found his voice, "Some way over there, aye."

"Then let us all go." There was a triumphant note to Snake's Bite's voice.

"All of us?"

He grinned evilly at me, "You especially, Shaman of the Bear. I have watched you and I do not like these conversations between you and Fears Water. I do not trust you. I will keep you in sight until we return to the snekke."

Erik's Clan

"Leave one of your brothers here with me. If we have to flee then it will be useful if the snekke is ready to leave. There may be pursuit."

I saw him debating and then he smiled, "Turn the boat around now and then, if we are followed you can launch it quickly. I want you within touching distance of my war spear. If there is treachery then you will be the first to die."

I turned the snekke around. Snake's Bite pointedly kept his spear at Fears Water's throat to prevent me from leaving. Once I had secured the boat Snake's Bite jabbed his spear in Fears Water's back, "You lead."

He and one brother followed Fears Water who seemed to have found the path up the bluff. The third brother walked next to me. I casually chose an arrow and held it next to the strung bow. I would bide my time but it was now clear to me that Fears Water and I were expendable. Indeed, it came to me that Eagle Claws might have decided that I was too much of a threat to the tribe and he wished me eliminated. I would have to use all my guile and cunning if I was to escape a grisly end. Equally important was the life of Fears Water. He did not deserve to be murdered. Almost a man, he had a family life planned out.

We had travelled about a mile along a twisting and well used path through the trees when I smelled smoke again. Would the knowledge that the camp was occupied make Snake's Bite cautious? He could, at that point, have left Fears Water and me and taken one of his brothers to scout out the camp. From what I had been told Eagle Claws wished to know if the village was still Powhatan or Moneton. I knew it was the latter but, for some reason, Eagle Claws wanted confirmation.

Fears Water was clearly terrified but that terror made him cautious and he was not moving quickly enough for Snake's Bite. When we heard the sound of voices then Snake's Bite and his brother strode ahead. I nocked my arrow for I erred on the side of caution. There were Moneton sentries and they were in the trees. Snake's Bite's brother suddenly sprouted an arrow. The brother next to me raced ahead to Snake's Bite as a cry went up from the trees.

"Fears Water, back to the snekke!"

I drew the bow back as warriors emerged from the trees and the village to race at the three brothers. To be fair to them they were resolute and even though one was wounded they faced their enemies and fought like stags at bay. I was grateful that they were buying us the time we needed. "Fears Water, get back to the snekke, untie her and prepare to lower the sail. I will delay pursuit."

He nodded and ran. The wounded brother fell as his skull was split by a stone club. The other two fought hard and died equally hard. Still watching but moving quickly I backed down the trail. When I heard a second death scream, I turned and ran. The third scream was followed by a roar of joy from the warriors. The voice that shouted out a command was almost like our death knell for I knew that they were following. By the time I reached the top of the bluff, I saw that Fears Water had reached the snekke. He had untied the fore rope and had the sail half hoisted but it was stuck. I turned and faced down the path. He needed the time to sort the problem and I had to buy him that time. One Moneton warrior, more eager than the rest was just thirty paces from me. I sent a flint tipped arrow into his chest and he tumbled to the ground. I nocked another. Fears Water needed more time and the sight of me hurtling down the path pursued by enemies might make him panic. He needed to be calm to free the sail. I sent a second arrow and a third at the next warriors and then I ran for the rest of the warriors, enraged to have been ambushed by me came down the path with death on their minds.

What I could not have known, although I suspect that had he not been terrified Fears Water might have remembered was that there was another path to the river and four young warriors appeared ahead of me. I knew that they would be between me and *'Gytha'*. Fears Water had the sail sorted and so I shouted, "Let the sail fly and sail home. The river will take you."

"I cannot leave you."

I was distracted or else I might have seen the arrow loosed at me. Before I could answer a stone-tipped arrow slammed into my right knee. "Fly!"

My command worked and he loosed the last rope. Despite the pain, I nocked another arrow and sent it toward the young warriors. I hit one in the chest and they slowed. They were coming at me from two sides and there was only one way out, the river. Slipping my bow over my shoulder I ran as fast as my damaged knee would carry me to the river. Without pause, I threw myself in. Luckily I was a good swimmer. Indeed I had almost died when the Penobscot had killed my brother and cousins but the water and Laughing Deer had saved me. I dived down and under the water. The current helped me and I held my breath as long as I could. The icy waters seemed to numb the pain in my knee. With my two arms like an arrowhead, I eventually rose. Turning on my back I saw the Moneton warriors searching the water but they were looking one hundred paces upstream from where I was. Taking another deep breath I dived beneath the water again. Five such breaths later and I was clear of danger. I turned on my back and I could not see them. As I turned to look south, I saw that I could not see the snekke either.

Had Moos Blood been at the helm of *'Gytha'* then he might have halted the snekke to wait for me. Fears Water could steer but that was about it. There would be no way he could slow the boat down. The best that I could hope was that he would manage to reach our home without wrecking the snekke. I would have to leave the river and make my own way home. I trod water, with my one functioning leg and my arms as I looked to see where I was. As much as I did not want to do so I would have to risk the Moneton shore. Firstly, I was not sure I could swim across the river for it was wide but secondly, I knew that our home was also on the Moneton side. I would have to risk a landing. The cold had numbed my injured knee and once I left the water I would be in for a world of pain. I stayed in the water but I just let the current take me and sculled with my arms, much as I might have done with the oars on the snekke. I was looking for a beach. I did not want to risk rocks for if my left knee or leg was hurt as well as my right then I would be in real trouble. I guess I had been in the water some hours and was feeling sleepy, a bad sign when I saw the small beach beneath the overhanging trees. I did not stand when I reached the sand but crawled until I was hidden from view and under the trees.

I turned to place my back against the bole of a large tree. Just turning brought paroxysms of pain to my knee and leg. I looked down and saw that the stone arrow had cut through to the bone. Now that I was out of the cold river the blood began to flow. I had intended to drink from my ale skin but I had to stem the bleeding. I took out one of the hide strips and tied it above my knee. When I tightened it, the pain was such that I thought I would pass out but I managed to both tie it and remain awake. I found myself shaking and I could not explain it. The river had been colder than the air around me; why was I shaking now? I had no seal skin cape to cover me and I would have to improvise. I drank some ale and then took out the jar of honey. I smeared a little on the wound. It would seal it and then not wishing to waste any I licked my fingers. My shaking began to diminish. Finally, I smeared some salve on the wound.

That done I took out some dried deer meat and began to chew a piece slowly. I had to make the food I had last a long time and I knew that my stomach needed food. As I ate, I began to plan. I was in trouble, I knew that and the last time I had been in such a predicament, Laughing Deer had been close by. Now I was more than a hundred miles from safety and with just one good leg. I would have to try to cross one hundred miles of unfamiliar territory pursued by a Moneton warband. I suddenly remembered my bow and I took it from my back. I unstrung it. I would need my bow sooner rather than later. I had two spare strings in my bag but I did not know how long I would be in this wild wilderness. I had found a good hideout. Looking at the beach I saw that the only tracks, except my own, were those of small white-tailed deer that had come to the river to drink. For the time being, I was safe. The Moneton would use their boats to search the river for me and I would be hidden when they passed this point. I needed to hide but I was loath to move too far from this beach until I had a better plan. I compromised. I found a piece of driftwood and I cleared my tracks. Then, using the wood to help me, I moved behind the tree. Its bole was enough to hide me and yet I was still close to the river. The river had saved me and I did not want to move too far from it, yet.

    I forced myself to look at my wound. The river had helped to clean it but something had been damaged. Would I be able to use it? I was frightened. I had endured much since I had left my home in the east but this seemed to me the most terrifying for hitherto I had been mobile. The Moneton warriors were hunting me and I had killed some of their warriors. They would wish vengeance. In the end, it was not my decision for I fell asleep. Perhaps that was the work of the spirits. Was Gytha still watching over me? I knew not but when I woke it was dark. What had woken me was not danger, but pain. My knee hurt so much that I feared I might cry out without meaning to. I loosened the hide above my knee and as the blood flowed the pain came again. I forced myself to look at the wound. The honey and salve were doing their job and little blood could be seen. I took out the jar of precious honey and smeared the tiniest portion where I saw the blood. Once again, I wasted none and licked my fingers. I drank some more ale and realised that I needed to make water. I used the tree and the driftwood crutch I had found to haul myself to my foot. I let my right leg hang. Once more I felt pain from it and I had not even risked grounding it. I made water to the side and then lowered myself to my bed. The canopy of leaves would have to be my blanket and I prayed to the Allfather and to the spirit of Gytha to watch over me. Had an animal come in the night then I was helpless. I slept.

An instantly recognisable figure came toward me. It was Gytha. Her face was indistinct but her hair and hands were unmistakable. It was as though she was wreathed in smoke. When she spoke it was as though the words were in my head. They were comforting for they seemed to sing to me and were both gentle and reassuring. "Erik, you are not meant to die here. Your days of exploring are not yet done. The river is dangerous. Leave it and head for the high ground. I cannot heal your leg and you must do so. Nature will help you if you use your eyes to see.

You need to walk. I will visit Moos Blood and hope that he heeds my words. Erik, we will watch over you but your survival depends upon you." The voice drifted off and then all was blackness.

Chapter 6

When I woke it was still dark and, as the last time, it was my knee that woke me. I just wanted to cry out and relieve the pain but that would have meant death. Gytha's words had been both a comfort and a shock. I had to navigate through forest and hills whilst avoiding trails and with a leg I could not use. Gytha had ever been my friend and guide and I would trust to her spirit. I ate and I drank. They helped me to think. Looking around I saw a piece of driftwood washed up amongst the trees. It was straight and the length of my right leg. I took it and forced myself to slide up the bole of the tree. Although I did it carefully each time my knee was touched it was as though someone had poked a red-hot sliver of wood into the wound. I placed the wood next to my leg and braced myself for the pain when the wood touched. The pain came but I was prepared. I tied four of the hide strips around the leg and risked standing on it. I could not and almost passed out with the pain. I reached down and picked up the piece of driftwood I had first used to mask my tracks. The curve on it fitted under my arm and I tested it. It held. I moved just two paces and found that I could let my right leg hang. Even so, I was sweating with the exertion.

It was at that moment that I heard the sound of paddles in the water. I turned and saw, through the overhanging branches, birchbark boats filled with warriors. The Moneton warriors were still seeking me. Gytha had been right, the river was not safe. I waited until they had passed and then picked up my bow. I donned my bjorr skin hat and looked for the trail. I found it. It was not a human-made trail but one made by the deer coming to drink at the river. I had the river as a guide and I followed the trail that led, as far as I could tell south and east. Those first five or six steps were the hardest I had ever taken. I learned from my mistakes. I learned to plant the driftwood in the ground, move my good leg and then swing, with a slightly bent knee, my right leg. I learned to look at the ground for even a pebble in the wrong place might be a disaster. I had no way to measure time for the canopy of trees that hid me from sight, also hid the sun. I counted steps. After a thousand steps, I was so exhausted that I had to stop. I might want to hurry but my body would not allow it. I remembered Gytha's words. I would let my body be my master.

By the time the sun began to set I had walked a thousand paces eight times. When I found the small beck that I knew must run to the Patawomke I stopped. I needed rest. I had seen no signs of animals or people. I suspect that I was making enough noise to scare off any animals. As I looked at my diminishing supply of food then I knew I had to forage for some. It was as I cupped my hand to drink from the stream that I saw hope. In the water were small creatures. At home, they lived in the sea in the rocks around Orkneyjar and we called them crays. These were black and looked to be of a similar size to their seawater cousins. They moved when my hand cupped the water but when I had drunk, they returned. I plunged my hand in and grabbed one. It had claws and tried to nip me but I bit off the body and it stopped. I was about to discard the rest when I realised it was all food. I put the claws and head to one side and fished another four before the crays decided to find another place to hunt. By the time I had used my seax to open the claws and suck out the meat from them and their heads I felt a little more satisfied. I drank a mouthful of ale and resisted the temptation to delve further into my diminishing supply of dried meat. I had been lucky finding the crays and I knew not if I would find more.

Once again, I had a restless and disturbed night. Gytha did not return but that was, perhaps, because my sleep was so disturbed and was a shallow pain-filled sleep. It rested my body and that was about all. I woke in the dark. Over the previous day and overnight my already swollen knee had doubled in size. It felt warm, almost hot to the touch. I was neither volva nor galdramenn but it seemed to me that I needed to release the pressure. I took my seax and risked a cut. I almost passed out when the tip entered the flesh at the side of the wound but the yellow and green pus that oozed out, mixed with the blood told me that I had done the right thing. I did not use the honey but this time took out the jar of salve. It was then, as I began to withdraw the stopper that Gytha's words came back to me, *'Nature will help you if you use your eyes to see.'* There, before me, on the north side of a tree was some moss. The Mi'kmaq had used the moss which they believed had healing properties. I scraped the moss off with my seax and packed it around the new wound. That done I lay back against the tree and completed my sleep. This time exhaustion took over and I slept.

When I awoke the sun was rising and that told me which way was east. I put my hand to the new wound and the wound was merely warm and not hot. The swelling was not as bad as it had been. I went to the stream and managed to find another two crays. I ate them and, with something inside me, headed off down the trail. The rising sun and the direction of the beck, which I crossed, gave me my direction.

That second day was a trial for the trail rose. I had seen, from the river a ridge of hills that looked to be almost blue to the west of the Patawomke and I guessed I was climbing it. I did not want to but the alternative was the river and the Moneton were there. I had to trust in Gytha. Surprisingly, even though I was heading uphill I found that I was able to walk further. I gritted my teeth through the pain and managed ten one thousand steps by noon. Then I was forced to stop and eat. I ate sparingly, husbanding my food supply. I also had to drink some of my ale for there was no water nearby. However, as I sat back against a tree, resting my leg I spied, in the trees above me, squirrels. I had been so still that they had ignored me. I took my bow and, making small movements, strung it. It had never taken me as long to do so before. I still had eight arrows and they were all flint tipped. The feathers were damp but that could not be helped. I used the bole of the tree to slowly rise. The squirrels were too busy squabbling in the branches to notice and I manage to rise and nock an arrow. Loosing an arrow with my back against a tree was far from perfect but I had little choice. I was patient and waited until one was just thirty paces from me and I loosed. I was lucky for instead of pinning it to the tree, beyond my reach, the arrow knocked it to the ground. Its companions fled. It took some time to reach the dead animal for it was off the trail but when I retrieved it, I removed the arrow and put the dead animal in my bag. I would save it for the evening.

    Returning to the trail I continued on my way. I was becoming worried that I had not found any more water and my ale skin was half empty when the ground began to descend and the trail became a little wider. It was late afternoon when I found the spring that bubbled from the rocks and made a small pool. I knew that I would not be lucky enough to find crays but I had water and I drank deeply. As I looked around, I saw that just above me was a large rock. I wondered if the overhang might provide shelter. Thus far it had not rained but I knew it could. Using my crutch I hobbled up to it. I paused halfway there partly because I was exhausted but also because I found more moss. The first moss I had used, although it had worked, had fallen off while I walked. I took a handful and put it in my satchel.

    As I neared the rock there was a sudden flaring of light as the sun dipped in the west. I spied a cave. I was not foolish enough to hobble straight in for it might contain animals but I knocked the arrow I had used to kill the squirrel and headed towards it. I sniffed but did not detect an animal smell and I was not greeted by the angry growl of a bear who might not wish to share his home. I had to dip my head beneath the roof but, inside, I was able to stand. I had a sanctuary for the night and I smiled, "Thank you Gytha, for guiding me here."

    I laid down my bow, quiver, satchel and ale skin and went back outside to seek kindling. There was plenty, and after returning to the cave, I made a fire and used my flint to light it. I fed the fire until it blazed and illuminated the interior. I saw fur and knew that a bear had used it. I gathered the fur to keep and use to start my next fire. I went outside to find more wood and was gratified to see that the fire could not be seen from without. With enough firewood for the night, I took out the squirrel. I skinned it and laid the pelt to one side, I had plans for it. Jointing the carcass I stuck the pieces on sticks and by using rocks I found on the floor put the food to cook. I placed the squirrel skin close enough to the fire so that the inside would cure. Then I applied the moss to the wound. The swelling was going down and the knee did not feel as hot as it had.

It was as I turned the squirrel meat to cook it on all sides that I made another discovery. The rocks I had used to rest the meat upon were iron ore. The Norns had been spinning or perhaps Gytha had guided me here. Whatever the reason I now had iron and I could make arrowheads and weapons. The meal I enjoyed was even sweeter thanks to my discovery.

The squirrel was not a large one but I only ate half. I had rations for the next day. The squirrel pelt had dried and I used it, fur side down, to make a bandage for my knee. It would hold the moss in place. I took the opportunity to remove the splint, fashion the bandage and then refasten the wood to my leg. I made a better job of it than I had when I had been by the river. After feeding the fire I lay down and for the first time since the attack actually had a reasonable sleep. My knee woke me but as the fire had almost burned itself out, I worked out that I had slept for most of the night. I made water, fed the fire, for I found that the warmth helped the wound, and went back to sleep. For the first time since the attack, it was after dawn when I woke. I confess that I was tempted to stay in the cave but then realised that would be a mistake. I placed the pieces of iron ore into my bag. They were a treasure and I would have to endure the weight. After eating half of the remaining squirrel I reluctantly left my haven and headed down the slope. I knew that I was on the other side of the ridge and closer to my home.

If I thought that going downhill would be easier, I was wrong. It was easier going uphill than coming down and I made less progress that first downhill day than on the day before. The iron ore I had taken meant that my satchel was heavier. That too slowed my progress but it also made me look about me to see what I could forage.

The small herd of white-tailed deer that were grazing did not smell me but I smelled them. They were too tempting a target for me to ignore although I knew that I would need luck to hit one. I was not mobile and I could not stalk. I would have to lay down my crutch and either stand on one leg or risk falling by trying to use my bad leg. I made my decision. Still using my crutch I took off my satchel, bjorr skin hat, waterskin and quiver. I took a deep breath and just using the toes of my right leg for support I lowered my crutch to the ground. My knee screamed in pain but only I heard it and I gritted my teeth. I strung my bow and did so more carefully and slowly than I had ever done before. Still, the deer did not seem to notice me. Perhaps my movements had been so slow that they had not seen me. I took a deep breath. I knew that the leg would only support me for so long and I nocked my arrow. I sighted the small deer I would take. It looked to be an old female who, like me, had a bad leg. I drew back and it was as I did so that the stag raised his head. I released and the herd fled. It was lucky I chose the injured deer for she was slow to move but, even so, she staggered on for some steps before falling. I picked up my bags and hat and using my crutch headed towards her. She fell a few steps from where I hit her.

Kneeling was impossible and so after slinging my bow around my back I used my left hand to lift the carcass and drop it in the cleft of two branches of the nearest tree. It was an effort to do so but the relief when I managed it made me smile. I put the crutch down and used my left arm to support my body as I slit open the animal's belly with my seax. The guts tumbled out. I reached down to take the heart. I bit into it. It was still warm. I forced myself to eat it for I knew that I needed it. That done I left the carcass to hang for a while I went to the nearby stream to wash away the blood from my hands and drink. I did not want flies following me. I was too exposed here to risk a fire and so I slung the deer across my shoulders. I knew that the next miles I trekked would be the hardest for I had the weight of the animal on my shoulders.

The animal trail led me, by late afternoon, to a dell by what I assumed was the same stream where I had washed. What I had seen no evidence of was humans. There were neither footprints nor faeces. I did not know how far I was from Moneton land but I knew that I was close to Powhatan ground. I decided to risk a fire but I made sure that I lit it where it was sheltered by rocks and bushes. I was not a fool and knew that the smell would carry but I needed the food. The squirrel meat was all gone and I had just my emergency dried meat left. While the fire grew, I skinned the deer. It was not the neatest of jobs. I then butchered the animal. I placed the fillet on a rock closest to the fire. The other joints I hung from wood. I would eat the fillet and let the fire, overnight, cook and dry the rest. I would not need to hunt again. I reckoned that I must be a lot closer to my home. That might take me five or six days but the deer would, just about, last until then.

Erik's Clan

The fillet was delicious and I ate it when it was still slightly pink in the middle. I drank a mouthful of my ale as a celebration and then, after turning the meat, I left my camp. I had to empty my bowels as well as make water and I wanted to do so as far from my camp as I could. I had my strung bow with me for the last thing I needed was to be caught by a wild cat or whatever creatures hunted in this forest. It took me longer to empty my bowels than I had expected. By the time I had finished, I was worried that the deer meat would be burning. With an arrow nocked I headed back to the camp. I was thirty paces from it when I heard the voices. They were speaking a language I did not understand. As much as it pained me, I had to lower my crutch so that I could hold my bow in two hands. As I listened, I realised that there were two people and I guessed that they were warriors. I could not see them and so, even though I was wracked with pain, I stood.

The two Moneton warriors must have been kneeling, examining my tracks for they suddenly rose. I was lucky that I recognised them for what they were. I had one chance. I had to strike first. I was thirty paces from them and hidden by the dark. They were illuminated by my fire. I loosed an arrow and even as it struck one in the chest I had another nocked. The second warrior ducked and I drew back as he raced through the dark towards me. He was just two paces from me when he rose with a war axe in his hand. The flint tipped arrow smashed through his face and emerged from the back of his skull. I took my crutch and hurried to the fire. The first warrior I had hit had managed to crawl two paces before dying.

I put down my bow and dragged the body to join his companion. It took me longer than I might have wished. I forced myself to sit and drink something. My hands were shaking. They were no longer hunting me on the river but on the land. Gytha's advice had been good but now I needed to get to the river. I also needed sleep. I reasoned that these two were scouts. That meant a hunting party was nearby but when would the two men be missed? They had been drawn by my fire and so I doused the fire by the simple expedient of making water on it. The meat would have to do as it was. I lay down and tried to sleep. I dozed rather than slept but I rested and the rest, as all the other nights of rest had done, seemed to improve my leg.

I rose in the dark and put the meat in the skinned hide and made a bag from the skin to hang around my back. I took one of the legs to eat as I walked. I headed, not for the river but for the place I had emptied my bowels. Then I followed the natural slope until I came to a beck. What I did next was the riskiest thing I had done thus far. I walked along the beck following it down to what I hoped was the Patawomke.

Erik's Clan

It was risky as not only was the water icy cold but I could not see the bottom and any stone might prove to be disastrous. I hoped that I would lose my pursuers by doing so. By the time dawn had come the stream was wider and deeper. I had to leave it. I stepped out of it and felt the blood rush to my feet. It hurt my knee too. I had walked another two thousand paces when I heard, in the distance, a cry. It was too far away to make it out but I deduced that the hunting party had found the bodies. I had bought myself some time but eventually, they would work out that I had gone downstream. I forced myself through the pain as I hurried down the slope. I was no longer being careful and I stubbed my right foot on more than one occasion. It could not be helped but the pain almost made me weep.

It was when I heard the roar of water that my spirits rose. It was either a waterfall or the Patawomke. If it was the former then I might have somewhere to hide and the latter meant there was a chance I could emulate Brave Eagle and Fears Water and find a log to float me home. Each time my right foot touched something the pain went straight from my knee and raced up my body. I was learning the true meaning of agony but if I was to live then I had to endure it. Since I had used the squirrel skin bandage, I had not examined the wound. I hoped I was not causing irreparable damage. I did not turn when I heard the noise of pursuit. With an injured knee that would have spelt disaster. I had the hide bag about my back and if they loosed arrows or sent spears at me I would trust to that. I saw the water through the trees. I had, at least, made the river. Water had ever been my friend and when I spied it hope grew and I hurried on. I had to deviate around trees and bushes to reach the river and there was a patch of sand. To my horror, the sand was devoid of any driftwood. How would I get down the river? I made the beach and peered downstream. I was hoping that I would see a snekke seeking me but downstream the river was empty. I heard the Moneton and I turned,

If I was to die then I would take some of them with me. So long as I lived then there was hope. I strung my bow and nocked an arrow. I had but four left. I did not fully draw the bow but watched for the wild warriors to get closer. There were six of them in a line and as with the first time I had seen them it was the younger warriors who were closer. I pulled back and released at the warrior who was thirty paces from me. Even as he fell, I nocked a second and sent it at the warrior behind. It was hurriedly released and hit his arm and not his chest. My third arrow was more successful for the warrior was ten paces away and hurried or perhaps his chest was simply too big a target for me to miss. It knocked him back. Then I saw more warriors heading through the trees. I had one arrow left and the warrior was so close that although I drew the flint arrow, I could not nock it. I rammed it into his eye even as he speared my left shoulder. I dropped my bow and held my crutch before me. It was then I remembered my seax. I swung the driftwood crutch like a club as I knelt to pull the blade from my boot. I felt the blood dripping down my shoulder. My swing did not deter the warrior who raised his stone war club to smash down on my head. I had to put my weight on my right knee to try to block the blow and I failed. I sank to the ground and the pain was excruciating. The fall, however, saved me for the stone club missed my head and I lunged up with my seax, gutting him.

The next warriors were too many for me to fight. I used the crutch to rise, pain screaming in my knee and leg as I did so and backed towards the river. It was then I heard Moos Blood's voice. It was coming from upstream. I turned and saw the two snekke, crewed by my sons, Fears Water, Brave Eagle and White Fox. "Father, get in the water!"

Their arrival distracted the Moneton. After slipping my seax into my boot I hurried, as fast as my leg would allow me to the water. Once the water came to my waist, I threw myself into the river. The current grabbed me and although I tried to swim upstream to my sons the wound in my arm, allied to my weak leg and the current meant that it was a hopeless task. I went with the flow and turned on my back. It was a risk, I knew for there might be obstacles ahead that might cave in my skull but this way I would be able to see my sons.

It was Moos Blood in *'Doe'* who reached me. Brave Cub was steering and Brave Eagle was sending arrows towards the shore and the Moneton. My son was leaning as far out as he could get for Brave Cub did not wish to hit me with *'Doe's'* hull. I could not rely on my left arm and I grabbed for the arm. The effort made my head sink below the water but I felt Moos Blood's fingers grab my arm and I heard his voice, muffled by the river shout, "Brave Eagle, I need help, I am losing him." I felt myself sinking into the water. The weight of the satchel, still filled with rocks, deer hide and meat not to mention the boots that were now filled with water meant I was losing the battle to survive. The arms pulled me but suddenly my head cracked against the hull and all went black.

Erik's Clan

Chapter 7

In the blackness, I saw and heard Gytha. For the first time in a long time, I saw her face and behind her, I caught vague glimpses of my brother, father and cousin but they were indistinct. Her hand reached out to me. 'Erik, you are dying, come back. Now is not your time. Erik, there are new lands for you to see. Sail to the bend in the river. Erik. When you see it you will know. Seek the setting sun.'

Suddenly the blackness went and I looked up and saw Laughing Deer, "Erik, come back. We cannot lose you. Erik, come back."

I smiled and tried to speak. My voice came out cracked, "I am here."

I heard Little White Dove, her voice seemingly far away shout, "He lives! He lives!" And I heard a cheer from without the yehakin.

My wife shook her head, "You are lucky. Your knee was poisoned. Running Antelope has spent the last four nights tending to you. She said that the fever would break today or you would die."

I closed my eyes and nodded. I knew that it was more than luck. A combination of the Norns, the spirits and my stubborn refusal to die had been the reason. Gytha's last words came to me. *'Sail to the bend in the river.'* Which river? The Shenandoah or the Patawomke. The setting sun suggested the former.

"I am hungry."

"And that is no surprise, I will fetch some soup. Little White Dove, Moos Blood, sit with your father."

My children came and sat on either side of me. They each took a hand. I saw that Little White Dove was weeping. "All is well, Little White Dove, and I live."

"But you almost died. Had not Running Antelope used all her magic then you would have done. We cannot lose you, father. You must take more care." Her head dropped to my chest and she sobbed. I let her for I knew that it was necessary.

"Moos Blood, what happened?"

"When Fears Water returned and told us what happened it was dark and too late to look for you. The next morning Hides Alone went to tell Eagle Claws of the fate of his warriors and we set sail to find you. Each day we sailed north to look for you on the banks of the river. It was slow work but we gradually worked our way, each day, further upstream. We were heading back south to return home when we saw you. The Moneton were not expecting us."

"You did not see their birchbark boats?" He shook his head. "I spied them not long after I was pursued and I left the river." I smiled, "I found iron stones."

He did not seem impressed by that and continued, "Father, what is to be done? Eagle Claws has said that he wishes to make war on the Moneton. Brave Eagle spoke to us when we were on the snekke. He has an impossible decision to make. He either makes war on the Moneton or on our people."

"I know. He has to fight with Eagle Claws as will we but once that war is over then we will leave this land. We will sail beyond the land of the Moneton up the river Fears Water calls the Shenandoah and we will find a home of our own. Gytha has spoken."

Little White Dove had ceased crying and said, "But you will take months to heal. Running Antelope said so."

I nodded, "And soon it will be winter. Even here, in this land, warriors do not fight in winter. The war will come with the new grass and I will be ready."

"You cannot fight, father!"

"Little White Dove, I do not fight for Eagle Claws but this clan and my family. I am a tough old bird and as the Moneton discovered, hard to kill. While I breathe, I will defend my family."

Just then Laughing Deer and the rest of my family, along with Fears Water came in with the soup. My wife fed me and silence filled the yehakin. Sometimes silence can be oppressive but that was not the case. It was comforting. I felt the love from my whole family and I was touched by the fear that they had thought they had lost me. When I had eaten, I tried to sit up but my left arm was bandaged and I could not. Moos Blood and Brave Cub helped me.

"Family, I have spoken to Moos Blood and know that war is coming. We will fight not for Eagle Claws but for the clan and for us. When that is done, I will not live here where a chief like Eagle Claws makes decisions of which I do not approve. When I left the Moneton land I found a land that was without people. I found animal tracks but no sign of people. If we sail along the Shenandoah, we will look for such a place."

Brave Cub said, "And what of Brave Eagle?"

"I will speak with him. We have both been close to death and there are no secrets between us. I do not fear him but Eagle Claws is a different matter. However, that is a river we will cross when the time is right."

"And now your father needs sleep. Leave us." My wife's voice brooked no objection.

"Moos Blood, I would have a steam hut built. I need to speak with the spirits."

He smiled, "It will be done."

I slept a dreamless sleep but one that was interrupted by agony as my knee woke me. I tried not to disturb Laughing Deer but failed. She smiled and said, "Running Antelope said there would be pain." She rubbed a salve on the knee and the pain diminished. It did not disappear but became a warm ache. I endured it and went back to sleep.

Brave Eagle and Running Antelope came to see me the next day. Running Antelope examined my wounds and pronounced that she was satisfied. "Thank you, Running Antelope. I owe my life to you."

She rose and shook her head, "Erik, Shaman of the Bear, my family would have nothing had you not rescued us. If I were to save your life ten times then it would still not pay back what we owe you." She turned to Brave Eagle, "Keep this brief. He needs time to recover." She left. Like my wife Running Antelope's word was law.

"Your son has told me of your plans." I frowned. "Do not be angry with him. He is now a man and a warrior. You can be proud of him." I nodded for he was right. My son was of my blood and he had done and said that which I might have. "We will be sorry to see you leave but I know that you must. My wife is right. We owe all to you. I will put myself in your debt once more. Do you think we should fight the Moneton?"

I nodded, "You have no choice. Eagle Claws wants a war. If you did not then he would use the opportunity to make war on us and we would lose."

"You are right."

"The plan was for the three brothers to kill Fears Water and me. I do not think that Eagle Claws thought that the Moneton would still be where Fears Water said they would be. I think they thought they would find an empty camp and that would be where we would be slain. The Norns spun and they died. I cannot stay here for Eagle Claws fears both me and our boats. Long Spear also feared them but he was old and was happy to allow us to exist. Eagle Claws wishes power." I then told him of Sweyn Forkbeard and his ambitions. "The Powhatan are a powerful confederacy of clans. Long Spear was happy for them to exist in peace but I think Eagle Claws has the worm of ambition eating into his heart. When it gets there, it will completely change him. He will make war on all your neighbours."

"Then it is right that you will leave." Brave Eagle and I understood each other as only men who have fought together and been on the brink of death can do.

Erik's Clan

Little White Dove tended to my wounds every day and her attention helped me to heal. She chattered on about how Moos Blood and Fears Water were paying close attention to two young maids. She told me all the gossip in the clan and her words helped me to come back to the clan. I left the yehakin a week after Brave Eagle and I spoke. The warmth of the welcome from the rest of the clan was touching. My leg had healed but I still needed the support of a staff. Golden Bear and Brave Cub accompanied me for my eldest son and Fears Water were fishing. The days seeking me and my recovery meant that the clan was running out of food. I could not be idle and after I had spoken to, seemingly everyone in the village, I set my sons the task of making arrowhead moulds. I could have done it but I knew that I had to pass on the skills I had. The cave where I had found the iron stones had not only saved my life but given me something I thought I would never have again, iron. I knew that the stones had nearly drowned me but they would be necessary to our survival when we left this clan. While they carved the arrowheads, I made the mould for the seaxes I would make. The arrowheads would simply be cast and then cleaned and sharpened. A seax or a sword normally needed to be cast as an iron blank and then beaten, heated, beaten and reheated until it was tempered. I had no iron tools to do that and so I would cast the seaxes. They would never be as strong as those made by a weaponsmith but they would be better than anything else we encountered in this land. I calculated that I could make two seaxes and twenty heads from the iron stone. I knew that having found iron once when we left the clan and found a new home, I would seek more iron. Before the cave, I had not known that it existed in this new world. Now that I knew it did then all was well.

The next day I went with my sons to **'Gytha'**. "Father you are not yet ready to sail the snekke."

"No, Moos Blood, and I do not go to do so. I go to find treasure in the bottom of the snekke."

I had them intrigued but I did not enlighten them immediately. I had them lift the deck on the snekke and then I rummaged around in the ballast. I found what I was looking for and as my left arm was still bandaged, I had my sons retrieve the two large rocks. I had dreamed that they had been there for I vaguely remembered seeing them when we had left Bear Island.

"Rocks?"

"Yes, Brave Cub, but not just any rocks. These came from the land of Ice and Fire. There they were spewed forth from a mountain whose fire was hot enough to melt these rocks. If we are to melt the iron, we need a rock that can stand the heat. Carry them back to the yehakin and we will make an oven. Then we will make charcoal. We need hotter heat than normal."

It gave my sons and Fears Water a purpose and I was passing on skills. I had never made a seax before but I had seen swords made. The best weaponsmiths mixed a little charcoal with the iron when it was melted and I planned on doing the same. We still had the bellows we had made when I had made the trenails. It took many days for us to make the charcoal and carve the spout in the firestone. We then had to make a support for the firestone and fire of charcoal beneath. Brave Eagle and his sons came to watch what was to them, magic. I do not think that they believed we could melt stones. My sons had used stone clubs to break down the iron stone to make it easier to melt. I knew that there would be waste and slag, but I hoped that there would not be too much. I was sure that we would find a use for the slag. With my sons working the bellows we set to melt the iron. It aided us when we poured it, I had used my driftwood crutch to fashion a lever so that we could tip the precious iron out without spilling too much. When the stone began to melt and become liquid everyone but me clutched their amulets. I just smiled.

"Moos Blood, take the seax moulds and place them close to the fire."

He did so and I began to lever up the stone. The spout we had carved did its job and the molten metal flowed into the moulds. I returned the stone to the heat.

"Carefully move the wooden moulds out of the way and Brave Cub place the first of the arrow moulds where Moos Blood put the seaxes."

I smiled as he chose one of the moulds he had made. By the time we had filled his and Golden Bear's, there was still some molten metal left. Unwilling to waste it I had Golden Bear fetch the moulds we had used for the trenails. I poured the last of the molten metal into them.

The metal began to cool and Brave Eagle put his hand out to touch the metal. "Do not do that, my friend, you could lose a finger. It will take time to cool."

He nodded, "Come, we should speak."

Leaving my sons and Fears Water to guard the precious treasure I went with Brave Eagle towards the river. I still used a staff but I did not really need it. The knee would support my weight but with my shoulder still bandaged, the staff gave me more confidence.

We sat on the bank and watched the two snekke bob up and down with the current. "The Moneton did not take kindly to our attack." He smiled, "You killed too many of their warriors and they remembered the snekke. They have begun to not only attack but also to destroy the

Powhatan villages that lie to the north of us close to the river. Survivors have been flooding into Eagle Claws' village."

"Eagle Claw's village?"

He nodded, "Long Spear died after we rescued you. Eagle Claws is now the chief. He has ordered warriors from the rest of the tribe to gather when the new grass has come." I did a mental calculation and worked out that would be in a month's time. By then I should have healed sufficiently for me to use a weapon.

"And he has a plan?"

"He seems to be willing to lose the land to the north for the villages there are small and he is counting on defeating them here."

It came to me as clearly as a picture drawn in the sand, "You mean our village?" He nodded. "We are bait."

"The Moneton must know that your snekke need to be close to the water and it is your boats they wish to destroy."

I could not risk the snekke. "Then we must find somewhere to the south of us where we can hide them and you, Brave Eagle, must do as we did when we fought the Penobscot at the camp of Wandering Moos. You must make the village like a fortress."

"You are right. Eagle Claws will see this as an opportunity to rid himself of two thorns at once, the Moneton and us. He will let the weight of the Moneton fall on us and bring his warriors to defeat them when they are engaged." I nodded. "Then you have a month to hide your snekke and we have a month to make us hard to swallow!"

I left with my sons and Fears Water the next morning and we sailed south. I already had an idea where I would moor the snekke. We had sailed up and down the river enough times to be familiar with it. There was another stream just a mile south of our village but it was largely hidden by overhanging trees. I had the boys scull the two snekke while Moos Blood and I took down the mast. I then led the two snekke under the trees. It was hard paddling, especially for Fears Water and Golden Bear who were my only crew but we made it under the trees. The stream was fairly shallow and narrowed but that made it perfect for us. We turned the snekke and then secured them to the trees that lined the banks. We left the masts on the mast fish so that, with the undergrowth, the two snekke melded into the river bank. That done we headed back to our camp. The boys were eager to take the metal from the moulds and see their handiwork.

I think that they were slightly disappointed with the results but I was not. "Brave Cub, go and fill these two sacks with sand. Golden Bear help him."

Erik's Clan

I used a stone knife to remove the slag and tendrils of hardened metal that were not needed from the heads and the weapons. It improved the looks of the seaxes and the arrowheads a little. When the sandbags were brought back, I put the metal in them and said, "Now they need to be shaken."

They looked at me in surprise, "That is all, shaken?"

"Yes, Fears Water. The sand will smooth off the rough edges and then we can sharpen them."

While the four of them did that I went to examine the new defences. Brave Eagle had the warriors and children digging a ditch all the way around the camp. We would place bridges over it for us to use but when danger threatened then the ditch would be covered in grass to disguise it. In the bottom were small, sharpened stakes.

I stood with Brave Eagle who smiled, "When we returned here from the north, I did not think we would have to do this."

"Nor me. It seems to me that fleeing from danger is not always the best choice." I pointed to the north, "How will you have a warning of an attack?"

"I have my sons building two platforms in the trees. We will have men watching from there. It will be good for the young warriors who are yet to be blooded to learn the discipline of simply watching and waiting."

"Arrows?"

"Ah, Erik, I am pleased that you mention arrows. Although we might wish them, we know that you will want to keep your magic iron arrows for yourself but you have a great skill in making flint arrows. While your leg and arm heal, I hoped you might make such arrowheads."

I nodded, "And I would be more than happy to do so."

So while others prepared defences I became a weaponsmith. Between making flint arrows with my sons I finished first the two seaxes and then the arrows. I used a whetstone to put an edge on the seaxes and arrowheads and then, while my sons fitted them to newly fletched arrow shafts, I made the hilts for the seaxes. We had slain, when we lived in the land of Ice and Fire, a walrus. I still had the ivory from one tusk and when I had napped enough flint, I made four ivory pieces to fit on the tang of the seaxes. I used trenails to fasten the two sides and my hatchet head was used to flatten the sharp end. Bound with leather they were both fine weapons. I secreted the two knives and returned to my napping.

That night, after we had eaten. I produced, like a magician, the two knives. Moos Blood already had a seax and I handed one to Fears Water and one to Brave Cub. "Here are weapons that might well save your lives. Care for them and make a scabbard so that the blades are protected. Find a whetstone and keep them sharp."

The two were so amazed at the gift that they had no words. Golden Bear smiled his cheeky smile, "And when you find more iron, father, then I shall have my gift too?"

Ruffling his unruly hair I said, "Perhaps."

Before we went to bed I said, "Moos Blood, tomorrow I will use the steam hut you made. My body feels as though it is almost healed and I need to dream. If any wishes then they can join me but I must warn you that the experience can be frightening."

Moos Blood said, eagerly, "I hoped that I would be invited and I for one will brave the terrors."

I saw him look at Fears Water. Since they had begun courting two village girls, they had become close. Fears Water smiled too, "Having overcome my fear of water I shall see if steam is as frightening."

We lit the fire before we went to bed. By the time morning came, it was hot and when we added the water and herbs then the hut filled with aromatic steam. Moos Blood and I were already naked and with our pipes in our hands entered the hut. Moos Blood sat cross-legged but that position was now impossible for me. I had my right leg held out before me. Fears Water entered and I saw him cough with the heat as his breath was taken away.

"Just breathe and close your eyes. Moos Blood and I will smoke a pipe and then we will enter the dream world."

Before we had used the steam hut on Bear Island, we had not smoked tobacco. I found it enhanced the experience and made dreams more likely. I smoked a pipe as did Moos Blood and when it went out after putting more water and herbs to create steam, I closed my eyes. Each person experienced something different in the steam hut. I knew I would dream but what I was not expecting was the easing of the ache in my knee and my shoulder. The lack of pain relaxed me and soon darkness overcame me.

I saw a bubbling piece of water and there were jagged rocks beneath it. A white cloud turned into Gytha and as she wove over the water, pointing with her long and elegant finger, I saw the passage. Once beyond the bubbling water, all was calm. Fish leapt from its surface. I spied a bluff above the water and suddenly found myself standing on its top. The ground was flat and trees shaded it on one side. I saw corn growing and apples. In fact, there were so many apples it looked as though the Allfather himself had planted them. White-tailed deer grazed beneath the trees. It was a perfect place. The next thing I knew I was high in the sky looking down on the bubbling water and the orchard. As I peered to the north I saw a blue line. It was the hills where I had found the cave. It looked so close that I felt I could touch them. 'Seek the valley and seek the hills.' Gytha's words confirmed that this would be our new home. When the time came, I would seek the bubbling waters.

I opened my eyes and saw that both my companions were still in the dream world. I did not disturb them. Instead, I enjoyed the freedom from pain. Moos Blood awoke first and he just smiled. I nodded and we awaited Fears Water. When he awoke, his body bathed in sweat, he looked at us in amazement. "I saw the dead. I saw my father and my brothers." We just nodded. "My mother is dead also. They smiled, Erik, Shaman of the Bear, and looked happy, how can that be?"

"I do not know for sure but perhaps they are happy that you live. Did you speak with them?"

He shook his head, "I was too frightened."

"We will do this again for it helps my wounds. Next time try to smoke the pipe as we did and do not be afraid to speak." I turned to Moos Blood. "And you?"

"I saw warriors dressed and armed like you. One looked like you but he was bigger and fiercer. They slew many warriors and when they saw me, they banged their shields and chanted my name. How can that be?"

"Where did the battle take place?"

"At the top of a waterfall."

I smiled, "That was my brother and my cousin. They all died together in the land of the Penobscot. They know your name because they are in Valhalla and I believe that they can see our lives." I shrugged, "I do not know for certain but I do not think it is a bad thing that they know your name. You were not afraid were you?"

He smiled, "No, for it was like being with a warband made up of warriors just like you."

From that day my wounds healed far quicker than before and even Running Antelope was impressed. I was able to go out in the snekke more regularly. The walk to the new moorings was a long one but now I found that I could do it easily although when I overdid it the knee complained. The escape from the Moneton had improved Fears Water's skill as a helmsman and I was able to study the riverbanks as we sailed. I knew that I had to get to know the land. Hitherto I had just looked for fish and the river. The trees and the banks would be even more important from now on.

I spoke with Brave Eagle. The month had passed quickly and while our defences were now stronger, we still had work to do. "Brave Eagle, when I leave, I would take two of the birchbark boats we captured when we found the salt."

He nodded, "They are yours. You still plan on leaving?"

"You know it is the right thing to do. It may not be for a year or two, that depends upon Eagle Claws, but one day, perhaps after the boys have married, we will find a new home."

"We will miss you and your mind."

I smiled, "And my mind has been working. I can see a way to improve our defences. We will know when they are coming for our sentries will spot them and the ditch and traps will be a barrier but we could do more before they reach our ditch."

I could see he was intrigued, "In the forest?"

"I do not think that they will just come along the paths. Even the Penobscot did not do that. They will expect us to watch the paths. What if we laid traps between the trees away from the paths? It would slow them down and, more importantly, make them wary and nervous."

"It cannot hurt and we have spare boys now who would enjoy such an activity."

And so we made traps and placed trip ropes where our people did not go. By the time the Moneton came, the undergrowth would have grown back and they would not see them.

We had almost finished when Eagle Claws arrived in our camp with one hundred warriors. War was coming.

Chapter 8

It was lucky that he came down the main path from his village otherwise he might have fallen foul of the new traps. I saw that the warriors looked different from Brave Eagle's. Eagle Claws and his warriors wore more feathers. Many had shaved part of their heads and marked their skulls with colours, mainly reds and blues although some were yellow. All were heavily armed and they each wore a look of arrogant superiority. I felt White Fox and Hides Alone bristling with indignation. So far, the warriors of Eagle Claws had not fought. Hides Alone and White Fox had fought many battles and knew how to fight.

The warriors strode into the centre of the village and Eagle Claws spoke as though he owned it and all of those within it, "I have brought my warriors to save this village from the wrath of the Moneton." If Eagle Claws thought his words would bring a cheer he was mistaken. The village was angry at the food tax as well as the new leadership of the tribe. His face lost some of its arrogance and he waved to Brave Eagle and to me to close with him. "Where are your boats? The ones that fly across the water."

I was not about to divulge their position to a man I did not trust. "They are well hidden and safe from any that would take them."

"They are a weapon and we should use them against our foes." He pointed to the river. "We have come here because the Moneton have been making their way down the river. They have destroyed three Powhatan villages that lay close to the river." I knew the ones he meant. Had Moos Blood not come for me I would have made for them to seek refuge. "They have many birchbark boats carrying warriors down the river and others who march through the forest. They are heading for here. You, Shaman of the Bear, should lead the warriors of this village to the river and fight the boats."

The man was a fool and I knew that not only would that not work, but it was also the best way to eliminate the best warriors in the village not to mention my snekke and me. Brave Eagle answered for me, "We will defend our village. You and your warriors are welcome to fight alongside us but you should know that this," he spread his arm around the village centre, "will be our battleground."

The new Powhatan chief looked around incredulously, "This? But why not use the forest?"

Brave Eagle smiled, "By the time the Moneton come, the forest and the traps we have made will already have thinned their numbers."

Erik's Clan

"You risk your women and your children."

"No, we do not for they will fight. They know that if they do not fight then they will become slaves and many endured the cruelty of the Penobscot. Better to die fighting so that some of the clan might live."

"Perhaps I should leave you to your fate, Brave Eagle, as you seemed determined to destroy your clan."

"We had already decided to fight before you came. Your news helps us, Eagle Claws, and if you stay then so will your numbers but we have warriors who have been blooded. While they might be fewer in number, we know their quality." He lowered his voice, "Can you say the same of the men you lead?"

I added my thoughts, "Eagle Claws, the brothers you sent as scouts were brave men but they were like maidens in war. They died well but did not slay many. I killed four at their village and others later. I think the brothers killed just two. I tell you this not as a boast but as confirmation that we know what we are doing. We will fight in an organised way and use the whole of the clan to fight. When a people are united then they will win."

He stared at me and I saw the anger and hatred for me in his eyes, "When I heard you were lost, along with my warriors, I was pleased. You are not of our tribe and should not be here. Your blood mixed with ours weakens it."

He was goading me and I felt Brave Eagle bridle next to me. I restrained his hand, "You may be right but my wife is not Powhatan, she is Mi'kmaq. We are here as guests."

Brave Eagle growled, "And their blood when it is mixed with ours, will only make it stronger."

I could see that Eagle Claws was not convinced but he dismissed the arguments with a wave of his hand, "We have a battle to fight and when that is over, we will discuss the position of those who are not Powhatan."

I thought Brave Eagle was going to argue and I said, "Come, Brave Eagle, let us organise our defences while Eagle Claws and his warriors find places to sleep."

As we headed towards White Fox and the warriors I said, "Well at least we know my position, Brave Eagle. Eagle Claws does not want me here and I now know that he sought my death when he sent me hence."

"But we want you here, Erik. You are part of this clan."

"But not, it seems, the tribe. He is right in one respect, we need to fight a battle before anything can be resolved and his news was useful. If they come by water and by land then we need to come up with a plan to face two attacks."

Erik's Clan

White Fox's face was filled with anger and Brave Eagle held up his hand, "I know, my son, you like not these allies but they are allies and if they fight with us then, perhaps, fewer of our men will die. Save your anger for the Moneton. They come by boat and by land."

Hides Alone smiled, "Then it is good that we put a ditch all the way around the village."

I nodded, "Aye, but we only put sentries facing north. There are none to the east and the river." His face fell, "Fear not, my sons and I will be the sentries on that side."

"I want every boy ready to hurl stones and I want every warrior armed with a bow." Brave Eagle waved a dismissive hand at Eagle Claws and his men. They had brought spears, shields and clubs. Few had bows. "I care not what they do but we will send a wall of arrows at them. I would rather kill them before they get close."

I nodded, "Remember the Powhatans who came with us to rescue your family, Hides Alone. They sought glory and they found death. Your father is right. Thin out their numbers before they get close. Our flint arrows will kill." I rubbed my knee, "The stone arrows cause a wound but, as the Moneton discovered when they pursued me, they do not kill."

I gathered my sons and stepson and went down the path that led directly to the river. There was a small beach there and, when we were at peace, the birchbark boats were left there. Now the boats had been stacked in the village. If the Moneton came by water they would come from this direction. The entrance to the mooring place for the snekke was disguised. They would find it at some stage but the easiest place to land would be the beach.

"We need to put obstacles in their way and as no one will be using the path until after they have attacked, we can make the trail a hazard. We will work backwards from the water."

We had brought spades and the boys dug holes and planted stakes in the bottom. I could not help as I was unable to put pressure on my knee. I could walk but rising to my feet was hard and I did not trust my knee, yet, to hold my weight. I largely supervised what they were doing. My arms, however, could be used and I wielded a flint axe to hack almost through a tree. We rigged it so that if a Moneton was careless and stepped into the cord he would bring down the tree. At best it might maim or kill and at the very least it would both block the path and make them wary of more traps. It took all afternoon to make the trail and the woods from the river if not a death trap, then an obstacle-strewn danger zone through which they could not pass quickly. We hacked at the briars that grew there, winding them into the gaps to increase their size.

They would be an impenetrable wall of thorns and would force the Moneton to pass our traps. When the battle was over then we could easily repair our trail to the beach and leave the rest as a permanent defence. I used my hatchet to cut some saplings. We buried them in the ground at an angle so that they would strike the groin of any warrior who ran without care. I sharpened the tips and then we disguised them with small branches and foliage. If they avoided the briars then they would not be able to avoid the stakes.

When all was done, we went to the trail and, avoiding our own traps, walked back towards the village. I pointed to the ditch. "We will place more stakes pointing outwards here and this is where we will wait for our enemies."

It did not take long to embed saplings in the side of the ditch and for me to sharpen them. When we returned to our yehakin I would put an edge on my hatchet, seax and sword.

As we headed back to our yehakin my eldest son asked, "Do we watch overnight, father?"

I shook my head, "No, Moos Blood, for they would be bold indeed if they risked the river and an accurate landing at night. We have had our boats fishing regularly and so far we have not seen scouts. If they have taken the villages north of here then they are more likely to learn of our beach from the people they have taken. Better that we have a good night of rest and then, on the morrow get into the forest before dawn and wait." I looked at all four of them, "We have to do what, in a perfect world, would be done by twenty warriors. I am honoured that Brave Eagle trusts us to do this alone."

"Can we hold them, father?"

I heard the fear in Golden Bear's voice and I smiled to calm those fears, "We do not have to hold them. We slow them until we reach the ditch we have dug and there we will join others to slay them as they emerge from the trees and try to cross the trap-filled ditch."

Since we had dug the ditches and planted the stakes warriors had been emptying their bowels on the stakes. When this was all over the ditch and the stakes would be buried but until then any wound would not only be painful but poisoned as well.

Little White Dove and Laughing Deer had worked hard all day preparing food and we ate well that night. After we had eaten and while we were seated around the fire the two girls that Moos Blood and Fears Water had been courting came to sit with us. The boys had done everything as they should have done and the two fathers of the girls, Beaver's Teeth and Fighting Bird approved. I was honoured that they did so for I knew that I was seen as different and as such, to be feared.

Erik's Clan

The girls, Sings Softly and Blue Feather, sat next to Fears Water and Moos Blood. I smiled as the girls, shyly and surreptitiously, held the hands of my son and stepson. I had a small clan. When I came to leave then both the boys and their prospective brides would have a decision to make: to come with me or to stay in Brave Eagle's village. That was a battle away and, for the moment, I basked in the peace and harmony of a family fire and a full belly.

My knee ensured that I did not enjoy a good night's sleep and poor Laughing Deer had to endure my moans of pain while I slept. I woke before dawn and went to the ditch closest to the river to make water. Brave Eagle had sentries out and Kicking Deer waved to me as I neared the ditch.

"A quiet watch?"

He nodded, "Just the owls and the creatures of the night." He gestured at the sleeping warriors brought by Eagle Claws, "They made more noise, snoring and breaking wind. They might be Powhatan but I do not like them. How can that be?"

I thought of my people and knew that it was the same wherever you were. You might be of the same tribe, race, or people, but that didn't mean you liked everyone. "You are lucky, Kicking Deer, this is a good clan and Brave Eagle a good chief."

He lowered his voice, "Then perhaps he should be chief of the whole tribe. Long Spear was a better chief than his son."

"Those are dangerous words, Kicking Deer. Are you really ready to go to war with Eagle Claws? I know that man for man our clan has better warriors but we both know that numbers count for much." I waved at the sleeping warriors, "And they have the numbers."

I went back to the yehakin and roused the fire into life. Trimming stakes had ensured that we had plenty of kindling. By the time dawn broke then the whole clan was awake. The ditches would begin to stink by noon. We ate in silence for we all knew that either this day or the next would see a battle. I wondered if the Moneton war chief was trying to play games with our minds. Having been seen he would know that we anticipated his arrival. Was he trying to make us do something foolish? That idea gained credence when Eagle Claws summoned Brave Eagle and me to a meeting with his leading warriors.

"We have spoken and I have decided that we will not wait for the Moneton to attack. We will seek them out and bring them to battle."

Brave Eagle nodded, "If that is your decision then we will watch for your return."

It took a moment for Brave Eagle's words to sink in and when they did Eagle Claws was incredulous, "You would squat here behind your defences and let us fight for you?"

Brave Eagle shook his head, "No, we would have you wait here with us and follow a battle plan that has some chance of success rather than foolishly seeking glory." He pointed to the river, "You said they would come by water and by land. When you go to find them in the forest who will there be to defend the village from the river?"

It was clear he had not thought it through. However pride took over and he reacted aggressively, "You and your clan are cowards. We will stay in the village for I do not think you are worth the loss of even one life."

Brave Eagle was seething with anger and his voice was cold as he replied, "When you sent your scouts to find the Moneton, then you woke the sleeping bear. Had you not done so then they would not now be here, making war on my village. They might be attacking your home but my people would be safe. You began this war. It was your ambition that led us here. A man has to live with his decisions, no matter how foolish."

I saw Eagle Claws' hand go to this stone club and I know not would have happened had not the sentry in the trees to the north shouted, "The Moneton. They come!"

We waited for no orders. We hurried to the yehakins. My sons ran and I lumbered. I donned my head protector and helmet. I put my freshly sharpened sword and hatchet in my belt and my seax in my boot. Finally, I strung my bow and grabbed the quiver with twenty arrows. I would not need metal ones. The flint ones would be good enough. The last item I donned was my bearskin. It covered my helmet and made me appear bigger than I was. As well as shocking the Moneton I hoped I would draw their weapons to me.

I was the last to be ready and my sons awaited me. I saw the fear in Laughing Deer's eyes. Golden Bear was still young. He was too young to be a warrior and yet such was the degree of danger that we would need him and his sling. I smiled at my wife, "I will send Golden Bear back if we need anything." The words seemed innocent enough but my wife knew that I meant I would send him back rather than risk his life.

"Thank you, husband. You are a good father."

"Let us hope that I am still a good warrior despite these injuries." This would be a test not only of my skill but of the shoulder and knee which would have to be used no matter how much pain they caused.

Chapter 9

Brave Eagle had already organised our clan and now he pointed out where he needed Eagle Claws and his men to stand. I saw Brave Eagle point to us. When Eagle Claws ignored the request, I knew that my sons and I would be alone. Eagle Claws and his warriors were seeking glory and they stood behind the northern ditch. My sons and I might have to face one-third of the Moneton. I turned to Golden Bear, "If we are in danger of being breached then I will send you to Brave Eagle for reinforcements. You must do as I say instantly."

Moos Blood said, "Aye, little brother, and it will not be easy for Brave Eagle will be in the thick of the fighting."

My youngest son grew before my eyes, "I will not let my father and brothers down. You can trust me." He patted the flint knife in his belt. It was, perforce small but very sharp and any Moneton who thought that someone so small had no bite was in for a shock.

We had cut some undergrowth down the night before and after placing some of it over the ditch had made a barrier with the rest so that we had a little protection. We spread ourselves out so that I was in the centre, in the middle of the trail. Golden Bear was to my left, Brave Cub to my right. Moos Blood guarded the extreme right of our line and Fears Water the left. We had four bows and a sling. I was not sure how long I would be able to use the bow for the wound in my shoulder, whilst healed, had yet to be truly tested.

"Whatever happens ignore the noises from behind us. We have one battle to fight and that is here. We deny our enemy the path into the village. We rely on no one but each other."

I selected an arrow. I had made all of them and they were all excellent but the first arrow had to be the best and I chose the one with the best flint arrowhead, the straightest shaft and the fletch that was pure white. I nocked it and looked to my left and right to see that my sons had done the same. Golden Bear held his sling loosely. I doubted that he would hit anyone but I had endured an attack by slingers and knew that there was always a fear that one might hit you and any distraction would increase the chances that a warrior might trip a trap.

We heard the crash followed by the cries and knew that the path was blocked. They had felled the tree trap. Orders were shouted and I said, "They will be coming through the forest. Do not loose until I give a command. I want them to think that we are unguarded. We know that this path is the only way in. We make it a killing ground. If they risk the stakes and the ditch then all the better."

There were more noises and shouts that suggested our traps were working. It was maddening not to be able to see the results of our work but as the sounds of battle behind us grew I knew that our defences had delayed their flank attack. We had done our job already. The screams and crashes at the main battle suggested that it was a bloody affair. I would not risk my sons in such a battle here. When we were in danger of being overwhelmed, I would fall back and keep them at bay with our bows. I just hoped that my knee would allow me to move quickly and that my shoulder would be strong enough to keep up a good rate of arrows.

They came along the path, when come they did, piecemeal. I had expected a mob and I had intended to use all our bows at the same time. One warrior darted from the undergrowth onto the path. He shouted something and raised his spear. It was clear that we were hidden from view by the tangle of dead undergrowth before us. The range was no more than thirty paces and my arrow slammed into his neck, spinning him around and throwing him into the undergrowth.

"I thought we were waiting for your command, father."

"And you still are, Moos Blood. Hopefully, the next warriors will not look to the side."

That our traps had worked became clear when no more warriors arrived for a few moments. I knew that my sons would be nervous but there was nothing I could do. They did not know the sagas and chants that helped to put steel into a man in a shield wall and besides that would alert the Moneton. We had to remain silent and, in the case of the boys, fearful.

It became clear that the Moneton knew that someone was waiting. I heard less noise from the woods. I guessed that they were using hand signals. When they came it was with a fearful roar and a wall of warriors. We had held them already longer than Brave Eagle might have hoped but now we would have to fight and I would need to make the decision soon about when to send Golden Bear for help.

I only waited for a few heartbeats before I shouted, "Loose!" I had to draw the bow through the screaming pain of a shoulder that did not want to be worked so hard. Every arrow struck a warrior, even Golden Bear's stone took out a warrior and I heard the squeal of excitement when he did so. Warriors fell but others took their places. The speed and concentration of their attack were working.

"Golden Bear, fetch help."

Erik's Clan

I did not look down but I heard him say, "Aye, Father." I felt Fears Water slide closer to me. Soon we would have to leave the wall of undergrowth to allow us to continue to use our bows. I did not think that my sons were trained enough for close combat. When the nearest Moneton was ten paces from us I shouted, "Fall back twenty paces." I waited until they moved and, after sending a last arrow, joined them.

The ditch and the embedded stakes caught them unawares and I heard their screams of exultation turn to shouts of pain as they found the traps. They had to come through the gap and that made it easier for us. Two arrows struck the first warrior who tried it. A second held his shield before him and so I loosed an arrow at his thigh. When he involuntarily moved his shield hand down to the wound Moos Blood slew him with a well-aimed arrow. The dead, dying and wounded helped them to make a bridge of corpses over the ditch and they spread out to run at us. They would use the sheer weight of numbers to overcome us.

"Behind me!"

I would use my body to protect my sons until help arrived. I saw a chief organising the attack. Perhaps we had slain the hotter heads and now it was the ones with ice in their veins who worked out how to defeat us. There were at least twenty warriors before us and they each held a shield. I saw that they did not hold them close to their bodies but before them. While an arrow might penetrate the shield it would be unlikely to cause a serious wound.

"Go for their legs." Although a harder hit I knew, from painful experience, that it would hurt and slow them down. I could hear, behind me, Golden Bear shouting something and I hoped for help. The chief saw his chance and launched his men at us in five groups of four. They would overcome us. I loosed an arrow and then dropped my bow for the other three who came at me were less than ten paces from me. I drew my sword and my hatchet. The bearskin had not made them pause but the sword and hatchet, their shiny sharpened blades glittering in the morning light did. I had not intended it but as I raised my sword it had caught a shaft of sunlight and dazzled them. The others paused too and that allowed each of my sons to hit another.

"Fall back and guard my back!"

They moved and I was grateful for I needed to be able to swing my arms. My injured knee meant I could not move easily and I would have to be a rock until Golden Bear brought help. The initial shock having gone, the three men who had advanced towards me resumed their attack. They had spears and tomahawks. Two spears came at me at the same time. Instinct took over and my weary left arm lifted the hatchet to fend off one spear while I hacked through the shaft of the second. The warrior with the tomahawk saw his chance and he threw it at me. I had learned that the warriors of this land prided themselves on their throwing skill and they could throw a tomahawk or stone club with great accuracy. My injured knee meant I could not run or even turn quickly but I could move my head. The tomahawk was in the corner of my eye when I moved my head to the side. The stone weapon hit my bearskin and helmet on the side. It was a good strike and without my defences, I would have been felled but the skin, helmet and head protector meant I was not hurt and I lunged with my sword at the warrior with the unbroken spear, gutting him while I brought my hatchet down on the other spearman. He raised his shield but hide does not stop a sharpened metal hatchet and I hacked into his bone. Once more the third warrior saw his chance and he drew his stone dagger to lunge at my unprotected middle. The stone that smacked into his skull hit him in the middle of the forehead. I saw his eyes roll as he fell and knew that he was dead.

Suddenly a shower of stones struck the remaining warriors. Golden Bear had brought the boy slingers. Allied to my sons' arrows we now outnumbered the enemy and while they faced boys and not warriors, they were unable to protect themselves. The chief shouted something and the ten surviving warriors headed back to the trees. I risked looking around. There were just twelve boys with Golden Bear but they had broken the back of the attack. Eagle Claws and Brave Eagle and their men were still engaged with the larger force of Moneton that had come from the north. I saw now how clever the Moneton plan had been. Had we not prepared for a waterborne attack then a second warband would have fallen on the rear of our warriors and the battle would be over.

"Thank you, Golden Bear, thank you, boys. Now return to the main battle and help Brave Eagle claim the victory."

They nodded and seeing no more warriors they could hit they ran. Golden Bear remained, "You too, Golden Bear."

He turned and ran after the others. "What do we do. Father?" I saw that Brave Cub's hands were shaking.

"A grisly task but a necessary one. We check that the ones who remain in our village are dead and then we follow the others to the river. I want to ensure that they are gone."

Moos Blood asked, "And if they ambush us?"

"I do not think that they will but I shall go first in any case."

There were seven bodies left between us and the path. All were dead. There were blood trails showing where wounded men had fled. There were five men at the ditch. Four were dead and one was dying. I gave him a warrior's death for he did not deserve a lingering one with his guts hanging out. The trail seemed dark and dangerous. I held my sword and hatchet before me. My injured knee meant that I had to be both slow and cautious. The need for speed was gone. We found two more dead warriors. One had managed to make it from the village before Moos Blood's arrow in his back had finished its work and killed him. We glimpsed others lying in the undergrowth to the side of the path. I had the boys send an arrow into each one in case they were feigning death but the corpses remained still even when an arrow slammed into them.

When we reached the fallen tree then we had to be even more cautious. There were neither dead nor wounded there but the tree, until we removed it, would be an obstacle. I could have climbed over but I did not trust my knee. "Moos Blood, climb over the tree and ensure that no one awaits us."

The other three drew back on their bows as he climbed over. He shook his head, "There are none here."

I had to be helped over the tree and I did not enjoy the experience, especially as I jarred my knee. I gritted my teeth.

There were just three birchbark boats on the beach and the other ten were paddling north. There were more than ten warriors paddling and I guessed that they had wounded paddling too. I sheathed my sword and put the hatchet in my belt. "We have done well, better, I think, than any could have expected. We will shift the log and then return to the battle."

Fears Water said as we laboured to remove the log, "Should we not hurry and help the rest of the clan?"

I shook my head. "Your weapons are not for close combat. I would not have any of you loose at a Moneton and hit a Powhatan and besides, I am weary."

"I thought, father, that when the tomahawk hit you that you were a dead man."

I smiled, "Aye, Brave Cub, and without my helmet and bearskin, I would have been. It is why my clan, when we fought the Skraelings won at first."

We shifted the log and headed back up the trail. When we reached the village, the battle was largely over. Women were tending our wounded and Brave Eagle and Eagle Claws had left to pursue the survivors. The boys were ensuring that the Moneton who remained were dead. I looked at the sun. The battle had lasted almost three hours. The pursuit would not be a long one as our warriors would be exhausted. Laughing Deer and Little White Dove ran towards us. I was covered in blood but that did not stop them as they hurled their arms around me.

"We thought you dead when they came at you."

I smiled, "Laughing Deer, I know how to fight but I hope that this is my last battle."

I looked at the dead in the village. The battle had been fierce and I counted at least twenty Moneton dead. I saw some of the clan dead but the largest number of Powhatan corpses belonged to the warriors that Eagle Claws had brought. He would now learn that it was not the quantity of warriors that counted but quality. The ones who survived would be better for the battle but he would have fewer. Would it curb his ambitions?

I knew that the battle had taken more out of me than the others. I was not totally healed yet and I had fought hard using both my arms and both of my legs. I was no longer the young warrior who had fought for longer and harder. I would need to choose my battles. In an ideal world, I would not have to fight in battles. I took off my bearskin and helmet first. The helmet had a dent in it but I decided not to repair it. A repair might weaken the metal. I cleaned and sharpened my weapons and put them in my chest. Then I ate and I drank. I felt no guilt that the rest of the warriors were still hunting Moneton. My sons and I had held off almost a third of the enemy warriors and had done so unaided.

My sons and stepson could not restrain themselves and despite my wife's glowering looks continued to speak of every blow and arrow in the battle. I did not stop them. They needed to do so. I had been the same. In my clan, someone would have made a saga about the battle. Here the braves just spoke of their perception of the battle. Even Golden Bear was able to speak of how he had aided Brave Eagle until the chief had realised the danger we were in. He was proud of the fact that he had led the boy slingers and they had tipped the battle in our favour.

The women, their men tended to, cooked for the warriors, like we were, would be very hungry indeed. They began to return just before dark. The Powhatan led by Eagle Claws returned first. They looked battered and bruised. As he passed my yehakin Eagle Claws glared over at me. I waved back, good-naturedly. His scowl increased. The last to return were Brave Eagle and his sons. I had been worried but when they walked in, as far as I could tell unwounded and with heads held high, I stood with my sons and we beat the handles of our daggers against our shields as we chanted, "Brave Eagle!"

I knew that it would not endear me to Eagle Claws especially when all but his warriors joined in the acclamation. My old comrade in arms came over to me and, even though he was bloody, hugged me. I hugged him back. "Truly, Erik, Shaman of the Bear, you and your sons earned much glory this day. You held off such numbers that had they attacked us then we would have lost."

I shrugged, "You are my clan and I will do all that I must to keep you safe. They are defeated?"

"They left a trail of dead all the way to the north. Carrion will feast on their bones. If they do return then they will need a much larger army. I think we were too big a morsel for them to eat."

"We were lucky, Brave Eagle." I pointed to the handful of bodies.

"I know and I am guessing that Eagle Claws will not be happy at his losses. More than half of his warriors fell." I looked at the bodies in the centre of the village. "Not here but when we chased them some raced ahead, still eager for glory and the Moneton turned and butchered them. It was only when Eagle Claws forbade them to go alone that the losses stopped."

We felt safe that night as there were still traps in the forests and while the creatures of the night prowled and began to devour the corpses it was doubtful that any Moneton would risk a night attack. I lay with laughing Deer in my arms, "You know, my love, that we may have to leave this village and this river."

She was silent for a while and then said, "Although I am happy here, I believe that you are right. The looks that Eagle Claws gave you when he returned were those of an enemy. I know that if he was just an ordinary warrior there would not be a problem but he is the chief." My wife was clever and her time as a slave with the Penobscot had given her wisdom.

"We will make preparations but I wonder if our son and my stepson will stay."

"That is out of our hands. When I left Stands Alone it broke my heart but it was right for her to do so. Moos Blood and Fears Water both have good hearts and will make wise decisions. We shall be together and I will be safe."

The next day we had the grisly task of collecting the corpses. Whilst the warriors we had lost were buried according to the Powhatan customs the Moneton were taken and burned. We made a pyre from the defences we had made. If there was another attack it would not be for some time and certainly not from the same direction. The dead were not mistreated but neither were words spoken over their corpses. As Brave Eagle said to me, "The honour we do will be when we spread their ashes on our fields so that the crops we grow will be better. When that food is eaten they will become part of our clan and there is the honour."

Eagle Claws did nothing to help with the disposal of the bodies but they did prepare to leave. The fire was licking around the first of the bodies when, with his men lined up behind him, Eagle Claws waved over Brave Eagle, his sons and me.

"The Moneton are defeated and will not return but this is not over. Those who fled the villages that were taken will return and I will make new chiefs for those villages. They will become stronger. This time next year you and the other clans will have made more warriors and we will head north to make war on the Moneton and teach them the folly of fighting our tribe." It was clear to me that any chiefs appointed by Eagle Claws would be his men and follow his orders blindly.

Brave Eagle shook his head, "You have already done that, Eagle Claws." He pointed to the spiralling smoke from the funeral fire, "They lost far more than we did. They took wounded back who will not relish fighting us again."

"I lost warriors who were close to me and I will have vengeance."

It was clear to me that the war had nothing to do with the clan and all to do with Eagle Claws' ambition. I knew, at that moment, that I did not have the luxury of a couple of years living with the clan. I would have to leave sooner rather than later.

"You will be ready to join us when I send a war arrow to you." Brave Eagle could only nod. Eagle Claws turned to me, "And you, Erik, Shaman of the Bear, have weapons that the chief of the tribe should have. The helmet, sword and hatchet should be mine and I would have them."

Before Brave Eagle could come to my defence I said, "You have said before, Eagle Claws, that I am not Powhatan so how can the weapons of a foreigner be yours? There is magic in them and I understand that magic. You do not. In my hands, they wield death to my foes but in another's…?"

I saw fear in his eyes. As much as he wanted the weapons, he feared their magic. My title of Shaman of the Bear and my skill with the snekke were something he did not understand. They were unknown and he feared the unknown. He feared that I would curse the weapons if I was forced to hand them over.

"When we attack the Moneton, next year, you will lead our warriors. You will use your magic to bring us victory."

I nodded knowing that I would not be here.

He said, "Come, we go."

After they had marched out along the now cleared trail Brave Eagle said, "He would have you dead and then he will claim your weapons."

"That is his plan."

He gave me a curious look, "And yet you are not afraid." His eyes lit up in enlightenment, "You will not be here. You still plan on leaving."

"Keep that to yourself, Brave Eagle, I have plans to make. Only Laughing Deer knows of my full intention." Pain replaced the enlightenment. "It is like it was with the Mi'kmaq, my presence brings danger to the clan and you would not want that, would you?" He shook his head. "As much as I would like to stay here, I cannot do so. I dreamed."

"And the witch came to you?"

"Gytha came to me and told me that I should leave. I have delayed for many reasons and perhaps that delay was necessary but Eagle Claws' words are a clear warning to me. One way or another if I remain here then my family and I will be in danger." I smiled, "Do not worry, old friend, my time for leaving is not imminent. I will not leave in winter."

We spent the rest of that day collecting the snekke and sailing them back to their berth. From now on we would have to treat them with care and attention. When we left, they would be our lifeline to a new life. We threw ourselves into the old routine we had enjoyed before Eagle Claws' had asserted power. We fished each day but I now did so with a view to gathering what we might need for our new lives. I felt guilty that I had not told my sons the fullness of my plans but they did not mind. I think I had given them enough hints to know we would be leaving and they just awaited the decision on the timing. We went to sea and caught the fierce finny fish whose bones were so useful. We returned to Salt Island to make salt, not for the clan but for us. We were there but two days and by the time we were discovered *'Gytha'* was already heading north. Laughing Deer and Little White Dove busily turned the hide from the animals we hunted into usable lengths and preserved. Laughing Deer and I were as one. Each night we spoke of what we might need for our new lives. It was almost like being newlyweds again as we spoke each night of our plans for the future. I thought that we had been clever and disguised our intentions but our sons and the villagers who knew us best knew that something was amiss.

It was Moos Blood, now grown to be almost a man, who bearded us. It was close to the day when the sun burned the longest and we had just enjoyed a feast. He and his brothers had hunted and slain a white-tailed deer. The animal was hanging from the rack and Brave Cub had just regaled us with the story of how his arrow had been the first to strike the deer when Moos Blood looked at Fears Water and said, "So, father, there are no secrets from us. Yet you and our mother are hiding your thoughts from us."

Laughing Deer gave me a guilty look and I tried to smile my way out of it, "What do you mean? There are no secrets."

"We are not fools, father. Since the war, you and Laughing Deer have behaved differently. When you took us to collect the salt then I knew something was amiss. When the clan went to collect it, we almost lost warriors yet you were willing to risk that fate. We have spoken and we think that you plan to leave the clan." He nodded his head towards White Fox's yehakin, "White Fox thinks so too. We are your family and we need to hear the truth. Do you plan on leaving the clan, as you said when you were still ill and suffering from the wound? And…" he waved a hand at his siblings and Fears Water, "us?"

Brave Cub said, "When no more was said and after the war, we thought you had forgotten the idea. We did not like the secrecy. When you were wounded and could not rise because of your injuries we thought you meant to leave the clan but since then you have not mentioned it." He smiled, "We are not stupid, father. Did you not think we would know something was amiss?"

"You are right we have been planning to leave but we said nothing for the time we leave is not yet decided and as for leaving you… we would not do so but we know that Sings Softly and Blue Feather are now part of your lives. You have decisions to make. We wanted to give you as much time with the clan as we could before we told you of our decision. That was wrong and I am sorry. I planted the idea in your heads and I should have remembered that." I looked at Brave Cub, Little White Dove and Golden Bear, "You are all older now and might not wish to come with your mother and me. So, let me put it to you now and you can all make your own decisions. Sometime after winter is over your mother and I will sail north along the Patawomke. I intend to sail along the Shenandoah and find somewhere without people where we can begin a new life."

I took a piece of fish from the platter and began to eat it. Laughing Deer's hand touched my leg and she smiled, "We hope that you might wish to come with us and begin a new life but your father is right. What he did not tell you is that so long as we stay here then Eagle Claws will make not only our lives hard but also the clan's for he fears your father. This journey is not one made for no reason and we have kept it from you for it has been a hard one to make."

Brave Cub said, triumphantly, "See, I told you it was to do with Eagle Claws." He turned to me, "I will come with you."

Erik's Clan

Golden Bear was the only one who could still be considered a child and he said, "And I."

Little White Dove smiled, "And I cannot let my father leave without me. Who would tend to him when he hurts himself…again?"

Moos Blood said, "Fears Water and I know that we have ties here. We have spoken to Sings Softly and Blue Feather. They would come with us." He smiled, "You see, that while it might have been many months ago and much has happened, we did not forget your words, father. We need to speak to Beaver's Teeth and Fighting Bird. We will be married before we leave."

That talk with my family was like the kindling of a fire. As soon as the boys spoke with Beaver's Teeth and Fighting Bird then the flames were fanned and the whole village knew of our plans. The two warriors understood that they were losing their daughters and that made them sad but they did not oppose the move. Of course, once the news was out then everyone demanded more information. When would the weddings take place? When would we leave? It was like trying to steer a snekke over a waterfall for we had not made all the decisions yet.

Running Antelope was not just the wife of Brave Eagle she was also seen as the wise woman of the clan. I knew that she was a skilled healer but when she came to speak to Laughing Deer and me then I knew she had some of Gytha in her.

"We know that you are leaving and that is sad but we need to celebrate your time with us. When the crops are gathered and we celebrate the bounty of this land will be a good time to be married. Brave Eagle and I will arrange it. As for the time you leave… I know, Erik, that Eagle Claws is the reason you are leaving and it is his return that will determine when you leave. He will not wish to make war until the new grass has come and winter is over. Leave when we plant the corn."

"And if he comes early or sends for me?"

"Then those sisters you speak of will have spun." She shrugged, "We would keep you here as long as we can. The clan would fight Eagle Claws to protect you."

Laughing Deer shook her head, "But we would not wish any to die for us. Yours is a good plan, Running Antelope, and we will do as you suggest."

We should have known that the Norns were spinning. The summer came and went and the wedding feast was planned. My sons and I hauled the snekke from the river, cleaned their hulls and painted pine tar on them. We ensured that the birchbark boats we would be taking were sound and each day was filled from dawn until dusk. My eyes were close to the ground and I did not see all. I confess that my wounds now healed, I worked harder than any and I was more exhausted each night. The result was that I did not see everything as clearly as I might have done.

I had seen Powhatan weddings before but these two were special for the whole clan had an interest and the presents that were given astounded me. It was almost like an outpouring of love from a people who had not known us until a few years ago. *Wyrd*. Inevitably there were tears but that was to be expected. There was great feasting. Eagle Claws appeared to have forgotten his demand that we send food to him. Since the war, we had sent nothing and there had been no recriminations. We ate and drank well. I confess that I drank more beer than I should have and felt a little tipsy. I should have known something was up when my sons and Brave Eagle all grinned at me as a young warrior, Humming Bird, approached. I knew the youth. He had fought like a warrior against the Moneton and killed two of their warriors. He was a pleasant youth and a friend of Brave Cub.

"Humming Bird, a fine feast eh?"

He nodded nervously, "It is Erik, Shaman of the Bear." He looked around and I saw Brave Cub nod. "I have something to ask."

Since the battle, many young warriors had come to ask me to make them a seax and as he was a friend of Brave Cub I assumed that was the reason he was speaking, "You should know, Humming Bird, that until I find more iron stone I cannot make weapons but as you are a friend of Brave Cub's then the first blades I make shall be for you and Golden Bear."

I saw Brave Eagle laugh and shot him a sharp look.

"No, Shaman of the Bear, I wish to marry your daughter, Little White Dove."

My mouth dropped open. I felt such a fool for it was clear that everyone else knew of this. Laughing Deer had no surprise on her face and Little White Dove leapt to her feet and held Humming Bird's hand. "Say that we can be wed, father, for Humming Bird is happy to come with us and I do love him."

I looked from face to face. Laughing Deer came and held my hand, "I am sorry we kept this secret from you but you were working so hard we wished no distraction. Answer your daughter and her husband to be and then we can plan another wedding."

I was losing my daughter and gaining another son. All was good and I smiled, "Of course, you may marry. Welcome to my clan, Humming Bird."

Chapter 10

The wedding was a moon later. We had built two yehakin for Moos Blood and Fears Water. Laughing Deer and I moved into the large yehakin with Brave Cub and Golden Bear and so Humming Bird and Little White Dove had their own home. As the leaves dropped and the nights grew longer the village settled into a winter routine and each day I sat with my sons, Humming Bird now included, and we planned our journey. It was not as easy as I had thought. We had two snekke and plenty of birchbark boats but the four women could not travel in the boats. They would have to be in the snekke. The two captains were obvious, Moos Blood and me. As much as Brave Cub and Golden Bear wished to be in the same boat the weight of the elder boys determined that Golden Bear would travel with Fears Water. The other two birchbark boats would contain what we would need for our new lives. I feared that we would be overloaded. I had not planned on my daughter being married. It was a good thing for we now had one more warrior and I was realistic enough to know that we might have to fight for a place along the river. I hoped that we would not and we would not seek a fight but we would be prepared.

Fears Water had visited and indeed hunted along the Shenandoah. He told us that it was hotter in summer and colder in winter than Brave Eagle's village but that there were, in his opinion, fewer villages. As the river sometimes flooded, the villages were on the higher ground. We would need tools to clear the land and so we made flint axes, to use to break up the ground and to hew down the trees. We also made more arrows. The boys had become more proficient at napping flint and we had less waste.

When the nights were at their longest and the cold weather came, we huddled in our yehakin and went over our plans to see what we had not yet thought of. During those cold, shorter days I spent a great deal of time with Brave Eagle and his sons. We were close and our parting would be hard.

"How far do you travel, Erik?"

I knew what was on Brave Eagle's mind, "You would visit?" He nodded. "From what Fears Water has told me the river, when it empties into the Patawomke, is a fierce one. I think that the snekke can sail it successfully but paddled boats might struggle. I would guess that if you wished to visit us you would carry your boats from one river to the next. As for where we shall live. That depends upon what we find but what I can say is that we will be close to the river and on the southern bank. It took us many days to sail up the Patawomke to find Fears Water's village. It would take you longer." His face fell. "When we are settled and time allows, I may well visit here to tell you of our new life. I seek a home where there are no neighbours. I wish for peace. You know better than any, Brave Eagle, how my life has been filled with war, fighting and death. I am no longer a young man and I would like to see grandchildren and be as Long Spear and Wandering Moos. I would sit and watch my family grow."

He smiled and nodded, "It will be hard for you, I know, Erik, but harder for us. You bring so much to the clan. Since you arrived none have gone hungry. The arrows and weapons you have made make us stronger. You have taught us how to fight as a clan. We shall miss you."

"And you will still have those skills." We had both avoided speaking of the most dangerous problem and so I brought it up, "Eagle Claws will be angry when he learns I have gone."

"That he will but that will not be your problem. I will speak the truth and tell him that you left rather than fight for him. If he asks where you went, I will just tell him you left by the river." He frowned, "Will that be too much information? Will he not follow you?"

"He might but we will have to take that chance. We could sail downriver and I could return to the land of the Mi'kmaq or we could settle by the coast. Upriver there are many places where we could live and the Patawomke is a long river."

"Aye, you are right and you are wise. You are still Erik the Navigator. I believe that if you chose to, then you could sail all the way back across the seas to your home in the east."

I shook my head, "My snekke would both die on the journey and my family with them. No, my home is here in your world and my old one is lost to me." I tapped my head, "Except here for when I sleep, I see my family and that comforts me."

Our preparations went on apace. Before winter had really set in, we had hunted. It was a good time to take bjorr and their fur was warm. In addition, their flesh was tasty. We had feasted well on their meat and now, as cold winds blew and flurries of snow-flecked rain made the warm yehakin a better prospect we all sat with flint scrapers and seaxes to scrape the furs ready to be sewn. If the Shenandoah was, as Fears Water had said, colder in winter then we had to be prepared. The others were able to scrape cross-legged but my knee would still not bend completely and so I scraped with my right leg straight out. It was a comfortable silence in the yehakins as the only sound to be heard was the scraping of the blades. The seax was a more efficient scraper than

Erik's Clan

the flint and I knew that once we found iron stone again, we would have to make more seaxes. I had already placed the stone from the land of Ice and Fire back in the hold of **'Gytha'**.

I know not why but words came to me and in the silence of the scraping I began to sing. It had been many years since I had sung. Snorri Long Fingers had been the singer and it seemed to me that it was his voice in my head. I know not what my new son in law and daughters-in-laws thought for they could not yet speak Norse well but as I sang, I saw a smile on the faces of my wife and sons in our yehakin. The song would carry to the others.

The Norns had spun, their spell was cast
The clan's enemies came at last
The Moneton came by river and land
A vengeful tribe, a fierce warband
The clan prepared to fight for life
In a land of peace free from strife
Erik's clan was by the water
The Moneton they would slaughter

With Viking sword and sharp seax
Erik's clan sent the Moneton to hel
Erik's clan was like a Norseman's axe
Their hearts were true they fought as one
The clan of the bear that day was born
Golden Bear and Brave Cub
Fears Water and Moos Blood
With Erik the Bear together they stood

The walls were made, the five they waited
To see the traps that they had baited
The Moneton found death and pain
Still they came again and again
The arrows flew, stones found bone
But the five of them were alone

With Viking sword and sharp seax
Erik's clan sent the Moneton to hel
Erik's clan was like a Norseman's axe
Their hearts were true they fought as one
The clan of the bear that day was born
Golden Bear and Brave Cub

Erik's Clan

Fears Water and Moos Blood
With Erik the Bear together they stood

Golden Bear was but a bairn
With the slingers he did return
The stones they threw and arrows sent
Broke the charge the Moneton were spent
Brave Eagle and his doughty clan
Defeated the Moneton as was their plan
Warriors were made on that bloody day
They held the Moneton carrion at bay
With the blood of Lars the clan fought well

With Viking sword and sharp seax
Erik's clan sent the Moneton to hel
Erik's clan was like a Norseman's axe
Their hearts were true they fought as one
The clan of the bear that day was born
Golden Bear and Brave Cub
Fears Water and Moos Blood
With Erik the Bear together they stood

A short while after I had finished Fears Water came into our yehakin and asked, "That was a mighty song but who is Lars?"

"Lars was my father and we are of his blood."

He nodded, "Humming Bird and I are not of his blood."

"True, but as you showed in the battle you have his heart."

"Would you sing it again? I should like to learn it."

And so I sang it again and did so while we worked. It seemed to help the work and the boys, Laughing Deer and Little White Dove all joined in. Eventually, the others would learn it and, when times became perilous, we would sing it. The anthem was comforting.

When we emerged from the yehakin to cook our meal Brave Eagle and some of the other warriors came over. "We heard a song. Was it a song of death?"

I shook my head, "No, it was the song of what my sons and I did in the battle." I waved a hand at them. "When I am dead and gone and they have children of their own, they can sing the song and that day will live on. It is how my people tell our stories."

He and his sons nodded, "And what did the words say?"

"I will put them in Powhatan words but they will not sound the same."

Erik's Clan

When I had finished, they nodded. Brave Eagles said, "Yet you did not name yourself and we all know that it was you who drew the Moneton to you."

"A maker of songs does not praise himself. When my sons and daughter teach that song they can, if they choose, add words that tell of me. That is what we do with our songs, they are living things and they grow. They tell our history."

White Fox said, "I like the idea, father. Perhaps we should try to do the same."

He nodded, "Aye, they will not be the same for our words are different but they will serve the same purpose."

The next day as we worked, I heard the rest of the clan as they tried to sing their songs. The music in the village settled hearts and minds and eased the pain of deaths and wounds like snow covers the hurts of a land. The snow that covered our land came just a week after the shortest day of the year. It did not last long but while it did, it cast a blanket over the land. The skies cleared and as I looked north and west, I saw the line of hills where I had found the iron stone. I was being reminded that we would be leaving this land and this clan where we were happy. I had to heed Gytha's voice for she had ever guided us true. The hills were only there for one day and then clouds came to hide them and bring rain that slowly rid us of the blanket of snow. It was a sign to begin preparations in earnest.

We took the snekke out to fish and to teach Humming Bird how to sail. We would be a small clan when we found our new home and each of the men had to be able to do all that the others could. Golden Bear had to learn too. We did not risk the sea but fished the Patawomke. We had to have supplies of brined fish to take with us when we left and the clan of Brave Eagle would miss the catches we had brought in. The days were never long enough. We were up with the sun and when darkness fell we too collapsed into the fur beds of our yehakin.

The messenger from Eagle Claws came earlier than we had expected or perhaps the Norns had been spinning. Whatever the cause we were almost a moon shy of being ready for our departure. I think part of that unpreparedness was our unwillingness to leave what had been our home for many years. The children had grown up here. They had memories of the Mi'kmaq village but they were fading for we did not speak of them. The messenger said that the tribe was going to war and Erik Shaman of the Bear had to bring his weapons to fight for the tribe.

I spoke to Brave Eagle, "We will have to leave and do so by tomorrow."

I saw the disappointment on his face, "That soon?"

"I do not wish there to be trouble and bloodshed. Our presence here ensures that there might be violence. Eagle Claws wants me dead in order to take my weapons and snekke. I will not go quietly and I will fight. You do not want that."

He nodded, knowing that I was right, "It may not always be so. Eagle Claws is not popular."

"No, but his father was and in the time of Long Spear the tribe did not go to war and they have forgotten how to fight. Your clan are the warriors but you do not have the numbers." I held a hand up to the skies, "The Norns spin, Brave Eagle, even for your people and we cannot see into the future. I know that I am meant to leave and we have only stayed this long for we are content here and amongst friends."

He clasped my forearm, "We wanted to hold a great feast for you."

Shaking my head I said, "By dawn, we will have slipped away. Any goodbyes must be today but the boys and I will be loading the snekke and birchbark boats all day."

Everything was ready but the loading of the snekke and the boats would take care and I stayed by the boats with Moos Blood while the others fetched the things we would need. I had removed the decks and some of the ballast so that we could put some items there. They would be the heavy things we would need in our new home but not on the journey. The pile grew next to the snekke for I did not rush. When Fears Water and Humming Bird came to tell me that we had all that had been in the yehakin they had incredulous looks on their faces as they saw the pile still to be loaded.

I smiled, "Do not fear, all will fit. Soon we will refit the deck and then arrange other things on the snekke. Your wives will have a cosy nest on these vessels." I pointed to the birchbark boats. "It is you four boys in the boats that cause me concern."

We had spoken of this over the winter. There were four birchbark boats and each one would have one of the boys with a paddle. Golden Bear and Humming Bird would be in the boats tied to the snekke as they were the least experienced. Brave Cub and Fears Water would be in the last vessels.

"You will need to paddle hard when we set off and then keep using the paddles regularly to ensure that we make good time. You will tire and if you think the ropes are in danger of shearing then you must shout."

"Will that not attract attention?"

I smiled, "Humming Bird, the snekke will be the strangest things on this river. We will be noticed and that is why we will find places to camp that are safe. Now let us waste no more time with words. We have boats to load."

Unlike the time we had loaded the drekar and headed away from the land of Ice and Fire, we had no animals with us. There would be no room. Now we used the baled furs we had collected over the winter to provide shelter for the women. Pots of dried meat and brined fish would also be on the snekke. The birchbark boats had spare woods for any repairs we might need for the snekke. Pots of pine tar and coiled ropes were also aboard. The birchbark boats had the bulky items but most of them were not heavy. Golden Bear, being the lightest, had the pine tar and I had told him that if the pine tar was too heavy and he was in danger he could ditch it overboard. We could always make more. By the time the sun was setting the two snekke were facing the right way and the birchbark boats were tethered. We wearily trudged back to the village for the last time.

Brave Eagle and his clan awaited us and stood in a half-circle to greet us. Running Antelope held out her hands, "You did not think we would simply let you sail away, did you, Erik, Shaman of the Bear? There would be no clan in this village had you not come with my husband and sons to rescue us and we all know that without you they would have failed. Tonight we tend on you."

It was a tearful night for the mothers of those who had married my children and knew that they might never see their children again. There might be grandchildren but they would never see them. Laughing Deer was not Powhatan but she had been popular and brought new skills to the clan. The women would miss her. As for me and my sons? Warriors who had come north with me to hunt the captives knew of my skills. The battle with the Moneton had also shown that my clan was a formidable force. They each asked to touch the sword or wear the helmet. The two were beneath the decks of *'Gytha'* and they had to make do with the hatchet and seax. The bearskin was also seen as a magic totem. The hunting of a bear was a dangerous thing for a band of warriors and for one man to have slain a bear was seen as magical. The bearskin would be with me on the snekke and so they asked to touch it and feel the rents of weapons. The cut on the head of the skin had saved my skull and they marvelled at that.

It was with great reluctance that I rose, somewhat stiffly for my knee was still not functioning as it might and bade farewell to the clan. A tearful Laughing Deer came with me as we went to the yehakin we would use for the last time. We said not a word but lay down and thought of the happy times we had enjoyed.

Erik's Clan

I woke early. It was a combination of the need to make water and the pain from my knee that woke me. After I had emptied my bladder, I went to wake my sons. I was awake and there was no reason not to leave. There was food left over from the night before and we ate as we carried the last of our belongings to the boats.

We passed Red Feather, the night sentry, and he nodded, "We will miss you and your family, Erik, Shaman of the Bear. It is sad that Long Spear no longer leads the tribe."

"Aye, Red Feather, but this is meant to be. The clan is stronger now than when I came and has warriors who can defend this land."

"And you, will you have to fight to carve out a land for you and your clan?"

I shook my head, "We will search until we find a place where there is no danger. The spirits will guide us."

Red Feather was voicing the fears that many, including my family, had expressed. I knew that Gytha and the spirits would not let me down and although I did not know where we would eventually settle, I knew that settle we would.

The sun was peering through the trees by the time the family was settled in their positions. Blue Feather and Sings Softly were particularly fearful. We had not had the opportunity to sail with them. Little White Dove was with Blue Feather in *'Doe'* and Sings Softly was in my snekke with my wife. I knew that in a world that I had fashioned I would have one of the boys with me in the snekke to work the sails. My wife and daughter would have to be the sailors. I smiled as I remembered the voyage from the land of Ice and Fire, then the women had learned how to be sailors and they had coped.

The passage to the river would be the hardest and I half lowered the sail and then told my wife and Sings Softly to use the two paddles we had made and help us to the river. There was little point in forcing it for we had two birch bark boats in tow but the current aided us and as Brave Eagle and his family came to wave us off *'Gytha'* began to tug and pull as the slight breeze from astern helped us. I called to Moos Blood, "The wind helps us. We will steer north by east and use the far shore of the Patawomke until we have to turn east."

One advantage I had was that I had sailed upstream a number of times and I knew that the river took a sharp turn to the east fourteen or so miles ahead. Anything could happen to the wind in that time but while it was with us we would use it. As we emerged into the river I said, "Laughing Deer, loose the sail and tie it off." She had done so when we had sailed from the land of the Mi'kmaq and as soon as she tied it off and I put the steering board a little further over we flew and

Erik's Clan

Sings Softly gave a squeal. I was not sure if it was of joy or fear but I knew that my heart was filled with joy as Erik the Navigator led his small fleet of boats to a home as yet unknown and certainly many days away. I was heading for an adventure again and I wondered if this would be my final destination.

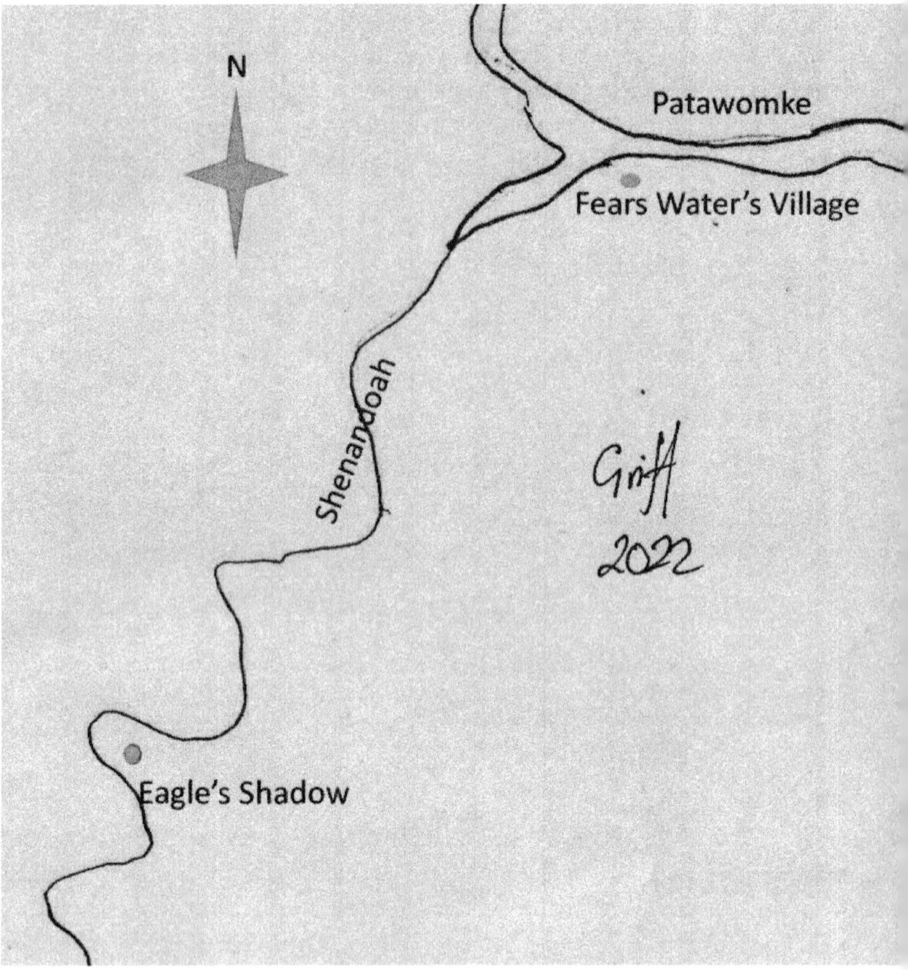
N
Patawomke
Fears Water’s Village
Shenandoah
Griff
2022
Eagle’s Shadow

Chapter 11

For the first mile or so I kept looking astern to see if the birchbark boats were coping and I was relieved to see that they were. *'Doe'* was newer and faster. Moos Blood soon caught up with me so that we could sail a course that was parallel to one another. It was safer and certainly more companionable. It meant my children could talk to each other and I know, from Sings Softly's face, that it made her relax.

The river appeared empty but then it was early. There would be boats for I knew that the tribes who lived on the far shore used the river to fish. I had seen them before and they posed no threat but I was glad that we were, for the present, unobserved. Later we would be seen but I wanted the direction we had taken hidden from Eagle Claws for as long as possible. The ropes towing the birchbark boats were holding up well and the four boys had a rhythm to their paddling. It was not fast but each stroke dug in and was a long one. The boys had practised and used their paddles on the opposite side of the boat to their consort. It kept them straight. I knew we were not moving as quickly as normal but that was to be expected. We were heavily laden and we were towing. It took until the sun had passed noon before we reached the turn. I knew that the spirits favoured us when the wind shifted a point or two to blow directly from the south. It meant we did not have to tack. With the wind from the larboard, we made a better speed than I might have hoped.

Laughing Deer said after we had eaten, "We really need to make water, husband."

I nodded, "And you, my love, should remember how we do that. You will need to hold Sings Softly's hands when she makes water over the side and then, having learned, she can do the same for you. We cannot stop." The prospect of making water over the side did not appeal and the women endured the discomfort as I did.

Once we turned north again we fairly flew and made good time. I had an idea where we would camp for I remembered a small beach, completely surrounded by trees. As the sun started to dip to the west I spied the patch of white and I shouted, "Moos Blood, head for the beach."

He nodded and then had my daughter loose his sail a little more. Hitherto we had kept pace with each other but now he used the wind to race ahead of us. I could not blame him and I hoped that the beach would be empty but I still feared for him. It was dark when *'Gytha'* ground onto the white sand. Moos Blood and those with him had hauled the birchbark boats up onto the sand and as they helped us, he said, "I neither see nor smell danger. Can we risk a fire? The women will need its comfort."

I knew he was right and I nodded, "But you and I must take turns to watch this night." He nodded and I smiled, "It will be like the time I sailed the drekar from the land of Ice and Fire. Then I often went without sleep."

"And now, father, you have a son who can share the burden."

While Brave Cub began the fire I secured **'Gytha'**. Until we reached our new home **'Gytha'** and **'Doe'** were the two most important possessions. The women made water and Sings Softly said, "I will make sure that tomorrow I do not need to make water while on the magic boat."

"You did well. You all did but know that we have many more days of this. We have managed more miles than I expected but we know not what will happen upstream."

Moos Blood was right. The hot food and fire helped. I let Moos Blood have the first watch and Laughing Deer and I curled up in my bear fur. When I was shaken awake it was hard to leave the warmth of the fur. It was still early in the year and the nights were cold. To keep me warm I fed the fire and then went into the trees to make water. It was reassuringly silent. By that I mean I could hear the animals of the night and their death struggles. It meant that there were no humans close by.

We left the next morning and headed north along the Patawomke under a rain-laden sky. In the snekke, we were prepared for discomfort as we had seal skin capes that could be used to make shelters but the boys in the birchbark boats would have to make do with deer hide. Making the shelters occupied the women and I had the shelters rigged well before the rain fell. As I knew it would do the rain slowed us down. The birch bark boats became heavier as they took on water. It would not be enough to swamp them but more than enough to slow us. If it had not been for a benign wind, we would have made barely twenty miles but we managed to make the large island in the middle of the river before dark and this time there was no discussion about the wisdom of lighting a fire. The rain had long stopped but the four boys were chilled to the bone. Laughing Deer and the women made a fine hot stew and the boys ate well. We needed no watch that night for we were on an island and my knee benefitted from the sleep. The rain had made it ache but the warmth of Laughing Deer's body and the fur took away much of the pain.

Erik's Clan

When we woke to just a few scudding clouds I was content. We drained the water from the boats and set off once more. Soon we would be close to Fears Water's village. I knew not if the Moneton were still there but we would be more likely to be in danger soon and we all had weapons to hand.

It was that day we saw people for the first time. They were Moneton and they were on the northern shore of the Patawomke. They were not warriors but women and children foraging in the shallows. We had been seen and could do nothing about it. The women and children did not flee at the sight of us but we would be noted. To make matters worse the narrowing river made navigation more difficult. The river was as wide as it had ever been but there were more islands and rocks. We needed sharp eyes and quick reactions. I remembered the problems from the last voyage. It was with some relief that we found another island on which we could camp just before the sun finally set. We saw the beach by the glow of the setting sun. The channels on both sides were deep and while the beach was not huge it was big enough for us to draw our boats up and disguise them with undergrowth.

As we ate, I spoke with the boys. I pointed to the western bank of the Patawomke, "That was Powhatan land. Fears Water's village was just a few miles from here." Fears Water nodded in agreement. "Now we do not know who lives there but we should err on the side of caution. Tomorrow keep your bows close to hand. If we are attacked then the four of you can lay down your paddles and defend us. We will let our snekke do the work." They all nodded and I took them into my confidence, "I do not know what the mouth of the Shenandoah is like for I have not travelled it. Fears Water has only seen it from the land. Before I risk sailing up it, I would have a good look at it. To that end, Moos Blood, tomorrow I shall lead and you will have to curb *'Doe'*. Let the old lady that is *'Gytha'* sniff out danger."

"I am happy to do so."

Brave Cub shook his head, "And I will learn how to sail a snekke for I am heartily sick of paddling!"

The next morning we woke to a wind from the southeast. It was the first time we had enjoyed such a wind. It helped us push north. Fears Water called out when he began to recognise the land. I, too, found familiar landmarks and I had the women watch the two shores closely.

It was Moos Blood who saw the boats and called out the warning. Behind us were six Moneton birchbark boats and they each held four warriors. They were dressed for war and paddling after us. Even with the boys paddling our weight meant that they would catch us but I was determined to get as far upriver as I could before they did so. The two snekke responded well to both the wind and our hands. While the Moneton still gained it was like the time we had hunted whales near Bear Island. It was a slow gain. I saw the Shenandoah when the Moneton were a hundred paces from Moos Blood. My heart sank. While the river looked to be more than a hundred paces wide it was littered with rocks and the white flecked water told me that it would be a dangerous passage. I suppose that at times the river would be high enough to cover them but I saw that while there was a passage betwixt them it would not be an easy sail.

I shouted over my shoulder, "Keep sailing north. Prepare, Moos Blood, to come alongside me and we will use bows."

His voice carried on the wind, "Aye, father for they are now gaining."

Gradually **'Doe'** came abeam of us. I said, "The Shenandoah will be tricky, Moos Blood."

"I saw, father, but the Moneton are less than eighty paces from us."

"Then now is the time to stop paddling and empty their boats."

The four boys in the boats were glad to put down their paddles and pick up their bows. As soon as they ceased paddling the Moneton closed with us. It took some moments to string their bows and the Moneton came ever closer. The three leading boats would have their best warriors. I had a wide river ahead and I was able to watch my clan fight their first battle since we had left Brave Eagle. Golden Bear did not have a bow and he used his sling before the three bows were able to send an arrow. His first stone was long and he quickly adjusted and sent a stone to smack into the skull of the warrior at the prow of the leading boat. It rendered him unconscious and as his paddle fell into the river the boat began to slew around and that allowed three arrows to strike two of the paddlers. One boat was out of the battle but the others closed. Now, however, with the range down to forty paces, the four found flesh with each stone and arrow. The Moneton had to paddle and could neither defend themselves nor fight back. When the leading three boats all suffered wounds and the fourth had two paddlers struck with arrows, they gave up their pursuit and headed to the northern bank of the river. They would tend to their wounded.

"Well done!" I pointed to a bend in the river. The trees would hide us from the Moneton and we would be able to stop. Night was just a couple of hours away. "We will stop beyond the bend in the river."

As we headed around the long slow bend my mind was calculating. The Moneton warriors were hurt but not defeated. They knew the land better than we did and I had no doubt that they would send for reinforcements. They had seen us head north and I wanted them to search in that direction. We had to risk the rock-strewn mouth of the Shenandoah and to risk it soon. As soon as we rounded the bend of the river, I lowered the sail and let the wind hold us against the current.

Moos Blood brought his snekke next to mine and we each held the gunwale of the other. "We must risk the river in the dark."

I saw fear on Moos Blood's face, "You might be able to manage that, father, for you are Erik the Navigator, but can I?"

"You have my blood and, I think, my skill. Just keep your snekke on exactly the same line as me. Little White Dove has skills. Have her at the prow and she can guide you. We must make the Moneton think we are north of here. Having seen it for myself I know that only a fool would risk the Shenandoah at night and come the morning the river Patawomke will be filled with their boats as they seek us. The arrows and stones have added to the list of injuries that our two magical ships have inflicted on them. Let them think that we used our magic to disappear."

He nodded, "If you think I can do it then I can."

I explained to them all what we intended. "The passage will be bumpy. I want you women to hold on tightly to the gunwale. You boys must paddle. We are shallow draughted as are you but while we can endure the odd rock or two your boats cannot. Use your paddles to fend us from the rocks lest your hull is ripped from you. If you are swept overboard then the current will take you towards the Moneton. If you do capsize then hold on to the boat. It will save you." I hoisted the sail and prepared to turn the snekke, "And I pray that Gytha and the spirits of my clan watch over us."

Night fell quickly and the black water merged with the dark land. As we sailed with the current and against the wind, I realised that the spirits were with us. As we rounded the bend of the river, we were travelling so slowly that any watcher on the other bank would not see movement. I took in some of the sail to make us even harder to see. I had to trust that Little White Dove would tell my son and he would emulate me. As we neared the mouth of the Shenandoah, I saw that the spirits were also helping me by marking the rocks that guarded the river with white specks of water. Soon the wind would make us travel faster but first, we had to cross a treacherous stretch of water. We would have to sail up the river until we were well out of sight of the Moneton.

As soon as we turned to head south and west the snekke began to buck as the bow struck the waters of the Shenandoah. The river became noisier as the water rushed and bubbled over rocks. The sound would hide us from any watching Moneton.

"Laughing Deer, go to the prow and warn me of rocks."

My wife had helped me to sail when we had left the Mi'kmaq and she made her way to the prow. As soon as she got there, she waved an urgent hand to the right and I put the steering board hard over. Sings Softly gave a squeal as she was thrown to one side. She stayed in the snekke. The rock my wife had warned me of was the size of a moos.

"A rock to larboard!" The cry was for the boys in the boats and for Moos Blood.

Laughing Deer's next gesture was less dramatic. She waved me to larboard and I made a gentler turn. Laughing Deer held her hand directly above her head and I centred the steering board. The motion of the snekke was still uncomfortable for the river bubbled over shallows and rocks. If this was in daylight then the passage might be easier for I would see the stiller waters that showed safety. The Norns had spun and we were forced to take this action. Even as I realised that I also saw that while this was dangerous the Norns web meant that, if we survived the passage, then we would be more likely to have a safer home. The river was heading south and west. Laughing Deer made one more dramatic gesture and when I had turned to steerboard and then centred the steering board, the motion of the snekke became smoother.

Laughing Deer turned and I saw the beaming smile as she shouted, "The river is wider and I can see a pair of islands ahead."

I turned and shouted, "We will land soon, Moos Blood."

"Thank the Allfather for that." I heard the relief in his voice.

I did not use more sail and we edged gently up to the two islands. I landed us on the island to larboard as it looked larger and had a white line that suggested a beach rather than a rock. We pulled the boats up out of the water and then dragged the snekke up too.

"I know you are all tired and hungry but before we do anything I want the snekke and the boats disguised with undergrowth. When morning comes I would have us hidden from view. By my estimate, we are just over a mile from the mouth of the river. The two islands will hide us. We will camp here for a night and a day. We need the rest." After we had disguised the boats, I allowed a fire and hot food. Night would hide the smoke and the islands and boats hid the flames. "When we have eaten, we douse the flames. I want no sign of smoke when the morrow comes. The Moneton will look for us. Let us not give them any help."

I rose first and walked to the end of the island with my bearskin over me to watch the dawn. My knee ached for the night had been cold but I had to ensure that we were invisible. I watched the sun rise and I looked west. I could not detect either the boats or smoke. I headed back to the camp and laid fishing lines in the water. When the clan awoke, I smiled for I was pleased, "This is our home for a day and a night. We will light a fire tonight and until then we rest and eat cold fare."

Laughing Deer came and hugged me, "And you, my husband will not stir. Last night you moaned in your sleep and I know it was your knee. You have done the hard work. Today you rest and we will tend on you."

Moos Blood organized the men so that they kept watch on the river while my wife had the women prepare the food that we would eat when we had the luxury of a fire. I lay on my bearskin and dozed. It did my knee good to lie with the rays of the sun warming me. When darkness fell, we risked the fire and ate a stew of dried meat mixed with freshly caught fish. After a day of cold fare, it felt like a feast.

After we had eaten, I spoke to them, "Our new life begins tomorrow. None of us knows what to expect along this river. For all that I know, it may become unnavigable and we might be forced to stop. The Norns are spinning still and I will lead. Every eye must be on the land to the south. I know that it used to be Powhatan land but I want a home away from others. I need time for our clan to make a secure home. I want a hideaway. Gytha told me of a bend in the river and a high place. We seek that."

The smiles on all their faces were gratifying and after dousing the fire we all slept well. The next day would be the first day of our new lives.

Chapter 12

My fears almost came true just a mile or so down the river. We came across shallows and rocks that barred our way. Moos Blood asked, "Is this as far as we can go, Father?"

I shook my head, "I do not know. Gytha said to look for a bend in the river and high ground. This has neither. Perhaps it is just a test for us. Brave Cub, empty your boat and you and Humming Bird carry your boat over the rocks and see how far this barrier stretches."

He was eager to do so and after placing his cargo on dry land he and Humming Bird carried their birchbark boat over the shallows. They dropped it into deeper water and then paddled off. I let our passengers off and we let the snekke rest on a shelf of rock.

Laughing Deer said, "This looks like a pleasant enough place to make a home."

I shook my head, "It is too close to the mouth of the river. I would sail further upstream."

"But how can we? The birchbark boats can be emptied but not the snekke."

"Portage."

She looked confused at the word, "That is a word I have not heard you use, my husband. What does it mean?"

"We cut saplings and lay them across the rocks. We haul the snekke over them. If the boys pull then the women can keep moving the wood from behind to before the snekke. It will not be quick but, if the boys come back and say that the river is clear ahead then it will be worth it. These rocks would make any Moneton believe that we could not take out boats further upstream."

The boys soon came back. Brave Cub was younger than Humming Bird but he knew about sailing, "It is good deep water for the next mile or so."

"Good then take out the axes, we will portage our snekke," I explained what we would do. While the tools were readied, we carried the birchbark boats and laid them on the bank to the west of the rocks. Then we began to hew. With five of us cutting, we soon made enough rollers to move the snekke. Tying ropes to *'Gytha'* we began to haul. At first, it was hard until I remembered how we used to row. I began to chant and when the boys joined in, we started to move the snekke for we were working as one.

Erik's Clan

> ***Erik's clan sent the Moneton to hel***
> ***Erik's clan was like a Norseman's axe***
> ***Their hearts were true they fought as one***
> ***The clan of the bear that day was born***
> ***Golden Bear and Brave Cub***
> ***Fears Water and Moos Blood***

The women joined in the chant and soon had a rhythm of their own going as, in pairs, they picked up a roller and raced through the shallows to lay it before us. There was laughter in our voices as the clan worked as one. *'Doe'* was moved even easier and by the time the sun had reached its zenith we had moved all the boats.

"It is a shame to waste these rollers and we may need them again. Tie them to the side of the birchbark boats. They will make the boats more buoyant." It took time to do but we were in no hurry. The Moneton warriors, I hoped, were still seeking us on the Patawomke and it was better to get to the place Gytha had described than settle for second best.

We sailed down the Shenandoah and whilst we were vigilant and scoured the banks, we saw no sign of man. There were neither boats nor smoke. It was as evening approached and we came to a large loop in the river that we found more shallows but the setting sun helped us for it showed the passage past the rocks. I did not risk damaging the boats and we made a camp on the side of the river. Despite the problems, it had been a good day and the clan was in good spirits. I had noticed, as we sailed along the river, the ridge of hills to the south of us. I said nothing but I recognised them as the place I had found the iron stone. We were getting close to somewhere we could call home. There was a slope and loop in the river. Was this the place we had been meant to come to?

My knee had been hurting and that evening Laughing Deer insisted upon me drinking the last of the beer. We would brew more when we found a new home but beer helped ease the pain. It did more than that for that night Gytha came to me.

> ***When you see the rocks that bar your way you know you have found a home where you can live.***
> ***Make a home of turf and wood and use the river as your friend.***
> ***This home will be safe and there you can defend.***

Her words were so clear that I felt I was in the spirit world with her. The next morning I was eager to get going and I hurried the family to board the boats. As we approached another huge loop Laughing Deer shouted, "We shall need the rollers, husband, there is a wall of rock barring our progress."

Lowering the sail I put the steering board over and said, with laughter in my voice, "They are not a barrier, they are a marker." I pointed to the slope that led up from the river. "This is our new home. The spirits told me. We shall live here. This is where our clan shall flourish." There was a natural inlet and I put the snekke into it. "Tie *'Doe'* to *'Gytha'* and we will use this as a longphort until we can improve the landing."

"Longphort?" asked Humming Bird.

Moos Blood smiled, "A sort of bridge of boats. My father's people were very clever."

I stepped ashore and tied the snekke securely to a tree. I strung my bow and nocked an arrow. The place felt safe but I would take no chances. "Land, but do not move far until I have explored. Moos Blood, begin the unloading of the boats."

The land was thickly forested but the trees were of a good size and I was able to walk easily between them. The ground rose gently and I headed up the slope. As I moved away from the river I found that the trees became more open. Reaching the top I spied, through the trees the two pieces of the river. We would have water on three sides of us and I knew this was the place we had meant to find. I descended to where I could see one arm of the river. I headed north and counted my paces. All the time I walked I looked for tracks and saw only those of deer and animals. There was no sign of man. Three hundred and eighty paces later I reached the river. The water looked deep enough on the other side for the snekke. Retracing my steps I climbed the slope and then when I found my starting point counted again as I headed south. Four hundred and sixty paces later I found the river again. This time I set off to walk around the loop. It was not a straight route but a manageable one and I reached the landing site.

"This is good. There is a large loop and by my estimate, the neck of land is less than a thousand paces wide. We can defend this place." The looks of joy on their faces made me feel happy. The spirits had guided us once more. I pointed to the snekke. "This landing place is not large enough for the two snekke. I will take Humming Bird with me. Moos Blood I want you and the others to dig out the earth and use branches to strengthen it. I want an area the length of the two snekke where we can moor the ships."

He nodded, "And what will you do?"

"Humming Bird and I will take axes and begin to clear the place where we shall live."

Fears Water asked, "Will you make yehakin?"

Shaking my head I said, "No, we will have no shelter for some days. I will build a longhouse." When I saw Laughing Deer smile and nod her agreement I knew I had made the right decision. She had seen, on Bear Island, such a home and she approved of it. I picked up my wood axe and handed two flint axes to Humming Bird. With my whetstone in my pouch, I would be able to sharpen the metal axe I held.

"We will cook some food. Come." Laughing Deer took charge of the women. My sons' wives would be guided by her. She was now the mother of the clan and knew better than any the importance of such a role. When we reached the top of the slope, I pointed to the trees at the very top. There were six of them and each one had a bole the thickness of my leg. They would not be as much use as the trees lower down the slope that were much thicker but these needed to be cleared first.

"We take these six first. We will work together." My metal axe bit large chunks from the trees but Humming Bird was strong and skilled so that between us we took down the six trees quite quickly and as soon as the canopy of leaves and branches were removed then sunlight bathed us and showed me the potential for the house we would build. We would waste nothing and so we began to trim the smaller branches from the trunks. The trunks were laid neatly in a pile and the branches in another. I looked at the sun. It had passed noon some time ago and I was anxious to see the camp by the river.

The smell of food made me realise I was hungry. The sight of the boys, muddy and weary made me smile. Moos Blood had done well and there was now an inlet of muddy water. It was deep enough for the snekke and, more importantly, long enough for them both to be secured. They had taken down four spindly trees but left enough of their trunks to make posts that were used to secure the snekke. The four birchbark boats, having been emptied, were now drawn up on dry land. The belongings we had brought were neatly stacked too.

We laid our axes down and I said, "Come, I will show you our new home."

Fears Water asked, "We will not live here, by the water?"

I waved a hand at the ground that was flat, "When this is cleared of trees it will make a place we can plant our crops. The river will water it and it is flat. We will live higher up. I know not if this river floods but, if it does, then we shall be dry."

I took Laughing Deer's hand and led her up the slope. Soon our feet would mark a path and by the time winter came, we would have a good trail that we would use to get to the river. As soon as we reached the part we had cleared smiles told me that they approved.

"We will need to dig out the roots of these trees but that is good for we can make pine tar. I have a mind to paint the outside of our home with pine tar. We will cut and collect the turf and that will be our roof. We will all live in one building but we will use the wood we made as rollers to make rooms within the house. There will be a strong door and we will be able to defend it. What think you?"

My family, Golden Bear excepted, nodded for they had seen the house on Bear Island. The others could not visualise it. They soon would.

We returned down the hill. The boys cleaned themselves up while Humming Bird and I rigged shelters close to the fire. We ate our meal under a setting sun with the Shenandoah gently bubbling as it headed towards the Patawomke. I had been told to look for a sunset and the magnificent red sky in the west was confirmation. All was well. We were too weary for night guards but I trusted the spirits. Gytha had led us here and all that she had told me was true. I knew that there might be clans living somewhere in this area but we had smelled no woodsmoke and seen no signs. If they were in this valley then they were many miles hence. The two patches of shallows we had seen explained to me why this was an underused waterway. To me it offered safety. If we had to, we could transport the snekke over the rocks and so long as no other clan tried to claim this land, we would be safe.

In the morning we ate the left over food and then the whole clan ascended the hill. As we climbed, I saw an eagle flying overhead. It was hunting for food and made large circles in the sky. As we reached the top its shadow appeared on the ground that we had cleared and it gave a cry. It was as though the spirits were talking. "And our new home shall be Eagle's Shadow."

The nods told me that they liked the name. While the women began to cut the turf the boys and I dug out the stumps of the trees. We spread the soil out to flatten it and I saw that we had an area that was twenty paces by fifteen paces. It would do. I estimated the number of trees we would need for the wooden walls and worked out that we had enough within ten paces of the house. We would have space to build other buildings if we needed them. I wanted a log store, a shelter for the snekke and a steam hut. We then began the hard part of felling trees and making them into usable logs for the house. That first day we only hewed two but they were mighty trees. The women descended to begin to cook food and we spent the last hours of daylight trimming the branches and even splitting one of the trees.

The path to the water was clear cut now and we headed down buzzing with excitement. Eagle's Shadow already felt like a safe home.

"We will need to hunt soon, husband. We still have some dried and salted food but…"

My wife was right. "Moos Blood, I want you and Golden Bear to go hunting tomorrow." I pointed towards the neck of land, "Head that way. You can explore and hunt. I would have you make a map of this land."

Humming Bird asked, "A map?"

I nodded, "A piece of deer hide with marks upon it. It shows where animals are to be found as well as the river and paths. We used one when we came from the land of the Mi'kmaq."

Fears Water frowned. He had seen the sea, "A map of the water? Does it not all look the same?"

Moos Blood laughed, "No, it does not. My father is called a shaman but his real skill is in navigation. Trust us, the maps will be useful."

By the end of the next day, we had enough logs ready to begin to build the house. With notches cut in the ends of the logs, we made two sides of the house. When my sons returned with the deer they had hunted, they were impressed by the progress. We had not, however, achieved all that we had without setbacks. We had broken one of the flint axes. With, at the moment, no flint to hand we would have to use one of the stone axes the next day. It would do the job but not as efficiently as either the metal or the flint axes. With all the boys working on the house progress was quicker. Seven days after we had begun, we had four walls and were almost ready to start the roof. It had rained during the week and that had kept the turf moist but I knew that we needed the roof in place sooner rather than later. It was when we came to begin the roof that I realised I would not be able to help. My knee had improved but Laughing Deer would not risk me suffering greater injuries by allowing me to climb. Moos Blood and Brave Cub laid the turf on the branches we had laid to make an apex. I worked with Fears Water to build the chimney from river stones. We would have a fire in the house and we would be warm in winter. There was no door but as the last turf sod was laid on the roof we all felt satisfaction. Within a day or two, we would be able to move from our riverside camp to Eagle's Shadow.

When we had built the house on Bear Island, I had not taken much interest in the building but having defended it from attack when I was left alone I now had a better idea of how to make it better. As soon as I was satisfied with the door the others began to ferry our belongings up from the river. Moos Blood and I used the rollers to make the six sleeping chambers in the interior. We buried the roller poles in the ground and Moos Blood secured them to the roof trusses. The privacy would come when we fitted the walls. I used saplings bound with lianas and mud for mine. Moos Blood chose deer hide for his. Each family could make their own decision. The floor was already dry and as we walked on it, it became packed and hardened. When summer came we would cut rushes from the river, dry them and use them as cleaner flooring.

    A month after we had landed all was finished. The fire in the fireplace would be for winter and Laughing Deer and the women used the outside fire to cook. We dug a pit some fifteen paces from the longhouse and I made a tripod on which to hang the cooking pot. We built a simple shelter over the top so that the women could cook outside, even when it was raining. We were now desperate for food and so leaving Golden Bear and Fears Water to build a wood store I led the others to hunt and explore. Moos Blood had made the beginnings of a map and hunted some white-tailed deer but the map was rudimentary and we had already eaten the meat. I wanted to know what lay within five miles of our new home. I also wanted to head close to the ridge of hills where I knew I would find the iron I needed. The broken flint axe reinforced the need for metal. It would make our lives much easier. I let Moos Blood lead as he had already walked this land and he had made the map. I noticed where animals had grazed and their trails. I had asked him to lead us to the furthermost point he had explored. He led us to the place where they had hunted the two deer that they had slain. I took over. The ground rose slightly and I saw another animal trail. I nocked an arrow and headed along it. The lack of any signs of man was reassuring. We had not seen any evidence of the clearing of land for food. The absence of men also helped us for the animals were unused to being hunted. When I smelled the deer ahead, I raised my arm to halt us and waved for the other three to spread out. We stalked our prey.

    This was my clan and I led. I knew that the other three would only loose an arrow when I gave the word and when I saw the herd of deer ahead, I moved even more slowly. We had to get as many as we could. We needed to clear land for crops and I wanted one good hunt to feed the clan for a month or two. I waited until we were less than thirty paces from the herd. With the wind in our faces, I knew that they had not smelled us and the undergrowth hid us. They were grazing in a clearing. I did not risk getting closer and I drew back on the bow. I released at the large doe and I heard the other bowstrings. I nocked another arrow and managed to hit a second deer in the rump. Only one of the deer had been killed outright. We hurried after the wounded and dying animals, following the blood trail. We found them within two hundred paces of the clearing. After using my hatchet to cut small trees to carry them we headed back to the clearing.

Erik's Clan

It was when we reached the now empty clearing that I noticed what I had missed before. The clearing was man-made. I spied the stumps of the trees that had been felled. I saw why the deer were grazing for the stumps had signs of new growth and the soft shoots had been eaten. While the others gutted the animals to leave the entrails for the carrion, I explored the clearing. I found the marks where a dwelling had once been. It looked to me like a small number had stayed here. Were they hunters and had they made this a hunting camp? The other explanation was that this was a small clan who moved around the forest taking what they needed and moving on.

"Moos Blood, give me the map."

I took the map and, dipping my finger in the deer blood, made a mark where the clearing was. I used an X to do so. "What is that for father?"

I handed the map back to Moos Blood and said, "I think, Brave Cub, that there is another clan who lives in these woods. Those trees were not felled by animals. From now on we look for clearings like this and mark them on the map."

Carrying the carcasses on the poles we headed back to our new home. Already we had made our mark. The smoke that spiralled in the sky and the smell of food cooking showed where we lived. As we ate that night I explained to the women and the ones who had not been on the hunt, the significance of the clearing. "I do not think that this means danger but it means there might be others who live within a few miles of us. They may well fear us but I would, rather than fight them, speak to them."

Fears Water said, "And if they are Moneton?"

"I do not think that they are. I believe they are more likely to be Powhatan for the clearing was made some years ago and by a small number of people. Who knows, there may be people like us who, for one reason or another choose to live alone."

Moos Blood pointed to the river, "Perhaps we should explore upstream of here. We saw no settlements between the Patawomke and here. It would make sense if we discovered if there are clans upstream."

I nodded, "We will do so when we have cleared the trees by the river. We can use the timber for more buildings and plant the seeds that we brought."

Humming Bird shook his head, "It is too late in the season to plant, Erik."

I smiled, "We will not plant things like corn but we will plant those plants that grow quickly. As much as I enjoy a diet of fish and deer, I also like the variety that green plants bring. Besides which it will ready the soil for spring when we do plant." What I did not say was that we had brought cereals that would grow now and be harvested before winter settled in. They would allow Laughing Deer to make beer. I had drunk the last of our precious supply and we now relied on river water. While that was, generally wholesome, I knew that if the river flooded then it might become undrinkable. I did not wish to dig a well.

We cleared the field in seven days and then, while the land was tilled, I built an oven to burn the tree stumps and make pine tar. The stumps that were left would make charcoal and I still had plans to find iron. Once the tar was collected, we painted, first the hulls of the snekke and birchbark boats and then the walls of the longhouse. By the time it had dried we were ready to explore upstream. I went with my three sons in a birchbark boat. I left Fears Water and Humming Bird to guard our home and to fish from the river.

We had found another place to launch the birchbark boats upstream from the shallows and we paddled. I sat in the stern and steered whilst paddling. Both sides of the river were heavily forested. We spied deer and other animals at the waterside drinking but we saw no sign of man. The river twisted and turned and narrowed but at its narrowest, it was still more than eighty paces wide. More importantly, there were no more shallows. We could sail the snekke here if we wanted to. We turned the boat around when the sun was at its height. I had found what I needed to know. The land was safe, at least for the moment. We could prepare for the winter.

Erik's Clan

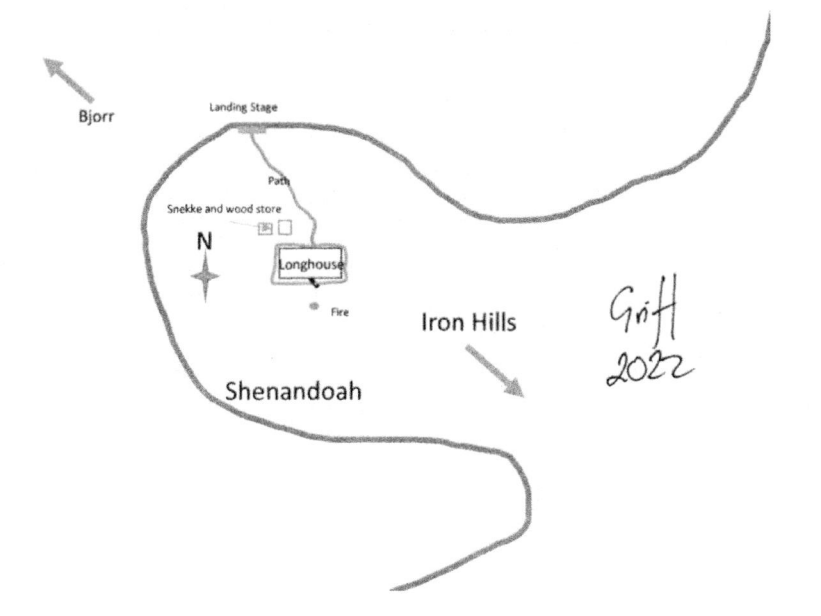

Bjorr

Landing Stage

Path

Snekke and wood store

N

Longhouse

Fire

Iron Hills

Shenandoah

Griff
2022

Chapter 13

By the time the days shortened again our cereals were growing well and the salad crops we had planted were ready for harvesting. We had hunted and fished and had more than enough food to last until the depths of winter. We also had three women with child. It was almost as though the Allfather had decided that when we planted our seed in the ground he would help Moos Blood, Fears Water and Humming Bird to plant theirs. I would be a grandfather. Laughing Deer reacted by insisting upon better conditions in the longhouse. We stripped the bark from the trees we had felled to augment the rushes on the floor. It gave the house a different sort of smell but ensured that the floor was slightly cleaner. The women worked to clean the hides from the animals we had hunted. As yet we had not found bjorr and we needed fur. I knew that my next expedition would be to find bjorr and hunt them before hibernation.

We were now more familiar with our little neck of land between the two arms of the river. We had walked the same routes and made paths. It gave us all more confidence and, leaving just Humming Bird and Fears Water to watch the camp and the ships, I left with my sons to find the bjorr. The iron hills were to the southeast and so we took a boat to cross the river. The land to the west was flatter and more likely to be the domain of the bjorr who liked to build dams where they could flood larger areas. We had seen few such streams during our exploration. We drew the boat up on a beach close to the mouth of a stream and walked up it. The fact that the stream looked wide and yet was shallow gave me a clue that it might be dammed. When we had sailed the drekar in the land of the Penobscot I had learned how to look for bjorr sign. I explained everything to my three sons for these were lessons that would help them when I was no longer here. I was aware, especially now that I was to become a grandfather, that I did not have years ahead of me.

We had with us flint spears as well as bows and arrows. Golden Bear was happy about that. he had begun to use a bow but did not yet have the strength to draw a powerful one like his brothers. He could, however, stab with a spear. I pointed to the dam that was just two hundred paces from us.

"That is where the bjorr lives."

"But it is just a jumble of trees and branches brought there by a flood."

Erik's Clan

I smiled, "No, Brave Cub. The bjorr is a clever builder. He fetches wood and makes a home much as we made our longhouse. Do not underestimate the bjorr and he is a tricky animal to hunt. His teeth are sharp enough to bring down a tree and would make short work of any hand placed too close to him."

We left the stream to come up to the bjorrs' home from the upwind side through the trees and undergrowth. The bjorr had cleared the trees there but there was new growth that would disguise us. We strung our bows and then stalked the stream and the dam. There were so many bjorr that it looked as though the water was alive with them. I had seen no sign of man and that meant that we were safe and, more importantly, the bjorr would not be used to being hunted. To Golden Bear's disappointment, I said, "Let us close with them and use arrows before they descend to the safety of their underwater home." He wanted to use his spear.

I knew there would be a sentry bjorr and I spied him on the trunk of a felled tree close to the land. He was a big one. I drew my bow back and the arrow slammed into him. I was lucky. He made not a sound and fell into the cleft of an old branch so that he did not even make a splash. The cry of the sentry bjorr would have been a loud one. The rest of the bjorr continued to work on the dam, adding small branches to make it more secure for the winter. Nocking another arrow I nodded as we closed with the bjorr. Three arrows struck three bjorr and even as we each sent another arrow at them there was a warning cry and they scurried for safety. We hit seven in all before the water emptied of the creatures.

We laid our bows and arrow bags on the bank and took the spears, "We must get close to the dam but try to stay on solid ground. The bjorr will think themselves safe underwater. When you strike in the water you have to do so harder than you think."

The bodies of the dead bjorr lay on the dam and in the water. We would have to risk walking in the dam to retrieve them.

Golden Bear was determined to emulate us and despite my attempts to restrain him, he was the first to find a bjorr. He jabbed down with his spear and the water bubbled and shook as he hit the bjorr.

"Hold on firmly with two hands."

As the bjorr tried to escape the spear Golden Bear began to tumble. I grabbed at his deer hide tunic and pulled back. The spearhead popped from the water and the wriggling bjorr came with it. The creature was mortally struck and as Golden Bear laid the animal on the bank it stopped moving.

"You were lucky, Golden Bear, and this is a lesson for you all. This is a dangerous place."

"Thank you, Father. I will be more careful."

By noon we had enough bjorr to be able to gather them in. Moos Blood was the best swimmer and naked, he went into the water to retrieve the carcasses. We did not want to damage the pelts too much and so we strung them on a spear skewered through their tails. They were heavy and Moos Blood and I carried two spears full of bjorr back to the boat. It was when we began to load the boat that I realised we should have brought two for the weight of the wet, dead bjorr, meant we had to paddle carefully for fear of capsizing. It was late afternoon when we reached our landing. Humming Bird and Fears Water came to our aid and then we began to skin the animals. The need for more iron was never clearer. The seaxes we had made short work of the pelts but the flint knives, good though they were, failed to skin as quickly as Moos Blood and me. We ate some of the bjorr tails that night. They were delicious. While most of the carcasses would be salted and brined, we would eat the tails fresh. The next day we pegged out the pelts to dry them. They would be made into furs that would keep us warm. Already, as the days became shorter, it felt cooler than it had at the same time of year in Brave Eagle's village. The signs were there that winter would be more challenging.

In anticipation of a harder winter than we were used to, I had the boys collect wood every day and we kept it dry beneath the roof of the wood store we had built. Moos Blood and I also improved the roof for the outside cooking fire; we made it bigger so that all the women could be accommodated The sides would be open and there would be an aperture for the smoke at the top but the women would be able to cook, even in winter, and be protected from rain. They enjoyed cooking and talking.

"We will move the snekke from the river." It was ten days since the bjorr hunt and I knew that we would not need the snekke again before spring. Moving them would take all of us. "We will take the masts from them and the steering boards. If we lift the decks and remove the ballast then they will be lighter." I pointed up the trail to the longhouse, the smoke spiralling from the roof, "I would have them by the house. We will build a shelter for them close to the wood store."

I heard Humming Bird groan, "Do we really need the snekke? This is a good home and the birchbark boats will suffice."

Before I could answer Moos Blood did, "Have you forgotten the effect of a snekke? We can sail faster than any birchbark boat and if we have to can return to the Patawomke easily and quickly. We do not discard the snekke." I approved of his assertive manner. He would lead the clan once I was dead.

Humming Bird was the only one who failed to realise the importance of the snekke. He had never been to sea in one and unlike Fears Water, his life had not been saved by one. We removed the ballast and we put them in a neat pile by the bank. The melting stone from the land of Ice and Fire would be taken to the longhouse. When we found iron, I would need that to melt the precious ore. We placed the two boats, decks, masts and steering boards upside down between the house and the wood store. When we had cleaned and coated the hull, we would build a roof over them. The air would get to them but neither the rain nor the snow. Once the snekke were moved we were able to moor our four birchbark boats in the berths on the landing stage they had vacated. They were far more secure.

As much as I wanted to head to the hills and their precious iron, I knew that would be a job for spring. The cave where I had found the ore would be the sort of place that a bear might choose for winter sleep. I had killed a bear once but it was not something I wanted to repeat. I contented myself with planning how we would make our way to the ridge and hills and how we might transport the iron back. I wanted more than a couple of stones. I intended to mine enough to make not only weapons but tools. I had seen iron pots once when we had lived close to Orkneyjar. If I could make one such pot then Laughing Deer's life would be easier. The clay pots we made and used rarely lasted longer than a season.

The snow came before the shortest day of the year. We had a warning of it for the skies became dark and threatening. The air was so cold that to step outside without a fur was foolish. As soon as the air warmed, when I rose in the dark of night to make water then I knew that snow would come. When we awoke it was to a world blanketed in white. Moos Blood and I were the first up and we cleared a path to the wood store. We had collected plenty of wood and stacked it under shelter. It seemed foolish to trudge through snow and bring wetness to our home. Mud could be scraped off before we entered.

"I will light the fire outside. Perhaps now we shall see how well we built the larger roof. Will it cope with the snow?"

The kindling was kept in the longhouse. Dried bark and old rushes were perfect. I returned to the ice world beyond our door and soon had a fire going. The roof worked and the smoke was drawn up through the hole. The snow that had accumulated on the roof began to melt and drip from the sides. I had not anticipated that. We would need some sort of gutter to take the water away. I was still studying the problem when

Laughing Deer joined me. She had some salted bjorr to make breakfast. The early cereals had been harvested and a few handfuls cooked with the bjorr meat would make a hearty meal.

She smiled, "The roof works. You are a clever man, Erik."

"Not clever enough for the melting snow drips."

"It is a small thing." She began to fill the pot and stir it. "You moaned in the night."

I nodded, "I am sorry. It was my knee."

"You should not have to apologise. I just wish there was something we could do to ease the pain."

"We should build a steam hut. When I last used one then I had less pain."

"You should have made one before now, before you built this!" She waved a hand at the roof.

"The steam hut would be for me. This is for the clan and I know which is more important."

She might have been right and it was too late now to think about making one. We would have to wait for a thaw. It then struck me that there might not be a thaw. In the land of Ice and Fire once the snow came it stayed all winter. There, of course, we had the warmth of the earth itself for there were hot springs that steamed and bubbled no matter how much snow and ice there was.

The snow meant that we stayed inside for a few days while a blizzard raged. When it blew itself out and blue though icy skies appeared, I went with Brave Cub and Moos Blood to see the effect of the snow. The first thing we discovered was the number of animals that lived within a few hundred paces of the longhouse. Their tracks crisscrossed the snow. Perhaps they had known of the impending storm for we found no dead animals caught out by the cold. They would be tucked beneath the ground. The clear skies meant that we were able to see as far as the tops of the hills. Now with a sprinkling of snow, they looked to be almost blue. We went down as far as the northern side of our land. While the river was not frozen there were pieces of ice floating down the river. If nothing else the snow showed us the natural contours of the land and I saw that we could if we wished, dig a channel between the two bends in the river and make our home an island. I had not seen enough danger yet to warrant such work but it was a thought. We made our way back to the landing and strung fishing lines with hooks made from the bjorr bones. We had gathered lots of food but the snow meant we might not have enough. With three pregnant women, we could not afford to have them go hungry.

Erik's Clan

The fishing provided a decent catch but they were not big enough to preserve. We used them in a stew with dried wild garlic and onions as well as greens and the last of the knobbly, seedless yellow fruits that grew close to the ground. Fresh meat was a distant memory. The last fresh meat we had enjoyed had been the bjorr and that seemed a lifetime ago.

As the three women grew larger so their three husbands wished to stay closer to the longhouse. On the first clear day when it neither snowed nor rained, I decided to take Golden Bear and Brave Cub to hunt beyond the bjorr dam. Animals that still grazed in winter would be more likely to be on lower ground and my knee did not relish a trek up the side of the hill that rose to the iron hills. We took a birchbark boat and paddled. Golden Bear had grown during the winter. He was rapidly catching up to Brave Cub who in contrast to his younger brother had filled out rather than grown taller. The result was that they were able to paddle well together. Golden Bear had his first bow and we had made arrows for him over the winter. I still had my sealskin cape while the boys had hide ones. They would keep them warm and unless we had a storm, dry. They were good but I preferred the sealskin that seemed to shed water and never became heavy. It was also a reminder of my former life. Wearing it made me feel Norse once more.

We hauled the boat onto the bank and I led. I still had the best eyes and ears although Moos Blood was becoming as good and would be able to take over from me soon. We followed the bjorr stream and looked for signs of grazing animals. We found the trail of deer a mile upstream from the dam. We strung our bows and nocked an arrow. The snow had a crust upon it. It was a sign that soon there would be a thaw but, for the moment it was a danger as it made a noise when we crunched through it. I took us into the stream. Our progress would be hindered but we would be silent and the icy waters would have to be endured. I smelled the deer before I saw them and as I rounded a bend saw them just thirty paces from us. My sons knew what to do. They made their way through the water until they flanked me. It was a larger herd than I had expected: a stag, a dozen hinds and then ten of the offspring born last year, the young. The boys knew to leave the stag alone. He was the herd's protection from other predators. They would also avoid the young. The three of us would aim for the older females. The meat would not be as tender but the animals might be slower and there would be more meat. As usual, the signal to loose was my arrow's flight. I caught an older hind in the shoulder. Brave Cub's hit another in the rump. To his chagrin Golden Bear missed for the hind at which he had aimed had moved. They fled into the safety of the trees.

There was no need for silence now and we left the icy river to head after the two wounded animals. The heavier blood trail was from the one I had hit. She was mortally stricken and we found her three hundred paces into the spindly trees. She had bled out and was dying even as we neared her. I took away her pain and we followed Brave Cub's strike. She managed almost half a mile before she stopped. Brave Cub nocked an arrow and sent it into the side of her head. She died.

"Your kill, Brave Cub. Gut her while I cut a pole for you and Golden Bear to use."

Golden Bear looked unhappy, "I missed."

"And I missed more than I hit when I was your age. It is how you learn. You will do better next time."

"I would have been better off using my sling."

"Perhaps but then you would never improve with a bow." My youngest son was learning valuable lessons.

I left him to help his brother and then went to cut a stave. I had my hatchet and I found a branch that was straight and looked to be the perfect length. I hacked it at the bottom and then trimmed the branches. It was as I was doing so that my eyes were drawn to prints in the snow. They had broken through the crust and were human. There was a jumble of them and they were confusing, at first, but I worked out that there was one adult, a small man or a woman, and three children. They headed to the south and east.

I returned to my sons. "Come we have to take these to the boats and then we have a puzzle."

As we carried the dead deer back to the first kill, I told them what I had found. Brave Cub shrugged, "You have found others, where is the surprise in that?"

"Did we smell the smoke of a camp?" He shook his head. "Then what are these doing alone in this land in the depths of winter? If this was summer there might be a reason. No, I do not like this and even though it will take us time I would have us investigate it. I do not think that a woman and children pose a problem but they are unexplained and I would like to get to the bottom of this."

By the time we had taken both carcasses back to the boat, it was noon and I made them run to return to the prints. My knee complained all the way and I knew that I would not sleep well that night. My wife was right. We needed a steam hut. When we found the tracks, I nocked an arrow and I led the way. The tracks, generally, followed the stream. The jumble of prints told me that the party was rushing. Had an animal pursued them? I had seen no signs of such a beast but they could have been stalked from the side. We did not have time to search a wider area.

I was curious to know what four people were doing out in the icy cold of winter alone.

When I saw blood in the snow my caution increased and I slowed down. The blood was not fresh and the wound not deep for there were just drops but what had caused the wound? We had been travelling for an hour and I knew we had to turn around soon but something drove me on. Then I heard the sounds of raised voices. I stopped and knelt knowing that my sons would do the same. I sniffed the air and smelled humans. They were ahead of us. The harsh angry voices were males and I heard weeping. I could have turned around then but I did not for the memory of finding Laughing Deer close to the Penobscot village filled my mind. I began to move closer to the voices. They appeared to be ahead of us and below. As the voices grew louder so my approach was slower and I made out the language. The voices were Moneton. I had not realised it but we had been rising up a small bluff close to the stream we were following and when we reached a line of thin trees and shrubs I stopped and peered through the undergrowth.

Below me were two Moneton warriors dressed in furs. There was a woman and three children: two girls and a boy. The boy had his right arm pressed to a wound on his left and the girls were crying. The mother was trying to protect the children with her body. From the words I heard from the woman, they were Powhatan. We could not leave them. The two warriors were forty paces from us. The furs they wore would be a problem as the flint arrows might not penetrate. Had I brought iron tipped ones then I could have guaranteed success. I turned to my sons and mimed for them to aim at the warrior to the right. I would take the one to the left. This was not a situation that could be resolved by talking. The Powhatans had been pursued and that was enough for me.

I rose and drew back on the bow. The movement was slow and gentle but the Moneton on the left must have heard the creak for he turned just as I released. His movement sealed his fate for it allowed my arrow to strike him in the chest. My sons' arrows also hit but they struck fur and were not fatal. I nocked another as the two warriors, both wounded ran at us. I aimed at the head of the one whose fur had been struck by arrows. The Allfather guided my hand for the flint arrow smashed into his skull. Dropping my bow I took out my hatchet and seax and slid down the bank. The warrior with the arrow in his chest had discarded his fur and drawn his own tomahawk and knife but he was wounded and my seax slashed away his blows and my hatchet ended the work begun by my arrow.

I said to the woman, "Are there any more Moneton?" I spoke in Powhatan and the woman shook her head. "Golden Bear, fetch my bow." I went to the bodies and took the furs from them. The woman and her children would need them. I dragged and rolled them into the river. I hoped that the melting snow would take them hence. Golden Bear handed me my bow and the three of us tried to disguise the blood by scraping snow over it.

"Come with us. We will take you to safety. Brave Cub, lead the way." I draped a Moneton fur over the woman and her injured child and Golden Bear placed the other over the two weeping girls. Their story would have to wait. The four were in shock and obeyed our commands.

We hurried but did not run. The woman was helping her children and my knee complained. I had done too much. I stayed at the rear in case there were others. I hoped that the two warriors we had slain had been alone. They would be missed but, I hoped, not for a while. When we reached the boat, we had a dilemma. We had too many people to ferry in one journey. I took a decision.

"Brave Cub you and Golden Bear take this family to our home. I will wait here with the deer." I saw the hesitation on his face. "Go, you two can do this and my knee aches. Let me sit on this rock."

The argument convinced them and, with an arrow ready to be nocked, I sat next to the two carcasses. The Norns had been spinning and sent us to find this family. They were Powhatan and, as such, almost kin. The Moneton, like the Penobscot, were enemies. It was not necessarily the world I wished but that was not life. The followers of the White Christ believed in a perfect place where peace reigned. They called it the garden of something. It was a noble idea and ideal but I knew no such place existed. Our clan had sought such a place in the land of Ice and Fire. We almost had it on Bear Island but my brother's frailties cost us dear. My thoughts and musings did not detract me from watching the woods. I saw animals. The deer were now grazing closer to the bjorr dam. Hunting birds swooped. Life was going on. There were Moneton and they were close enough to cause us harm. We would need to be even more vigilant in future.

I heard paddles in the water and turned to see Humming Bird and Moos Blood paddling toward me. They looked relieved that I was unharmed. When we had loaded the deer, they turned around and paddled down the river.

"The Norns have been spinning, Father."

"I know Moos Blood. They sent that family to us and we were handily placed to save them."

Erik's Clan

"There is more to it than that, Father, they are from Fears Water's clan. He knows them. They have been captives since he escaped."

"*Wyrd.*"

Humming Bird had learned our language in the time he had lived with us and he said, "Aye, Father, I now know exactly what that word means. The men you slew, will their deaths bring conflict?"

"I truly do not know but I hope not. As the Norns have spun this is out of our hands but we have a strong home and when the snow disappears, we can make it stronger." Before the death of the two warriors, I had already thought of digging a ditch around the house. Although we were on the top of a slope, when the first snows had melted they had made a muddy morass outside the door. By digging a ditch and building a removable bridge, as we had on Bear Island, we could be drier and have more protection.

The boys insisted on carrying the carcasses up the path to the house and I confess that I would have struggled. My knee ached so much that I wondered if I had burst the wound again.

I entered a longhouse filled with activity. The three pregnant women were feeding the two girls while my wife tended to the injured arm of the boy. Fears Water was speaking to the woman. I went straight to my bed and lay down. The relief from the pain in my knee almost made me sing with joy. I pulled the bearskin over me and closed my eyes. The next thing I knew I was asleep. I dreamed.

I was alone and I was wandering through a forest. I found a trail that climbed up the hills. It twisted and turned to afford me tantalising glimpses of the blue tops of the hills. When it began to rain, I ran and, surprisingly, my leg held me. I spied a cave and I ran into it for the rain was now pounding so hard that it hurt. As soon as I entered, I knew it was a mistake for there before me, was a black bear. Its eyes glowed in the dark. My hand went to my weapons but I halted when the bear spoke. Its voice was that of Gytha, "The bear means you no harm, Erik. I mean you no harm. You are still Clan of the Bear. When you slew the bear, you became part of the bear. You and your clan will be a solitary clan and you will wander but you will grow and we will watch over you." The bear moved to the back of the cave and I saw, on the floor the iron ore I sought. Gytha had guided me.

Laughing Deer shook me awake. She stroked my hair, "You have done too much, Erik. You are the chief of this clan and while the boys are young it is they who must shoulder some of the responsibility."

"But they are about to become fathers."

"And when I was with child, were you there?" I shook my head. "The women are stronger than you know."

"And what of the woman and her family?"

"She is Willow Leaf. Her husband was slain when the Moneton attacked and she was taken as a slave." My wife shook her head. I knew that she was remembering. "The boy who was injured, Bjorr Tooth, has seen ten summers and he was badly treated. The girls have seen eleven and twelve summers."

I looked up. That meant they were almost women.

"Aye, husband, and that is why, even though it was winter, Willow Leaf fled their camp for many of the Moneton youths had cast lascivious looks at the two maidens. Willow Leaf did not want them despoiled. It is many miles to the north of where you found them but they are close enough to cause us trouble. You should know that."

"I do and the Norns have spun. We will make our home stronger." I smiled, "We learned good lessons at Bear Island."

"Aye, we did. Would that we were back there now."

As much as I wished that dream, I knew the clan, small though it was, would be too big to take on snekke. We had been lucky on the first voyage and we could not guarantee safety. There was no going back for the Clan of the Bear. "Are they happy to stay with us or do they wish to go to Brave Eagle?"

I saw the surprise on her face, "You would take them there?" I nodded. She squeezed my hand, "You are truly a good man. They will stay here. They see the presence of Fears Water as a good sign and your skill with the bow and hatchet impressed them all. They see you as a great warrior."

I gave a sardonic laugh, "Aye, a great warrior who needs to sleep because his knee causes so much pain."

"We will build a steam hut. Now you rest while we butcher the deer. The three of you did well and the food will last us almost a moon if we husband it carefully."

"No, I will rise. The pain in the knee has lessened." I held her hand. "I dreamed." Her eyes widened. "Gytha showed me the way to a cave with iron stone within. We are meant to be here."

When I entered the main chamber of the longhouse the woman, Willow Leaf, dropped to her knees to kiss my hand. I lifted her up, "None of that. You are one of our clan now and we must make a chamber for you and your family." There was a space between Fears Water's sleeping platform and the end wall. It would only need a hide curtain to afford privacy. "Moos Blood and Humming Bird, fix a hide curtain there. Fears Water and Golden Bear, find furs to lay upon the ground." Our bjorr hunt meant we had enough to give comfort to them and yet keep the pregnant women warm. When the babies came, we would now have two women who could help with the delivery. *Wyrd*. As I sat at the table we had built and which occupied most of the remaining space in the longhouse, I marvelled at my clan. All made the four newcomers welcome and it was as though they were meant to be here. As I drank some of the ale we had brewed over the winter I reflected that while that was a good thing what was not so good was that we had alerted potential enemies to our presence. Even if the Moneton did not find the bodies they would still wonder and all it took was one hunting party to head towards the river and see the smoke in the sky. We would need to be even more vigilant and careful.

When we awoke the next day, the snow had begun to melt. As I stepped out to make water the air felt unseasonably warm and the drips from our roof were larger than I might have expected. The wind was from the south and west. By noon the outside of the longhouse was a sticky, muddy mess.

"Boys, let us begin to dig a ditch."

The four of them looked unhappy at the prospect. "But the mud!"

I smiled, "Brave Cub, the mud means that the ground is soft and will be easier to dig. I will take Bjorr Tooth and the newest warrior in the clan can help me to make a bridge." They were not convinced. "Today we will be muddy. We can go to the river and bathe. Tomorrow there will be less mud as the water will lie in the bottom of the ditch." I paused and added pointedly, "The ditch will slow down any who tries to get into our home. Surely that peace of mind is worth a little mud."

Moos Blood nodded, "Aye, it is. Come let us get spades. How deep shall it be, Father?"

"Just the length of Bjorr Tooth's leg. I will explain how it will work when you are done." I had learned much at Bear Island. "Come Bjorr Tooth."

"But I can only use one arm."

I laughed, "And one of my legs does not function well. Let us see if, between us, we can be a whole."

We went to the wood store and I selected a dozen lengths of timber. They were all roughly the same size. The wood store had a roof and we were protected from the drips. Already the other four were soaked as meltwater continued to drip on them. I still had nails and I gambled that Gytha's dream meant I would find more iron. I would use the iron nails to make the bridge. Bjorr Tooth forgot that he only had one arm when I asked him to hold the plank while I drove in the metal nail with the hatchet head. He had never seen anything like it.

"Aieee, that is magic."

"Perhaps, but when the new grass comes and the babies are born, we can show you how to make such things." I nodded to the upturned snekke next to the wood store. "Those are boats that can sail without paddles."

His eyes widened, "Are you teasing me?"

"No, ask the others and when the snows have gone and we launch them again you shall travel on one."

We worked and he asked me questions. "Mother said that you are a shaman, the Shaman of the Bear. Fears Water told her."

"Your people call me that but I do not. I am a navigator."

I used the Norse word and he looked confused, "I do not know what that is."

I pointed to the east, "You have never seen it but out there is a piece of water so big that you could drop the whole of the land of the Powhatan into it and it would disappear. There is nothing but water as far as the eye can see. I can sail across it." I saw doubt in his eyes. "Ask my sons."

"You are not Powhatan yet you are chief of the Clan of the Bear."

"I had a clan and we came from the east. They sailed back there and left me here."

"And you collect those who are lost like you were."

I smiled, "I was never lost but I like the picture you paint. Aye, we welcome all those who are alone."

"My father was killed by the Moneton and I had friends and cousins who were slain. There are others who are still the slaves of the Moneton."

"And we are too small a clan to go to war. We will do what we can do but just as the bear, powerful though it is, hides in winter so we do not seek war. We hide from it but our claws," I held up a nail, "are sharper than our foes."

When we had finished, we took the bridge back to the longhouse. When we laid it across the ditch, we had a cleaner passage into the longhouse. The ditch was already filling with water and the boys had done well, digging the length of one wall. They stopped while I fitted the bridge.

"Eventually we will fit ropes so that in times of danger we can draw the bridge up to give us a second door. We will fix it at the bottom." I let them take that in. Humming Bird, Fears Water, Bjorr Tooth and even Golden Bear could not grasp it as clearly as my two sons who had seen Bear Island and knew what I meant. "There is no danger yet, at least I hope there is none, but when we fear that there is we embed stakes in the bottom of the ditch. If it is full of water then the stakes will be hidden."

Fears Water grinned, "As they were at Brave Eagle's camp! I see now how this will work." He smiled, "I will endure the mud, Shaman of the Bear for I now see a purpose."

Moos Blood shook his head, "My father never does anything without purpose. We may not see it but he sees all and that is why he is a chief and a shaman. Back to work, boys. Bjorr Tooth, we would have some beer."

Happy to be involved our newest member of the clan hurried indoors and, taking my bow I headed down to the river. It was already becoming slippery and went even more carefully than normal. I did not want to injure my knee but I was anxious to view the river. When I reached the landing, I saw that the river had already risen. The rocks that had barred our passage upriver were now under bubbling, white-flecked water. The thaw had begun upstream of us. I saw that the birchbark boats were in danger. I headed back up the path.

"Boys, cease this labour for we have another more urgent task. We are in danger of losing the boats. Let us go down and save them."

We could make more boats but saving the ones we had was a better idea. By the time we reached the river the four boats were straining at the ropes tethering them to the shore. We moved them two at a time to higher ground and then carried the four of them back up the slope. I did not think that the river would get high enough to threaten the house but I wanted the boats closer to us. The melting snow had been a warning of dangers I had not seen.

By the next morning, the river had burst its banks. The landing was hidden and the river was within a hundred paces of the house. The ditch was finished and had filled with meltwater. As the snow had now all gone and we were at the top of the hill I did not envisage it filling anymore but Moos Blood was impressed by my foresight.

"Can you truly see into the future, Father? Your decision to dig the ditch was timely."

I shook my head, "I had already planned the ditch when we rescued the family for I feared an attack. The melting snow and the floodwater means that our tracks are hidden. That does not mean we will be safe in the future but that, for the moment, we are."

The melting snow and the warm air meant that we could plant the seeds we had brought from Brave Eagle's village. With Willow Leaf and her family, we now had more people to work the fields. The whole clan toiled to clear and dig another field while the first one was planted. The trees we would use as building materials and firewood. Once the seeds were planted the men of the clan had our first hunt of the year. I did not risk crossing the river but, instead, we explored the land that led to the iron hills. It was now clear to me that while we had iron hills that were to the east, to the north was a mighty range of mountains. The Moneton would use that range as a boundary to the north and showed me that if they wished to expand, as they had once before, then they would come south.

We spent ten days exploring and hunting to the north of us, always looking for signs of the Moneton. We hunted mainly the white-tailed deer that were both small and plentiful but there were other creatures we hunted to give variety to our diet. We found the large game birds that made a strange gobbling sound and were incredibly hard to kill. Even when struck by a flint arrow sometimes the bird would continue to run. We found that chopping off the head was the only way to ensure that they were dead. The feathers were plentiful. The Moneton and the Powhatan used them as decoration. I suggested stuffing a hide with them to make a soft bed. My wife and Willow Leaf found the idea amusing but I was thinking of my sleep. The meat was good and we hunted them, as the new grass grew, more than the white-tailed deer.

Once we had hunted and while we weeded the crops my wife gave orders for a steam hut to be built. The hunt had given us food but made my knee ache and stopped me from sleeping. "Erik is the heart of this clan and we need to keep him as healthy as possible." The river had subsided and we had been able to move the birchbark boats back to the landing. We built the hut where we had stored the boats, close to the snekke.

At my suggestion, we made the steam hut from turf taken when we had cleared the field. With branches on the outside and a smoke hole, it was a more solid construction. Seven days after its building I used it for the first time. This time Laughing Deer joined me and, that night, I enjoyed a pain-free night. The next morning my wife told me that I would be using the hut every other day.

My first grandchild to be born was a grandson. Blue Feather had gone with Moos Blood to the river for on the day that my grandson was born we had a beautiful sunset and Blue Feather said that she wished to watch it. I went with the couple along with Laughing Deer and Willow Leaf. Willow Leaf had her own reasons for wanting to see the sunset. She had been held captive to the west and knew of other captives who were there. Whatever the reason all of us were by the water when Blue Feather's waters broke. I know that the Norns were spinning. The baby came so quickly that there was no time to make it back to the longhouse and Water Bird was born in the river. Laughing Deer said that the river would help the birth. She was right and it gave my grandson his name. He was healthy and screamed. We celebrated with freshly brewed beer.

It was a sign that the other babies would follow soon. My other two grandchildren, Brown Feather and Bird Song were born in the longhouse. My granddaughter, Bird Song was born at dawn to a chorus of birds in the trees outside. Her birth was more difficult and had begun in the dark of night. Humming Bird was relieved when his daughter finally emerged and screamed. Brown Feather came as quickly as Water Bird. Sings Softly's waters broke and less than an hour later my second grandson was born. In his excitement, Fears Water threw his arms in the air and knocked over a sack of gobbling bird feathers. They cascaded down and we had his name.

The three babies living in the longhouse were a joy and a trial at the same time. With three of them, you could guarantee that one or another would cry and bawl in the night. It was no longer my moans that woke the longhouse.

Chapter 14

As the new crops grew so did my restlessness. One evening in late spring as we sat outside enjoying yet another magnificent sunset, I spoke to the clan. "My people, the ones who lived on Bear Island, have certain traditions. This is my clan and I would like to use one now. When something important is to be decided then we hold a Thing." I used the Norse word and smiled when I saw the newcomers to the clan trying to get their mouths around the words. "At a Thing, anyone can speak but they cannot talk over anyone. When you speak and have said all that you wish to say then you say, 'that is all I have to say'. Do you understand?" They nodded. "I wish to travel to the blue iron hills to the south and east of us. I have dreamed and know that there is iron there. We need the iron for it makes us stronger. I cannot go alone and so I would need some of the men from the clan. That is all I have to say."

Fears Water spoke, "I have seen the iron and know its value but the arrival of Willow Leaf and her family has shown me that danger is ever-present. I would not be one to find the iron. I would stay close to my wife. That is all I have to say."

Having been the first it made it easier for Moos Blood and Humming Bird to voice the same fears. Laughing Deer said nothing and that meant the other women stayed silent too. Brave Cub had become a man over the winter. He had inherited my hair and flecks of a beard were there. "I will come with you, father, for there are warriors left to protect the longhouse. That is all that I have to say."

Golden Bear had also grown and whilst not yet a man was close enough. He was about the same age as when I had first sailed the snekke. He smiled, "This is simple enough. I will come. That is all I have to say."

I smiled. I could manage it with just the two of them.

"And I would come to. That is all I have to say." We all looked at Bjorr Tooth. Willow Leaf's hand went to her mouth.

"Are you sure, Bjorr Tooth? It will be a long walk and there may be danger."

"I am a man of the clan. True, I am not a warrior but I will shoulder my responsibility."

I saw that he was determined and so I nodded my agreement.

The planning followed. We needed supplies as well as tools and a means to transport the ore. I had thought of building a cart but dismissed the idea. A cart only worked where there were roads. We would be following tracks. Instead, the women sewed hide bags with straps that would enable us to carry them on our backs. Golden Bear now used a bow while Moos Blood had his seax. I took my hatchet and stone clubs that we carried in our hide bags. With spears and bows, we were ready. We left on the day that the night was shorter than the day and with my sealskin cape about my shoulders and bjorr skin hat upon my head we left for the blue iron hills.

We did not leave early for there was no need and better to go with all that we needed than discover we had forgotten something. I led with Bjorr Tooth behind me, Golden Bear behind him and Brave Cub at the rear. The first day's march was over familiar territory for we had hunted this far in the autumn. The animal trail we used inevitably followed water and when we found a place where a storm had uprooted a tree and made a sort of clearing close to water, we stopped. We used the half-fallen tree to make a cosy shelter and lit a fire. I had with me, one clay cooking pot. If we found iron and had to discard the pot then we would but we made a simple stew and, seated around a fire enjoyed a meal. We also took it easy that first day. I would be putting a great deal of pressure on my knee.

"Father, what I cannot understand is why no people are living in this forest. It teems with game and there is timber enough to build and burn."

I nodded, "I know, Brave Cub, and I have had those thoughts. The last time I used the steam hut I began to find answers. The ridge we seek is a natural barrier to the Powhatan lands. Fears Water and his people are Powhatan but they did not cross the ridge, they came up the river. The shallows at the mouth of the Shenandoah discourage boats from travelling. Did you ever visit the Shenandoah before you were taken, Bjorr Tooth?"

He shook his head, "Some of the men occasionally trekked to its mouth to fish but we used the Patawomke more. It was the Moneton who crossed the river to take us to their village."

I nodded for this was confirmation of my theory. "And that is why there has been no conflict between the Moneton and the Powhatan. Until they raided your village, they did not even know that Powhatans lived north of the ridge. To answer your question fully, Brave Cub, I am not sure that the ridge will ever have as many people as will live in our valley. When we crossed the river to hunt the bjorr the land was flatter and easier to cultivate. The floods will make the soil fertile. When we next cut down trees to make new fields it will be across the river."

Golden Bear asked, "You have thought this through?"

"I have. My dreams and the finding of Bjorr Tooth and his family have told me that this is our clan's home. We will settle here and we will grow. If we have to then we defend the land. I hope we do not have to but it is good land and worth defending."

The next day we moved more cautiously for this was new to all of us. When I had found the cave, I had come from the direction of the Patawomke. I knew there had to be a pass there that I had found, albeit accidentally. My wounds had meant I had not taken as much notice as I might but now, I had a specific purpose. We would have to leave the animal trails if we were to reach the cave I had seen in my dream. We headed south and I began to mark the trees with my hatchet as we climbed through what felt like a virgin forest. I wondered if any man had set foot where we were now walking. Certainly, the deer no longer climbed this ridge. We did not make as much progress as I might have liked for my route found a steep drop and we had to backtrack a little, however, it proved a fortuitous delay for we found a patch of water. It was the size of a tarn, a large pond and, once again, we found tracks of the deer. By my estimate, we were less than twenty miles from our home and the tarn, which I named Night's Rest, was close enough for us to use. There were fish and we ran out lines to catch some while we made an early camp. The fish had not been hunted and we caught one the length of my forearm. It had whiskers upon it and after we had gutted and cooked it, feasted on a fish that fed us all.

Brave Cub lay back against a tree and said, "I think that you are right, Father, this is a sign that there are no men close by for this would be a good place to live and yet there is no sign of men's feet."

"Then let us hope it stays that way."

I could see that we were getting close to the top of the ridge. In my dream, I had seen a bear in the cave. Had that been a real bear or had Gytha conjured one as a sign? Not long before noon, we stopped to drink from our ale skins. "Look for signs of bears."

Bjorr Tooth had an amulet around his neck, a bjorr tooth and he clutched it, "We actually seek a bear?"

Brave Cub laughed, "Before even my brother was born my father slew a bear. We are the clan of the bear and do not fear them. We respect them but they are not to be feared. My father needs signs of a bear for the spirits directed him to such a cave. In our clan, we trust the spirits."

"My son is right, Bjorr Tooth. We seek a cave where a bear might live. If he is at home, we will respect that and seek the stone of iron outside the cave."

Erik's Clan

It was Golden Bear who discovered the scratch marks on the tree. From their size, he was a huge beast and that fitted in with the dream I had. Once we found that we looked for signs of his feet. They were old but Brave Cub found some and we followed them up the slope, through the trees. I spied a jumble of rocks and I waved the others to fall in behind me. I held my spear in two hands. Hitherto it had been largely used as a staff but now it would be my defence should the bear, if this was his lair, be at home.

There was a small patch of flat ground and fallen rocks. I sniffed the air and I smelled death. Had the rocks fallen on some creature and killed it? I could not tell if it was a fresh fall or rocks or an ancient one. I signalled for the others to wait and then I headed closer to what I was sure, was a cave although it was not as big as the one in the dream. The one I had found before had been large enough to walk in upright. As I followed my nose and the stink, I saw that the entrance to this cave meant I would have to bend. There were rocks scattered around the exterior of the cave. I studied the interior but could only see a few paces and that did not help. As I looked at the rocks that had fallen, I realised that one of them was iron. My heart soared; this was the cave of my dreams. However, if it was Gytha's cave then there would be a bear. I whistled and Brave Cub and the others appeared at my side.

Golden Bear whispered, "What is that stink?"

I pointed to the rocks that surrounded the cave's mouth. "There has been a rock fall. Perhaps an animal was crushed beneath them."

"The bear?"

I shook my head, "No, Bjorr Tooth, for we would have seen the sign. Find me something I can light, dried grass and dead wood. I will light the interior. If there is a bear within then it will fear fire."

While they searched, I took off my hide bag and began to make a fire. No matter what I found within the cave this would be our camp for we had found the iron. I had the fire going by the time they had found enough pinecones, dead grass and an old fallen branch for me to fashion a brand. With my seax in my right hand, I entered the cave waving the brand before me. As soon as I ducked my head under the rock the smell and stink of death became more overpowering. The entrance was both narrower and lower than I had expected. Whilst I fitted through it, I could not see a bear managing it. Perhaps this was not the cave.

The bear was enormous and had been dead for some time. Rats get everywhere, even in such a remote cave and I saw evidence of their work. I went closer to the dead beast. As I looked back to the entrance, I saw what had happened. A storm had caused a landslide, trapping the bear within. That explained why the tracks were ancient. This was a bear's tomb.

I sheathed my seax and put my right hand on the bear's skin. "I am sorry that you died alone; no creature should ever die alone. Rest in peace. I am Erik, Chief of the clan of the Bear and we will honour you. You shall not be disturbed."

I heard from outside, Brave Cub, "Father, is all well?"

"It is and you may come in if you wish. It is a dead bear."

The three came in and stood in wonder at the huge beast. It must have been the king of this ridge. Perhaps he had once had a family but he had died alone. Had Laughing Deer not found me by the river in the land of the Penobscot that might have been my fate. It made me sad for the bear. He might have had a family but in the end, he had died of starvation and slowly at that.

"We cannot sleep in here but I have found the iron stone. We will camp without." I respected the bear and would leave him in his tomb.

We used fire for comfort. Although we were close to the top of the ridge the fallen rocks hid the firelight and even if the Moneton could see us they would be almost forty miles away. The smoke also helped to disguise the smell of the dead animal. We could not see the beast but it cast a pall over our camp. My thoughts were of the animal's suffering as it realised it was trapped and dying. To be so close to safety and still die did not bear thinking about. When the silence of the fire threatened to engulf us, I took out my seax and tapped the huge lump of stone close to Brave Cub. It was the size of a female deer. It rang.

"Iron stone. When you go to sleep this night put your minds to working out how we break down this lump of iron so that we can take it back with us."

Golden Bear waved his hand around, "There are smaller rocks here; could we not use them?"

I picked the closest one up and held it to the fire. "This is not iron, Golden Bear. Some may be iron and some may not. Even if we cannot take it all the odds are that it will be purer than any other iron we might find for it is so large."

Brave Cub nodded, "And Gytha sent us here. Father is right, little brother, and I will sleep and let my dreams conjure up a solution."

I did, of course, know how to break it up. I had spied a couple of pieces of hard rock such as we found in the land of Ice and Fire. They would be harder than the iron. By making cracks in the iron we could drive stone wedges into the cracks and split the rock. The danger would be we might damage our stone tools in the process. If we did then we would need to make more and that would mean staying here longer.

Erik's Clan

The fire had died when I awoke and the smell of the dead bear had returned. During the night I had heard the scurrying of tiny feet, telling me that the rats were still feasting. I wanted to spend as little time here as possible. After a cold breakfast, we broke out the tools. I selected stones for the wedges that were the right shape; narrower on one side. We were lucky in that there was a natural crack in the rock. I placed the wedges into the rock and then told the boys to stand well back and to protect their eyes. I did not know how far splinters might fly. I did not want them to lose an eye. When I used the stone club to strike the wedge sparks flew and the noise echoed against the stone walls above us. It was not a quick process and when I tired, I handed over to Brave Cub and stepped back to watch the progress. I saw that the fissure had begun to spread. I had been too close to see.

"You are almost there, Brave Cub."

My second son was strong and enthusiastic. Two strikes later a large lump fell from the top of the rock and the others gave a cheer. Emboldened with success Brave Cub hammered again until the rest of the rock fell. We now had three lumps of iron. Each was too large to carry but we could break them down. Even better was the sight of other cracks and fissures running through the rocks. By using our stone clubs we could all work, even Bjorr Tooth and Golden Bear. By noon we just had half of the original rock to break down. After we had eaten, I began to load the hide sacks we had brought. Bjorr Tooth and Golden Bear would not be able to carry as large a load as Brave Cub and me. By the time I had put just enough in theirs to carry I saw that we would not need to do much more work. We almost had enough for the last two bags. I was loath to leave stone here and as we worked through the afternoon to break down the last stubborn lumps I decided that we would pile the rest of the iron stone in the bear's cave. The dead animal would guard it for us.

That evening, after we had finished our work, we were weary beyond words. Even Brave Cub and I could feel our arms burning and the two smaller boys were almost weeping with the exertion. They would become stronger from the experience and I knew that the trek back to our home would bring different pain to them.

I had packed the bags for the boys but when they had hoisted them upon their backs, I rearranged the stones within each bag. I did not want them to be overbalanced. I had the heaviest load, of course, for I had all the tools we had brought. They were too valuable to lose. We left not long after dawn and began our descent. My injured knee had not really complained on the way up but it more than made up for it on the way down and I found each step to be agony. I began to seek a route that zig-zagged more than following the line of least resistance. We were making better time as we did not have to backtrack and we were drawn on by the tendril of smoke that rose in the sky: Eagle's Shadow. It was a slightly longer route that we took but easier both on my knee and for the younger boys who had been in danger of overbalancing and falling on the steep path I had originally selected. The route proved quicker than the more perilous once and as we approached the neck of land between the two loops of the river I realised that, with luck, we would be home not long after dark. We would not need to spend, as I had feared, another night in the forest. Already I was anticipating a night in a bed filled with gobbling bird feathers and the relief of a steam bath.

Darkness fell but by then we were on one of our paths. We were in familiar country and when we heard the wailing of a baby we knew that we were close to our home. The last five hundred paces were almost our undoing for although we had a good path to use it was uphill. We had not stopped to eat on the way back and weariness made each step an agony. I stopped to allow the others to pass me and to help Bjorr Tooth. He had not complained once but I saw the pain etched on his young face. He had never had to endure such agony before. It was not war but it would prepare him well for that day. A good warrior can keep on fighting beyond what he believes possible.

"You are doing well, Bjorr Tooth. I have asked you to do too much."

Even through his pain, he forced a smile, "It is for the clan, and besides I am honoured that you think I can manage this."

"Just another hundred or so steps and you can lay down your load." I knew that we could have put the bags down where we stood for we could have collected them in the morning but there was a pride within each of us. We would march into our home with the prized stone.

Perhaps it was the huffing and puffing or it may have been that Moos Blood was watching for us but whatever the reason as the shadow of the longhouse hove into view there was a flash of light as the door opened and my son, Fears Water and Humming Bird came out armed and ready to fight.

Brave Cub laughed, "Brother, you need not a weapon for if you used Laughing Deer's broom you could sweep us from this hill. Come, help our little brother and Bjorr Tooth. They carry a heavy load."

My wife appeared and her smile was as wide as her arms, "Aye, help them, Moos Blood, for the clan is back together and this night I will enjoy my sleep."

She was right. The clan was stronger when we were all together.

Chapter 15

After dropping the bags of stone close to the wood store we entered the longhouse. The family was eating and my wife went to fetch food for us. My knee was complaining so much that I simply sat with it stretched out and listened as I drank some freshly made ale. Brave Cub began the tale interrupted, much to his annoyance, by his little brother and Bjorr Tooth. I smiled as the size of both the bear and the iron stone we had broken grew with the tale. Moos Blood cocked an enquiring eye at me and smiling, I shrugged. The boys had earned the right to exaggerate.

It was after we had eaten and all the questions answered that I spoke. I waved a hand to the south, "We found no signs of any other clan to the south. We know from Fears Water and Willow Leaf that there are clans by the Patawomke but the land between here and the dead bear's cave can be hunted. The cave is a good day or more away from here but there are many deer signs betwixt here and there."

The others nodded for they knew what I meant. We did not want to over hunt the animals that were close to us. We had to be selective in our hunting. This way we would have to forage further but it would maintain the numbers of the animals close to us. The harsh winter had been a lesson. We might be trapped in our loop of land one day.

"And do we melt the iron straight away, Father?"

"No, Brave Cub. As much as I might want to, we need to put the snekke back on the river. When they are launched and we have the means to fish again then I will choose those who are to help me melt the stone."

Willow Leaf shook her head, "How can you melt stone?"

Laughing Deer put her hand on Willow Leaf's, "I, too, once thought it magic but my husband is clever. You will watch as the rock becomes liquid and then he makes it solid once more."

Our newest members of the clan had much to learn about us. I had forgotten the effect the snekke had on those who had never seen such a vessel. Willow Leaf and her family looked fearful as the masts were fitted and the newly repaired sails hoisted. My knee was still painful and so I allowed Moos Blood and Brave Cub, with Golden Bear and Fears Water, to sail them. It allowed me to examine the two snekke for flaws. There were none.

"Fish today and watch the riverbanks for any signs of Moneton. I will use the steam hut this day and be a lazy man."

Little White Dove, nursing Bird Song, laughed, "Father, you could not be lazy if you tried. You have men in the clan now who can take some of the load from your shoulders. Let them do so."

Her husband, Humming Bird, nodded and said, "Aye, come Golden Bear and Bjorr Tooth, let us see how your skills with the bow are developing. We will hunt."

And so I enjoyed a day of peace. I lit the fire in the steam hut and put the aromatic herbs and leaves on the fire. I still had some of the leaves we smoked in our pipes and I lit and enjoyed one. I did not dream but the peace seemed to ease the pain in my knee. After I emerged, I saw that the swelling, which had worsened on the iron hunt, had begun to go down. Perhaps my family was right and it was time for me to become like Long Spear and Wandering Moos. I could let others toil while I watched.

The boys were all successful in their endeavours. We had fish, deer and squirrels. I was content but the next morning when I awoke as usual before dawn, I knew that my nature would not allow me to sit by and let others work. We had iron to melt. I had time and space on my side. I had the time to build a forge that would be away from the longhouse and yet sheltered. I could make a permanent melting pot. I let the others go about their business and set myself the task of building what I hoped would be a perfect structure. I chose a flat piece of ground more than ten paces from the longhouse. That was the easy part. When we had cleared the land for the longhouse, we had unearthed many stones. I used those to build the foundations for the stone from the land of Ice and Fire. I used a beaker of water to tell me if it was level. I needed a slight angle for pouring but I decided to make the stone from the land of Ice and Fire flat first and then I would use stone wedges to give me the perfect angle for pouring. It took all morning until I was satisfied. The three new mothers were busy with their babies. They were still learning but Laughing Deer, Willow Leaf and her daughters were able to tend the fields. The birds had to be kept from them and the ground kept free from weeds. Even though I was at the top of the hill their laughter still carried up to me. It was good that they got on. Both had much in common and they each understood the pain the other had gone through. The two girls were also close enough in age to the three young mothers for there to be much common ground there too. When we had left Brave Eagle's village it had been with fear in our hearts for the unknown. Up until the present our fears had been groundless. The spirits had guided us well.

The afternoon's efforts took it out of me for I had much bending as I dug the holes for the posts and cut the timber to length. That was as far as I got. I lit the fire in the steam hut in the middle of the afternoon. When it was hot enough, I entered and felt the relief immediately. I fed the fire and used the herb-scented water to make me feel comfortable and I forgot the passage of time. Moos Blood and Fears Water appeared in the door, "May we join you, or would you prefer solitude, Father?"

I smiled and gestured for them to join me, "I never want solitude. I care not how many of you there are, you will always be welcome. I am not sure how many years the Allfather will allow me to live here so I will enjoy the company of my sons for as long as possible."

There was room for six adults in the hut and it was comfortable.

"How went the fishing?"

Moos Blood smiled, "Good. We went as far as the first shallows. There was much damage to the trees from the thaw. The river must have made its own dam. The passage to the Patawomke will be harder."

I nodded, "If we do sail the river, it will be in summer and I will send only one snekke to Brave Eagle. With a crew of four, we can portage the snekke easily enough."

Fears Water asked, "Why do you wish to return to the village? We have left it and it is now in the past."

I shook my head as I explained, "We were made welcome and we fought for the village. There are ties. If I could I would visit the Mi'kmaq village where we lived but that is too far. I know that we can sail to Brave Eagle's village in a couple of days and they will wonder if we survived. There are fathers there who know not that they are grandfathers. We owe it to them to tell them their good fortune."

Fears Water would not easily let it go, "But it is a danger. As soon as you return then all will have an idea where we live."

It was my turn to smile, "And do you think they would find it easy to travel where we came?"

Moos Blood nodded, "I know of no other who could have negotiated the mouth of the Shenandoah as our father did. He is right, Fears Water, Humming Bird, Sings Softly and Blue Feather have a family. Do you not think that your wife's father would wish to know that she was well? That he had a grandchild?"

"You are right but I still have fear hidden in here." He tapped his head.

I knew that the fear would never go away. It would make him suspicious of strangers and discourage him from wandering. Moos Blood might inherit my wanderlust but Fears Water would never leave this home. Eagle's Shadow would be as far as he would explore.

"And the place to melt the iron, Father, how goes that?"

"By tomorrow I will have the roof built and then we can begin to make the charcoal and then smelt the iron. I will need you all for that. We need to break down the iron into pieces that are as small as possible. That will be in three days from now."

I turfed the roof and I was satisfied that I had somewhere I could work in any weather. I had Golden Bear and Bjorr Tooth collect the wood we would use for the charcoal. I was specific about the size of the wood for I wanted the charcoal to burn evenly. I made the charcoal fire far from the house, almost in the trees and when it was made, it took all day for it to be completed to my satisfaction, I lit it. Under the pile of branches and earth, it would burn all night and the next day too. There was always a temptation to look in prematurely but to do so invited disaster. Instead, the next day when I rose I took Golden Bear and Bjorr Tooth to the river. It was time for them to begin to learn how to sail *'Gytha'*.

One major advantage of the relatively shallow Shenandoah was that it was safer than the Patawomke for those learning to sail. Mistakes could be more easily forgiven. Even so, I chose the widest part of the river and we spent the morning tacking back and forth. It made for quick reflexes as the boys had to adjust the stays and the sails. We pulled up on the shore to eat the raw fish we had caught with the trailing fish lines. I let them steer during the afternoon. As I had expected they both made the classic mistake of turning the steering board too severely and I smiled at their faces when we stalled into the wind. Steering any ship or boat with a steering board takes time but I was impressed by Golden Bear's natural ability. Poor Bjorr Tooth would never have that skill. It did not really matter as, when I ceased to be Erik the Navigator, there would be four of them who could steer the two snekke and that gave me comfort.

Despite his lack of skill Bjorr Tooth had been captivated by the experience and he bubbled like a mountain stream all the way back to the longhouse. He rushed into the main room and then gushed his words at a bemused Willow Leaf. As she listened, she looked over at me and gave me a smile of thanks. The rebuilding of Bjorr Tooth from the frightened and injured creature damaged by the Moneton was almost complete.

"Tomorrow, we see if we have made good charcoal. Come what may we will make more tomorrow and then the day after you can all watch as we make iron."

That invited questions, of course, especially from Humming Bird and Bjorr Tooth. I was patient as I explained, "I am no blacksmith but I have learned from my mistakes. A blacksmith would, when he wished to make a blade, cast an iron bar which would then be heated and beaten with an iron hammer. It would take many days but the result would be a sword such as mine. We have no iron hammer. If we can get more iron then perhaps I can make one. Until that time it means we use moulds to make the tools and weapons we need. They may not be as good as the ones I brought from over the ocean but they will be better than any stone weapon. I intend to make a seax for each of you and a blade for the women to use when they cook." I saw the nod of approval from Laughing Deer. She had been desperate for a tool that she could sharpen. "When that is done, we make more arrowheads, twenty. Whatever we have left after that we use to try to make a hatchet and then nails. We can never have too many nails."

Moos Blood was the cleverest of my children and had a quick mind, "You would make another snekke?"

"Perhaps. *'Gytha'* is getting old and when she is too old to sail, we may need to build another. I want the nails in case that day comes."

After starting the next charcoal fire the boys and I made the sand and clay moulds we would need. We used my original seax to make the first mould in clay. I had to take off the handle so that the tang was exposed. That was no bad thing as it meant I could fit a new handle. We did the same with the arrowheads. I still had arrows that had been made before we had sailed to the land of Ice and Fire. There were two of them and I had never used them. They were like a pair of lucky charms. They would make good blanks for the arrows. The nails, now that we had more iron, could be of varying lengths and thickness. We made more moulds than we would need. The hardest mould to make was the hatchet for we had to work out how to make a hole for the wooden handle.

Moos Blood suggested using a piece of wood. "I know that the heat of the iron will burn the wood but perhaps there will be enough of a hole to fit a wooden handle." He shrugged, "If it fails then we melt down the hatchet head and begin again."

I could think of no other method and we made the mould for the hatchet using my son's idea. It was as I took the handle from the hatchet that I wondered how the blacksmith in Larswick had made the hatchet. I had been less impressed with the gift than my sword and yet I had used the hatchet almost every day. The sword only came out of its scabbard when there was war.

If Bjorr Tooth thought the melting of the iron would be quick he was in for a disappointment. Despite the good work done by all to break down the iron it still took some melting. I had lit the fire at dawn and the boys took it in turn to work the bellows but the iron was still reluctant to melt. We had four wedge levers to tip the stone and pour the fiery liquid into the moulds and the four eldest warriors stood waiting as we neared the time for the pouring to begin. I was the one who would take the risks and ensure that the molten metal flowed well. When I deemed it ready, I placed the seax mould on the ground below the lip of the stone. The two boys on the bellows had done enough and I moved them away to a safe distance so that they did not risk a burn.

"Begin to tip but slowly." I had the mould ready and when the first seax had been filled I said, "Stop." I carefully moved the mould as slowly as I could so that they could pour the second and third seaxes. I was relieved when they were done. I moved the seax mould to cool and then put the arrow mould in place. By the time we came to the most difficult task, the hatchet, the four young men were sweating but had learned to work as one. It reminded me of the skill of rowing a drekar. We had more ore to melt if we needed it. I had kept enough so that we could make more tools but the Moos Blood idea had merit and if it worked then the number of tools we could make would increase.

The hatchet mould was different to the rest. We used clay and encased the clay in wood. It made both the pouring and the cooling processes easier but would have no idea if we had succeeded until we removed the wood and the clay.

"Pour." The molten iron hissed its way into the mould and I saw smoke. Had it ignited the wood already? Unlike the other efforts there was a surplus and it pooled on the top of the mould. We would be able to break that off and then use my axe head to beat into shape smaller iron items.

We were hot. Spring had come and brought warmer weather. I said, "Golden Bear, fetch the ale. The men of the Clan of the Bear have earned a drink."

Bjorr Tooth joined him and when they returned, he said, "You are truly a shaman for you turned the rock into liquid. You can make the wind move a boat. Is there anything beyond your powers?"

I laughed, "If you had seen a real galdramenn then you would know that I am not a magician."

Moos Blood had to explain what a galdramenn was and he told of how the spirits still spoke to me from beyond the grave. "Father is right, they are the ones who had real power for they transcended death and that is the greatest power."

The roof for the furnace proved more valuable than we had thought for that night, while the iron still cooled, it rained. I was unsure of the effect rainwater might have on cooling iron but my roof meant we did not have to find out. When we arose all were eager to see what we had.

The seaxes were sound enough but rough. I handed them to Humming Bird, Golden Bear and Brave Cub. I gave Brave Cub the knife that he would give to his mother to use when preparing food.

"They will need to be sharpened and shaped on the whetstone and then you will need to make a handle." They took them reverently for they each knew that they had a weapon that was superior to any enemy that they might face. The arrowheads would also need work and I gave them to Bjorr Tooth and Golden Bear. "You will need to shake these first in a bag of sand and then each one will need to have the hole for the shaft smoothed and the arrowhead sharpened." They were also delighted to be given such an important task. Moos Blood and I took on the task of cleaning up the nails. I think we were both nervous about opening the hatchet mould and chose the more mundane task of cleaning the nails. When the nails had been cleaned up and the poor ones returned to the stone to be remelted, we went, somewhat nervously to the hatchet mould. We unfastened the bindings and removed the wood. Using the back of my hatchet I carefully knocked off the clay from the hatchet. To our surprise, it looked like a hatchet but the real test would be the handle. The iron was still warm to the touch and the ash from the wood we had used, smoked. I took one of the longer trenails we had made and poked into the ash. To our joint delight, most of it came out.

"Your idea worked, Moos Blood. The hatchet will need work for I can see that the handle will take some carving to make it fit." I handed the tool to my son, "Here, this is yours."

His eyes lit up as though I had given him a chest of gold. He nodded, "It is not a sword but I know that if an enemy comes close, he will die."

I gave him a sad smile, "Then let us hope that you only have to use this as a tool and not a weapon."

Realisation dawned and he nodded. I collected the metal that had fallen from the top of the mould. I saw immediately that some could easily be fashioned into fishhooks while there was enough to make small metal scrapers that could be resharpened. The women would appreciate them. In the end, I discovered that we had little wastage and the poorer nails and arrows, along with the pieces of metal too small for anything else would remain on Thor's furnace until we made more iron.

Everyone was keen to use the new tools and the next day I took the men from the clan on a hunt. Bjorr Tooth had a new bow and I had given him two metal arrows. He was desperate to use them. The women were already sharpening their scrapers while Laughing Deer had honed her new knife so that it was sharp enough to shave with. We would all use metal arrows. As we were hunting, we could recover and reuse all of them. Flint arrows did kill but a sharpened metal arrow not only killed more efficiently but also suffered less damage when striking bone. We left at dawn for I wanted to take the band towards the land we had passed on the way to the iron cave. I hoped that the animals there would not be used to man and we might have good kills.

It was noon when we found the trail of the herd of white-tailed deer. By my estimate and from the rising ground, I put us to be eight miles or more from our home and just a few miles from the cave. The deer had descended through the trees towards what I assumed was a watercourse. We were hot and while we had water and ale skins the deer would need water. Using the wind to guide us, as well as the prints we stalked the herd. When we finally came upon them, I saw that the Allfather had smiled upon us. There were more than thirty animals. There were young deer born earlier that spring and they had grown well. The young males were still with the herd. I had spoken to both of the youngest warriors, Bjorr Tooth and Golden Bear, the night before, "Do not go for the stag or the females. Take the younger ones and do not be greedy." They had nodded their understanding.

As we neared the herd, I waved my arm to spread out the line. Bjorr Tooth and Golden Bear were in the centre and Moos Blood and I flanked the line. I had used crushed beetles to colour my white fletch red so that I would know my arrow. I nocked one and aimed at the older doe. I noticed that she favoured one leg and I would be doing the herd a favour if I slew her. I looked down the line and saw every eye upon me. We all had a quarter draw and, as I pulled back to the full draw I nodded. The arrow I sent was the most accurate that I could remember. I had the confidence to aim at the head and the metal arrow drove into the deer's skull, killing her instantly. I drew another arrow but the herd had been spooked and they were fleeing. I saw that at least five animals had been hit but not killed and they were trying to escape.

"Bjorr Tooth and Golden Bear. Recover the arrows and gut my kill and the other deer that were slain. The rest of you let us follow the wounded animals."

I was the only one who had a marked arrow and that meant none, save the archer themselves, knew which arrow had hit which animal. Four of the animals were found within a hundred paces of the attack. The last kept running. We had to catch it and finish it. The Allfather had delivered the herd to us and would not appreciate suffering to an animal. We found the animal two hundred paces later. It was a young buck and I saw the beginnings of antlers. It had hidden between two trees as it tried to pull the arrow from its side. The others drew back their bows but I said, "Hold. We cannot afford a miss." I took another red fletched arrow and drew back. The animal was less than forty paces from us but I would have to aim at the head again. "Allfather, guide my aim," I released and watched the arrow slam into the deer's skull. It fell dead.

We cut saplings to carry back our kills. We had done well. Although we were not certain if Golden Bear and Bjorr Tooth had made a kill I let them eat the heart of one of the deer. It meant they were blooded. We headed back to Eagle's Shadow and reached there after dark. We were weary but, for the first time, the clan had been as one and every one of us had been involved in the hunt. It was a good day.

Chapter 16

It took a week for us to butcher the animals and preserve the meat. It was then I realised that we were running out of salt. Although I had fetched more before we left we had used it heavily. The preserved food had kept us alive through the winter and had saved us. The animal skins were cleaned and pegged out to dry. The bones were boiled so that we could use them for tools. Nothing was wasted. This was the Allfather's bounty and we used it well. We had lost no arrows and the new weapons had proved themselves. The seaxes had gutted the animals easily and Humming Bird especially was impressed with the keenness of his new weapon. It was when we had finally finished with the carcasses that I raised the question of salt.

Neither Willow Leaf nor Fears Water knew of any local supplies of salt and that left us with two options: return to Brave Eagle and trade arrowheads for salt or go to the sea. Both involved at least four of us leaving Eagle's Shadow. I let the others speak for I had already made up my mind.

"We now have four warriors, Father, Golden Bear has proved that he is becoming a man and could either go with you or defend the village. Bjorr Tooth is resourceful and I suspect might relish a voyage down the Patawomke. Brave Cub can be a good helmsman."

My wife was shrewd and she said, "So Moos Blood, you can think of reasons why your father, your two younger brothers and the smallest member of the clan should leave but not why the three strongest warriors should do?"

He looked shamefaced, "I did not say that Mother, and if my father wishes me to go then I will as will Humming Bird and Fears Water."

I smiled at my son, "But you meant what you said, Moos Blood. I would rather you were honest. I would not want to travel with a crew that did not want to go. If I had to then I would go alone."

Little White Dove burst out, "No! There is too much danger in that. If I were a warrior and not a mother, I would go with you." She gave Moos Blood a look which, had it been an edged weapon, would have drawn blood.

"Let us be calm. Brave Cub, Golden Bear and Bjorr Tooth, Moos Blood mentioned your names and you have yet to speak. What think you?"

Brave Cub grinned, "A trip down the Patawomke? The chance to fish for the fierce finny fishes? I relish the opportunity."

Erik's Clan

Golden Bear said, "As do I. Besides, I may get the chance to sail the snekke on a real river."

I nodded, "Bjorr Tooth?"

"Like Golden Bear the voyage appeals but I would be leaving my mother and sisters. What if the Moneton came while we were away?"

He had voiced fears that were within me. Moos Blood answered. "Thus far we have seen no sign of your hated enemies, Bjorr Tooth. I am not saying that they will not come but if they do first they will send scouts and as their village is many days from here then we would spot their scouts and be prepared. It takes time to mount a slave raid. Our chief can sail to the sea and return in ten days. If he visits Brave Eagle, then perhaps twelve. Your family will be safe but if you are that worried then stay with us."

He nodded, "I will stay with you. There may be other voyages and I will be older then."

It was decided. I would sail the next morning and head for the Patawomke. The other warriors would follow in the birchbark boats with the rollers we had prepared to help us over the shallows. The journey downstream, to the shallows was faster than I had expected and having used the rollers once we found it easier the second time.

"How will you manage when you return, Father?"

"The same way as we did this time. I will wait with the snekke while Brave Cub and Golden Bear come to fetch you."

Anxious to reach the Patawomke as soon as possible we bade a swift goodbye and headed for the maelstrom of waters at the river's mouth. Surprisingly it was much easier in daylight and without birchbark boats to hold us back not to mention a second snekke to worry about, we sailed through and headed down the Patawomke. The current was strong and our passage swift. I took the decision to sail through the night, much as I had when steering the drekar. Moos Blood was competent and with reefed sails and sharp eyes, we would be able to cut a day, perhaps two from the voyage. Bjorr Tooth's words had worried me and I wanted to spend as short a time away from the clan as I could. I would visit with Brave Eagle on our return up the river.

I told my sons of my decision and they seemed happy enough. I knew the first part of the journey would be an easy one and so I let Brave Cub steer while I slept. It would give him confidence that I slept while he steered. I awoke in the late afternoon. After I had made water over the side, I studied the riverbank and worked out where we were. We had made excellent time.

As I went to the steering board Brave Cub said, "I allowed Golden Bear to steer, Father."

I smiled, "Good, for that is how your brother will learn. You and I will eat while he steers and then I will allow you two to sleep and I will take the night watch."

After the open ocean, even the wide Patawomke seemed tiny but I had enough confidence to sail a straight course. I remembered sailing down Fox Water at night and that had been much narrower than this mighty river. I was tired and stiff when dawn broke. My knee complained of the cold and the damp of the river air. I woke my sons and then lay down on my bearskin to sleep. Before I did so I said, "We are now close to where the other Powhatan clans lived and where the Moneton attacked. Keep to the centre of the river and if you see any danger then wake me. I will not think you foolish for doing so."

When I slept, I dreamt but it was not a dream of the future. Instead, my mind seemed to relive all the voyages I had taken. It made for a more pleasant sleep than I might have expected for it was filled with familiar faces. That most were dead was sad but also reassuring in that they visited me.

I awoke just in time to see, as the sun started to set, the river where we had so often fished. None of Brave Eagle's boats was on the water but I wondered if we had been seen. The river was now as wide as an ocean. I knew that I would smell the land when we neared Salt Island and that I might reach it before dawn. I warned the boys and then let them sleep. The water in the estuary made *'Gytha'* livelier but I was not discomfited. I now felt the snekke as though it was part of me. I steered and adjusted the sails almost without thinking. Brave Cub needed his brother to adjust the sails, I did not. The wind began to turn during the night and I knew that our passage would be slower. As dawn broke ahead of me, I saw the long spit of land beyond the island and the breakers on the beach. I had unerringly found Salt Island and I roused the boys.

"Come, the Allfather has timed our voyage to perfection. We can land in safety before any boats are out fishing." I had already decided to step the mast and disguise the snekke. We could not disguise our purpose. Any watcher would see the smoke from our fires as we made salt but they might think it was locals and not the boat that had slain so many of their warriors.

The pans for the salt were still there and it meant we would not have to rebuild them. I stepped the mast and disguised the snekke while my sons collected driftwood, lit the fire and then began hauling pails of seawater. Golden Bear was disappointed as we cooked the river fish, we had caught on the way south, "I hoped we might catch one of the fish with the red flesh."

I nodded, "And we might well do but we came for salt. That is our priority and with just three of us then we need everyone to gather as much salt as we can before we head upriver again. We can fish if you wish when we have salt beneath our hold and can outrun any boat that tries to interfere." I looked out to sea and saw heavy clouds rolling in. We were due for some unpleasant weather. The Allfather did not wish us to fish. More importantly, a storm would keep any birchbark boats ashore. Only a fool came into the estuary with a full-blown storm. In the event, the storm lasted for three days. We had the snekke and sealskin to cover us and we were protected a little. The water we were heating, however, did not evaporate as much as we might have liked.

Although the storm was windier than wetter it delayed our collection of the salt. By the time it had blown itself out we had just another four hours or so before we could scrape the salt from the pots and store it. We had enough for my family. The amount we collected would last us, judiciously used, for a couple of years. We collected the last of it on the morning we left. I had fitted the mast, sail and steering board during the night and so all we had to do was pack the salt and put the deck back in place. The river mouth was empty and, after the storm, calmer. I nodded to Brave Cub and Golden Bear, "Aye, we can fish but watch for boats."

In truth, I was keen to fish for we had some of the new iron fishhooks I had made. They were intended for large fish and were too big for river fish. The fierce finny fish with the red flesh would be the perfect prey to try them on. I let the boys bait their own lines and they threw them over the side as we headed towards the mouth of the river. The wind was against us and that helped for we were more stable. It was Brave Cub who had the first strike. His line pulled hard as the fish took the bait and tried to escape. He wrapped the line around the forestay stanchion and let the fish do the work. I turned the steering board so that the wind helped us and as we beat north the fish weakened until Brave Cub managed to haul him aboard and club him to death.

Golden Bear looked pleadingly at me and I nodded, "Just a short time and if you have not caught a fish then we head upstream while the wind is with us. Even a good and experienced fisherman does not catch a fish each time he throws a baited hook into the water."

He caught one but, to his great disappointment, it was not a large one and certainly not one like his brother's. It expired after a short fight and he was able to haul it aboard unaided. "I would have preferred one with more fight."

I laughed as I turned the snekke to head upriver, "You wanted to catch one and you succeeded; be thankful."

Erik's Clan

It was as he hurled the guts over the side for the sea birds to swoop upon that I saw the birchbark boats. The warriors had used Salt Island to approach unseen and even though they were too far away to make out I knew that they were the warriors we had met the last time we had visited. I was now grateful for the wind and the sail billowed but the boats were between us and our destination. The worst thing to do in such a situation was to panic.

"Golden Bear, you wished for a challenge and the Allfather has answered you. Take the steering board and keep the wind directly astern. Brave Cub, string your bow for we have a fight on our hands."

I changed positions with my youngest son. As I strung my bow, I saw that there were six boats in two groups of three and one group was paddling almost on a parallel course to ours. The difference was that they were two hundred paces upriver of us. The other three were coming directly for us, their oars powering into the water. My hope was that they would tire but their clever plan meant that the three boats that were far ahead of us would simply block our path and overcome us with numbers. Most of the boats looked to have five warriors but two just had four.

"Brave Cub, when we are close enough take the warrior at the prow of the first boat and I will take the steersman."

He said nothing but I knew he had the skill. His strength had grown. He had been on more hunts than any other in the clan and his eye was also good. I knew that when the clan had hunted the last time it was his arrow that had made a quick kill like mine. I had not said anything at the time but the both of us knew. I was proud that he did not take credit for a good kill. I liked his modesty. We had plenty of arrows in the snekke. I even had some metal tipped arrows, a gift for Brave Eagle but they would only be used as a last resort.

The three boats closest to us could see that they would reach us soon and the warriors paddled even harder keen, I suspect, to be the ones to kill the magic boat. The estuary, wind and their speed combined to do two things: their boats were not moving as smoothly as either they or we might have liked and the boats were shipping water as the bows dipped into the waves. We were one hundred paces when I loosed. Brave Cub's arrow followed a heartbeat later. We both nocked another arrow even as the first arrows were in the air. A warrior can see the flight of an arrow. In a battle, most arrows can be avoided so long as the warrior is not engaged in combat. On a birchbark boat, there was nowhere to hide. Brave Cub's arrow arced down and hit the warrior in the prow forcefully in the neck. Such was the power and the speed of the wind behind that the warrior tumbled over the side and the boat veered to the right. My arrow also had a plunging flight and hit the warrior who was steering in the shoulder. The paddle fell and the boat almost stopped. The two boats behind had to take avoiding action and at that moment, they lost their chance to take us. *'Gytha'* seemed to take flight and sped ahead.

That left the other three boats and, having seen what had happened astern of them they turned to make a barrier of boats. The Norns had been spinning. They had made us delay our return by making us fish and they had sent a surge of wind. They were not done yet. The boats would be able to form a single line to stop us. They expected us to deviate from our course and I saw that they had throwing spears, tipped with stone, ready to attack us.

"Golden Bear, steer for the middle boat."

"When do I turn?"

"You do not. *'Gytha'* is well made and we trust her construction." He nodded. "Brave Cub, your arrows are for the boat to the left and I will take the one to the right. They will send spears and stones at us." He nodded. There would be little that we could do about the spears but endure them. I was telling him that the two of us might be hurt in this little skirmish.

This time we were loosing into the wind. I waited until we were eighty paces before I sent the first arrow. It hit the warrior in the middle of the boat. Brave Cub had his own battle and we fought alone. My second arrow, when we were just fifty paces from them, hit a second warrior. Neither was dead but they had been hurt. Their spears and stones came at us when we were twenty paces away. My arrow slammed into the chest of the warrior who had risen to try to throw his spear and as he fell overboard, he unbalanced the boat and it capsized. I am not sure that these warriors had ever fought in the estuary with a wind behind. Our sail obscured Golden Bear and one spear hit the mast while another landed next to my youngest son.

The warriors on the boat that we had targetted realised, almost too late, what we intended. Three hurled their spears at what was an impossibly close range while the fourth hurled himself over our bow like a human arrow. He held a stone knife in his hand. As we crunched and cracked across the boat, severing it in two, he landed upon me. He was a big man and his body was coated in grease, I presumed as protection against the cold. My right hand was reaching for my seax even as my left held his knife hand. *'Gytha'* rose and fell as we destroyed their boat and that made the warrior fall to the side. I trusted in the spirits and my snekke. I drove the seax up under his ribs and as it scraped off the bone I twisted and when blood gushed over my hand, I knew he was dead. His extra weight was slowing us down and I pushed his body from me and over the gunwale.

I raised myself to my knees and saw that my sons were unhurt. Golden Bear looked terrified. I smiled, "Now you are a steersman, my son, you did well. You both did well."

As Brave Cub and I stared astern we saw the sharks begin to gather. The blood in the water attracted them. There would be no pursuit. Any thoughts of sailing through the night had ended with the attack. We needed to examine *'Gytha'* for damage and that meant finding land and a safe beach. When we had sailed this estuary before I had noticed that the first land on the larboard side was a swampy piece of earth where a shallow river spilt into the estuary. We had never seen anyone living there but there was a beach just to the north of it. I took over the steering board and headed for it. Imagination can be a dangerous thing and I was convinced, as we neared the surf, that we were holed. Brave Cub lowered the sail as we approached the soft sandy beach and we slid up onto it. I lifted the steering board from the boat and we hauled the snekke onto the sand. There was plenty of light for we had not had to sail far. I could still see Salt Island, a smudge on the horizon.

"Light a fire and we will cook the fish you caught. I will examine the hull." I knew there was a risk but I hoped that our enemies had lost enough men to deter them from a pointless pursuit.

As they hurried to gather kindling and driftwood, I knelt next to the figurehead. I ran my fingers down to the keel. I was seeking cracks. I had to scrape sand away but there appeared to be no damage to the central keel, the piece of wood that gave *'Gytha'* her strength. I then examined the strakes in case any had sprung. To my relief, they appeared sound. Birchbark boats are, by their very design, light. The warriors had unwittingly given us our best chance of escape. Had we struck a glancing blow they would not have sunk and they might have managed to board us with more warriors. Perhaps next time they would learn from that lesson.

The fire had just taken when I reached my sons. They were already skewering the fish for cooking. They looked up as I approached, "All is well and the hull is sound. We built well."

Golden Bear said, "I thought when that warrior leapt aboard that we were doomed."

"*'Gytha'* saved us for we knew her motion and he did not. We will camp here tonight and then sail without stopping for Brave Eagle and his village. We will eat this fine fish you have caught and that will sustain us on our voyage."

Erik's Clan

The next morning, as we left, the wind had shifted and although it pushed us against the current it was not as powerful as when we had fled our enemies. *Wyrd.* Now that Golden Bear had successfully steered it meant that there were three of us who could watch and that made life much easier. The voyage up the Patawomke was not the fastest I had ever made but it was one of the most enjoyable as I chatted with my youngest sons about sailing, the snekke and my life. Sailing makes a man reflective and as the three of us had come close to death we were closer and able to talk about life and death a little more dispassionately. I was almost sorry to see the entrance to our old mooring. It was late afternoon when we arrived but we sailed unerringly through the tiny gap that led to what had been our home for so many years.

Chapter 17

It was Otter's Claw who came to the river when he heard the boat brush the undergrowth. He must have been the sentry and he came armed and ready for war. His expression changed when he recognised, first the snekke and then us. "Shaman of the Bear! This is unexpected. I feared we had enemies to fight."

I frowned, "Enemies? The Moneton?"

He nodded, "Aye and others. Come, Brave Eagle will be pleased to see you." He shook his head, "This is no longer a happy village, Shaman."

"Golden Bear, fetch the rest of the fish. It will add to the food we will enjoy." I followed Otter's Claw with a sense of dread. Since I had been away enjoying our new life, I had feared the worst but hoped for the best.

The village was just awakening. Men were making water and fires were being kindled. I was spied as soon as we emerged from the undergrowth. The ditch was still in place and had been kept clean. I had to step over it. Otter's Claw waved to Brave Eagle's Yehakin and said, "I will return to my watch. It is good to see you."

I waited for my sons and then headed to the larger yehakin. Hides Alone saw me and hurried to me, "Erik, what brings you here? This is not good."

I frowned, "Not good for me to visit with my old friends? Has the world changed so much since we left?"

"It was your leaving that changed it. Come, get inside my father's yehakin before too many eyes see you although I fear that enough eyes have spied you to make that useless."

I was confused but I obeyed the warrior. Brave Eagle had aged and he struggled to rise as we entered. Running Antelope smiled, "I will fetch food, Erik."

Brave Eagle tried to rise but I could see he was in pain, "Sit, old friend, and I will join you on the ground and you can tell me why I am no longer welcome in my old home." I looked at Hides Alone, "Your son told me."

Brave Eagle gave an angry look to his son and then relented. "My son speaks the truth but the words might have come more gently from me.

"Aye, Father, and I will tell White Fox and Long Nose."

Erik's Clan

I sat gingerly, with my right leg out before me. I did not know Long Nose well and wondered why his name was included. He was a youth who had fought alongside Golden Bear with the slingers when we had defeated the Moneton.

Running Antelope poured the three of us some ale and said, "I will cook food."

Golden Bear handed her the fish, "We have not come empty handed, Running Antelope."

She smiled as she took the fish, "You have grown. Your new home is good for you. And how is your mother?"

Both Brave Eagle and I were anxious to speak but Running Antelope was not a woman to be baulked.

"She is well and my sister and brothers have all become parents. Our clan is growing."

"Good."

Brave Eagle said, "I am pleased that you prosper but your visit puts both you and my whole clan in danger."

"Eagle Claws?"

"Aye, he came back a day after you sailed and was angry beyond words. He said he wanted the magic boats and they were his by right for he was the war chief who had defeated the Moneton."

"That makes no sense."

"Little that Eagle Claws does makes sense. It is as though his father's death gave him power and it transformed him. He has surrounded himself with the best warriors from each clan and they make war on our own people to subjugate them. He asked for the best warriors from this clan but my son angered him when he said that they were with you. All the other clans sent men to be trained by Eagle Claws. It is as though his father restrained him and now that he is dead an evil spirit has been released." He shook his head, "I tried to bend and it availed us little. I did not think that we would gain anything from a war with Eagle Claws. He asked for warriors to follow him and none went. They all said that they would rather follow me and my path. So he reinstated the tax on food. We have to work twice as hard for half of the food. Without your boats collecting fish, we go hungry." The Norns had been spinning. While we had enjoyed a peaceful life those we had left had suffered because of us.

Just then White Fox and Long Nose entered. I saw that Long Nose, like Golden Bear, had grown. He beamed when he saw us.

Brave Eagle held up his hand, "Say nothing, Long Nose, for I have not yet spoken of your part in this. Sit and I will tell you when you may speak."

Erik's Clan

I noticed that White Fox looked bowed. When his family had been taken, he had been a fierce and angry warrior. Now he looked defeated.

Brave Eagle spoke and his voice was tinged with sadness and regret, "Perhaps we should have fought against the unfairness of the food tax but I had seen enough death. It was Long Nose's father, Owl's Feather and his friends, who took matters into their own hands. He and some of the other warriors stood up to Eagle Claws. They simply said that they wanted a return to the time of Long Spear and they did so without weapons in their hands. Unprovoked, Eagle Claw let loose his wild warriors and Owl's Feather, Climbs Trees and Raccoon were all butchered." I could not help but glance at Long Nose. Brave Eagle said, "The young warriors were all with my sons, hunting. It is a full-time occupation. The three warriors who died were the only ones in the village when Eagle Claws came for his tribute." He nodded at the young warrior. "Now you may speak."

Long Nose looked at me and I saw the pain in his eyes. "I would have chased after Eagle Claws and killed him for what he had done even though I know it would have resulted in my death, but my mother's hand stayed me and I did not leave. She died a month later and I would have sought and killed Eagle Claws then had not Brave Eagle counselled me. He put me to live with White Fox and said that he would give me a task that would hurt Eagle Claws more and I would live. I was supposed to leave the village soon and paddle up the Patawomke to find you. We have been preparing food so that I could do so."

Brave Eagle held up his hand and Long Nose nodded. "We delayed sending Long Nose for I knew he would need to be strong and have plenty of food. With three fewer warriors we never seemed to have enough. I wanted you to be warned to stay away." He gave me a sad smile, "I failed for you are here."

I smiled, "Brave Eagle, the Norns have spun and we both know that a man can do nothing about that."

"Aye, you are right but I fear that this sudden visit may be like a stone thrown into a pond and the ripples will keep on flowing beyond our sight."

"I can leave on the morrow and he will never know that I was here. I would not bring pain to your people."

"And that is the trouble, Erik, there are those in the village who will tell Eagle Claws that you have returned. They will do so to make life easier for themselves. He wants to know where you now live."

The Norns had been spinning. I had planned on defending my home against the Moneton and now, it seemed, it might be my old nemesis who was the danger. I nodded, "We will leave before dawn and when

Eagle Claws comes, Brave Eagle, you shall be the one to tell him where we live."

"But when he finds you are not where we say he will return and destroy us."

"You will tell him exactly where we live."

Running Antelope had returned with food and I saw the surprise on her face as she heard the words, "You would draw him to you?"

I smiled, "We found the journey hazardous enough and we had the snekke. He will not find it easy. Besides the three sisters have spun. My family and I could not live with the knowledge that we had hurt the clan. We will take whatever punishment Eagle Claws thinks that he can mete out and trust to our iron weapons and the home we have built. We have brought this pain to the clan and it is not right. If I can draw Eagle Claws to my home and we are prepared then we have the opportunity to end his ambitions once and for all." My sons both nodded making me as proud as a father could be. The blood of Lars ran through their veins. "We live beyond the ridge of blue hills. There is a pass. The river Shenandoah is not a deep river like the Patawomke. In places, it is barred by rocks. We found a home a couple of days' sailing up the Shenandoah. We live in a large loop in the river at the top of a slope."

"He will bring warriors."

"I know but it is a long way and the paths are hard. I hope he tries to come by water for the Moneton prowl the Patawomke. We slipped by unseen but then we can travel at night. If he comes by land he will travel across a wilderness without paths. At the very least when he comes his grip on the tribe will be lessened." I looked Brave Eagle in the eyes, "Brave Eagle, bowing down to a tyrant does no good. We left our home in Larswick because of Sweyn Forkbeard. You have nowhere to flee to. This is your home. When Eagle Claws leaves to follow us then you and your sons must rouse the clans and retake the tribes while he is away. Men will die but three of your clan died in any case. This way you have a chance. If you bend the knee and bow the head you have none."

Silence ensued and I began to eat.

White Fox said, "I think it is a good plan. I am sad that Erik and his family will die but they should not die in vain. The Shaman is right and we can fight."

Long Nose nodded, "And, if you will have me, Erik, I will join your clan. It will be one more warrior to help you fight this evil. My death might avenge my father."

I shook my head, "Do not be so eager to die, Long Nose. Come with us by all means but come to fight and obey my orders. I do not wish my new clan to perish."

Golden Bear grinned, "Aye, Long Nose," he took out his seax, "our clan have iron and our claws are sharp."

Brave Eagle sighed, "You are right and I have watched the sadness in our clan for too long. Better that we rouse ourselves. Your plan is a good one and does, at least, give us a chance of returning to the life we knew." He smiled, "I miss you, Erik, Shaman of the Bear. You bring hope where there is none but I agree with my son, you and your clan will die and sacrifice yourselves for us."

Now that there was no longer any need for secrecy, we left the yehakin and went amongst the clan. I went to the three fathers whose children lived with us. I told them of their grandchildren and the life they now lived. The mothers wept and the fathers looked proud. It was as I was wandering around and speaking to the clan that I saw what Brave Eagle had meant. There now appeared to be a rift in the clan. Some could not look me in the eye. They would be the ones who would tell Eagle Claw of our visit. Indeed, I suspected that some might have sent sons to run to Eagle Claws' village and tell him that I was within his grasp.

By late afternoon I had seen all those that I needed to. Long Nose had packed his belongings in the snekke and I had given the gifts of the iron arrowheads to Brave Eagle. The two of us were alone in his yehakin when I did so, "We shall, probably, never meet again, my friend."

I nodded and then tapped my heart, "But we fought together and you will always be in here and when we both fall then we will see each other in the spirit world."

He gave me a surprised look, "Will it be the same spirit world? I thought that yours would be in the world of your people."

I shrugged, "Since I have been in this new world my views on Valhalla have changed. When I sit in the steam hut and dream, I often go to the spirit world. It is not just my brothers, cousin and fellow warriors that I see but also the Mi'kmaq who died in battle."

Brave Eagle beamed, "Then that makes me happy for I would like to spend eternity talking to you, Erik."

"And I, you."

White Fox came as we ate our evening meal. The red-fleshed fish we had brought had fed us all well and we were feeling content. "Runs Far has left the village."

He was one of the young boys who had fought the Moneton.

Erik's Clan

Brave Eagle said, "His father will have sent him, Erik. He will seek to gain favour with the news of your arrival."

I nodded, "It is, as you said, to be expected and even if Eagle Claws and his warriors leave their village directly we will be long gone by the time he gets here. White Fox, send your son, Black Feather to give the news to Eagle Claws." Brave Eagle and his son gave me a surprised look and I smiled, "Two can play the game of deception. By sending your grandson, Brave Eagle, we deceive Eagle Claws. Hopefully, White Fox, your son will get there first and when Eagle Claws arrives you can tell him where my new home lies. We will wait for him there."

Black Feather was proud to be given the chance to do something for the clan and I knew that he would race to beat Runs Far. The web of the three sisters was indeed complicated. Threads connected each of us in ways we could not even start to comprehend.

We did not sneak away before dawn but left after the sun had risen. If there were watchers, I wanted them to see where we were headed. Once on the Patawomke, I would fear no one. We might be more heavily laden but we also had more defenders for the boat. I placed Long Nose and Golden Bear by the mast for my youngest son could explain to his friend what they needed to do. Brave Cub ran lines from the prow to enable us to fish. I had a wide-open river and a benign wind. As on the voyage south, we would not stop except when we reached the mouth of the Shenandoah. That way we would be home before Eagle Claws and his new army were close. I turned my mind to defeating Eagle Claws.

He would bring his best warriors and they would outnumber us. That meant we needed an early warning of his arrival. I had to assume he would come by land and that meant we had at least seven days to prepare. I would use the land and traps to defeat the warriors brought by Eagle Claws. The only paths he could follow would be the ones made by animals or those made by us. I intended to make our paths clearer. He would follow them as the best and quickest way to get to us. We could then use ambush and traps. I wanted to thin his numbers before he reached my longhouse as well as discourage his men. This would be a war of attrition. We would make his men bleed as they tried to get to us. That would put fear in their hearts and a warrior who has fear in his heart loses. I was the Shaman of the Bear and that would invoke fear in my enemies. My iron weapons were also feared by my enemies. That also helped us. The river protected us and we had been guided to the loop of the river. That narrow neck of land would funnel any attackers into a narrower killing ground and give us somewhere to defend.

"Golden Bear, come and steer while I speak with Brave Cub." He did so. I did not want Long Nose moving in the snekke until he was used to the snekke. I slid up to Brave Cub and explained what my thoughts were. He added ideas of his own and I nodded. "I will sleep now. Take over at the steering board when Golden Bear tires and as the sun sets, then wake me. This shall be my bed." Covering myself with my bear skin I was instantly asleep. The motion of the snekke always did that to me. As I dreamed, I dreamt of my land and I saw every fold and ditch. I felt every tree and leaf. I was as one with the land.

When my son woke me, he said he had seen Moneton boats but that they had not approached. As I sent him to sleep I counselled him to wake me if the same thing happened the next day. My part of the voyage seemed the most difficult, as I sailed up a dark river, but I felt I knew the Patawomke. I did not fear the Moneton but I knew that they could cause trouble. If word came that we were on the river they might try to follow us. The Allfather watched over us and after two days we were nearing the Shenandoah and the Moneton had not come close again.

I had the steering board and I spied the white flecked bubbling water that marked the mouth of the Shenandoah. I would not risk it in the dark but dawn was just an hour or so away. None would see us enter the river and that meant we would disappear. The Moneton might seek us but they would not find us. The magical boats they feared which disappeared would be another legend to be told around the campfires. I reefed the sail and woke Golden Bear. "Wake your brother. Make water, eat and be ready to ride the maelstrom."

He grinned, "Aye, Father, Long Nose is in for a surprise, is he not?"

I nodded, "Let us call it the initiation into the clan. You had better warn him to cling on to the snekke."

Dawn made life easier for me. With Brave Cub in the prow, guiding me as his mother had done, I headed into the river. It appeared to be deeper than the last time we had sailed it and that meant they had enjoyed rain to the north of us. The ridge of hills seemed to act as a barrier to rain. We had not had rain in the south. The extra water made life just a little easier for me. I was learning to read the river much as a clever man might read runes. I found myself making a turn before Brave Cub signalled me. Even so, it was a wild ride and the snekke tossed and turned. Long Nose clung to the mast for dear life but the wild waters did not last as long as they had on our first passage.

We made good time to the shallows and we moored the snekke. "Brave Cub, take your brother and fetch the warriors. Long Nose and I will wait here."

Erik's Clan

My sons loped off. Long Nose began to babble almost before they had left us. He could not stop talking about the waters we had crossed. When his words finally subsided he turned to me, "You must have great magic in you that you could sail that stretch of water, Shaman."

"One day Brave Cub and even Golden Bear will sail it. It is practice."

"I could never do that. I fear the river when I paddle a boat and yours has a magical power within it."

"You may be right. It takes time to build a snekke and our blood lies within the hull. We are part of it."

He nodded and studied the boat in silence.

I broached something that had been on my mind for some time. "Long Nose, while you live with us you will be part of our clan and I am chief." He nodded. "That means you obey every command. If you cannot swear to do that then I will leave you in the longhouse with the women."

"I swear that I will obey you, Erik, Shaman of the Bear."

"I do not want you to be reckless. Your father died and I would have you live. I do not say he was wrong to face up to Eagle Claws but there are ways for a man to fight that keep him safe. He paid for his mistake with his life. We only have one life, Long Nose, so do not throw yours away recklessly. We will fight Eagle Claws but we will do it my way. The Clan of the Bear has a particular way of fighting. When this is all over and the threat of Eagle Claws has gone then if you wish we will take you back to your home."

"There is nothing for me there. I have no family left and the village has memories that make me sad. This is a new world for me and I will make a new life with you and your clan if you will have me."

The boys arrived, in their boats, far faster than I had expected. Moos Blood's face told me that his brother had told him our news. We had no time to waste in debate. "Get the rollers under the snekke. We have more arms to pull. Let us see how fast we can do this."

"We have to talk, Father."

"And talk we will but not here. Time is in short supply. Golden Bear, Bjorr Tooth and Long Nose, you will carry the rollers from the rear and replace them at the bows. The rest of us will pull."

Perhaps it was the precarious situation we found ourselves in, I do not know but the snekke seemed to fly across the rocks as though they were not even there. Of course, the boys were exhausted when we finally reach the water where **'*Gytha*'** could float but that was a minor consideration.

Erik's Clan

"I will sail the snekke back with Bjorr Tooth. The rest of you paddle hard and get back to Eagle's Shadow. I want the birchbark boats hidden by the time we reach home."

It was noon when I finally saw our landing. The boys were there already. Their sweating bodies told me that they had worked hard.

"Our task is not yet done. While Bjorr Tooth, Golden Bear and Long Nose help me to unpack *'Gytha'* I want *'Doe'* taken up to the longhouse."

Moos Blood nodded, "Let us take down the mast."

My knee needed consideration and so I used the three youngest members of the clan to carry our precious goods to the longhouse. I took down the mast and removed the steering board so that by the time Moos Blood and the others returned *'Gytha'* was ready to be hidden. It was the late afternoon when I finally entered the longhouse. All the women in the clan looked expectantly at me.

"Tonight we eat outside and when my stomach is full then I will tell you all our news and I will give you my plan to defeat Eagle Claws." I smiled, "Fear not for the Clan of the Bear is more than ready to face this evil tyrant. I did not flee Sweyn Forkbeard to be defeated by a pathetic little glory hunter like Eagle Claws!" I tried to put as much confidence in my voice as I could. The smiles told me that I had succeeded. Now we had to put my plan into operation.

Chapter 18

The food helped me to focus my mind. Laughing Deer held my hand as I spoke. I told them all exactly how we would defeat Eagle Claws. "From tomorrow the men of this clan will spend every day, from dawn until dusk in the woods. We will be looking for signs of Eagle Claws and his men whilst also preparing traps. I want many deadly traps to be built. Once we know that he is coming then we will ambush them. I expect their numbers to be such that we cannot defeat them in one battle. I intend to whittle down both their numbers and their will. We will pull back and retire to the longhouse." I paused. The last part of the plan had come to me as I had sailed back and forth at the mouth of the Shenandoah. "Moos Blood will command the defence of the longhouse."

He looked surprised, "Why not you, Father?"

"Because I shall not be there. I will not fall back with you. I will become Ulfheonar."

The use of the strange word deflected their minds from my meaning. Moos Blood said, "Ulfheonar?"

"Warriors who dress in animal skins. There are few such men left in the world now. There is a legend, in the land of my birth, of a warrior called Dragonheart. He had a sword that was touched by the gods and he led a band of such warriors. They kept their land safe. They used the land and the skins of animals to hide from their enemies. I will use my bearskin and my sword to become as Dragonheart."

Brave Cub shouted, "I will be with you and do the same."

I shook my head, "I have done this before. Ask your mother."

All eyes looked to Laughing Deer, "Although I fear for your father's life, he is right. He can hide in plain sight and he is a fearful warrior." She turned to look at me, "But you now carry a wound and that wound might cause you to fail."

I had thought of this, "You are right but every warrior I slay will be one less for Moos Blood and the rest of the clan to fight. I have had a good life and if it is to end here then what better way." I waved a hand, "to save my clan," I held my wife's hand, "our clan and our grandchildren? When I am gone then the clan will survive and keep my memory alive through their blood."

She nodded, "You are right and I am content. Your father's plan is a good one. Let us all do what we can to help him succeed." Her words were the final argument. Even Moos Blood would not argue with his mother.

The decision had an instant effect on the family. The couples grew closer together and I saw that Brave Cub took charge of his young brother and the two new members of the clan. That was good. I took it all in for I knew not how long I would have with my family and clan. I was not a fool. I was no longer a young man and my weak knee might be my undoing but I knew that I could still make a difference. Eagle Claw and his warriors had never fought a Viking and one skill I enjoyed that even my brother had not was the ability to fight and defeat the warriors of this new world.

I was up before dawn and I gathered the tools and weapons I would need. It says much about my clan that they, too, all rose early and the warriors left for the neck of land between the rivers. I sent Moos Blood and Fears Water to one loop of the river and Brave Cub and Humming Bird to the other. "Dig a channel, as we did for the landing. I want the neck of land to be narrower. I wish the land to be flooded and impassable. Work all day and see how far you can get. The narrower we can make the land the easier our task will be."

I was left with the two newest members of the clan and Golden Bear. "Our task is to make the trees over there," I pointed to the land to the east, "filled with traps. I handed them some vines I had cut the previous day. "Tie these between trees at the height of an ankle. We begin on one side of the path and then complete the other. I will make the traps deadly."

While they tied the tough vines, I hammered stakes into the ground and then sharpened them with my seax. I covered them with leaves and grasses. The idea was to make the enemy trip and fall onto the stakes. Even if they avoided the vines they might step on the stakes and become injured. I wanted weakened men when we faced them. We would avoid the forest until the danger was over and I hoped that the warriors would trip and fall on the sharpened stakes. Any wound would weaken them. We stopped at noon to eat and as we did I pointed to the forest. "We have made but a start. By this afternoon I hope to have a hundred paces on either side of our path prepared but by the time the enemy comes, we will need to make the traps reach all the way to the ditches that the others are building. You must remember where we have laid the traps. Now, while you continue to put the vines in place, I will head down the path and look for signs of the enemy."

I walked down the path, reassured by the lack of footprints. I walked about two miles, almost to the path that led to the blue hills and then I returned to the two boys. As I walked, I looked at the path with new eyes. What would the scouts of Eagle Claws see? He would be wary and so I looked for places we would put obvious traps that he would find. I dug shallow pits and covered them with undergrowth. They would find them and, I hoped, become overconfident. As I drew nearer to the line of vines, I sought the place for the first real trap. I found it where the path turned around a huge tree that was the thickness of a man. The view along the path was obscured. I took the spade I had brought and began to dig. It was ankle-deep when Bjorr Tooth and Long Nose reappeared.

"We have used all the vines up, Chief."

I nodded, "We will cut more later on. For now, I want you to help to clear this soil. I want it spread around so that it is hidden in plain sight. When the hole is knee-deep, we can begin to make it into a trap."

It took an hour of hard digging but I was happy with the result. The hole was two paces long and more than a pace wide. We then went closer to the house to cut more stakes and branches. I buried the stakes in the hole and sharpened them. Then we laid a thin lattice of branches across it. I pointed down the path I had taken. "Now take these other branches and lay them along the path."

Golden Bear grinned, "You want them to think that there is a trap and when they move the branches and find none, they might ignore the last one."

I nodded, "The last one is hidden by the tree. They will turn the corner and I intend to attract their attention further down the path."

Bjorr Tooth asked, "How?"

"I make them think we intend to ambush them. While you do what I have asked I will create my illusion."

I walked down the path from the trap for twenty paces and then took the feathers and squirrel tail from my satchel. I attached them to the far side of the tree at head height. When I had finished, I walked back down the path to examine my handiwork. It looked like a warrior was making a poor attempt at hiding.

I hid behind a tree to watch and when the three boys returned, I saw them point and Bjorr Tooth shouted, "I can see you hiding, Shaman of the Bear."

When I stepped out behind them and said, "Really?" They jumped so high that I laughed. "Come let us see how the others are doing."

I led them through the forest making sure that I stayed to the west of the line of traps. When we reached Moos Blood I was pleased with his efforts. They had managed to dig a trench thirty paces long. Already the first ten paces were filled with water while the other twenty were a muddy morass. He shook his head ruefully, "We will need to bathe this night or Blue Feather will not allow me near her."

"You have done well. Do not step towards the east when you return to the longhouse. We have laid traps and only use the path close to the longhouse."

He nodded, "Have you seen any signs yet?"

I shook my head, "Nor would I expect to. Tomorrow the boys and I will complete the line of traps and wherever you have managed to dig to shall be our line of defence. I cannot count on more than one more day to prepare our defences."

That evening we were all filthy and weary. Laughing Deer had been prescient and the steam hut was lit. It was a tight but companionable squeeze as we all huddled inside and I told them of the traps we had made. "When they come the ambush will be where I have placed the feathers. Once you have hurt them, Moos Blood, you will fall back but do so in pairs. One will use a bow to deter pursuit and the other runs to ready an arrow. You will leapfrog through the trees. By then we will have made safe paths for us." I smiled, "We have some trees to hew for the last trap will be a pile of logs at the top of the slope. You, Moos Blood, will release them when the enemy tries to ascend the path. Then you will retire inside the longhouse, pull up the bridge and await the attack."

There was silence until Brave Cub said, "And what of you, father?"

"I will be the bear and I will whittle them down. With luck, they will be discouraged and leave."

"And if not? Do we stay inside and starve to death?"

"No, Humming Bird, once the attack stops then you know that they are either fled or waiting. One of you, one of the smaller warriors, will sneak out through the escape passage we built in the longhouse and see if they have gone." When we built the house, I was aware that one entrance might not be enough. We had built a trapdoor on the landing side. It came out in the ditch and was well disguised. "If they wait and there are few of them then you can come out and finish them off." I paused, "And if I have not survived then bury me here, on Eagle's Shadow."

Brave Cub said, "But you will not die, Father. You cannot."

"I will do all that I can but the Norns have spun and I know that I have enjoyed more luck than any man deserves. I am content that I now have a family and a clan who will make this valley their own." With those sombre words in their heads, we left the hut and went for a meal that was long overdue.

Erik's Clan

I felt confident enough the next day to allow Golden Bear to supervise the last of the traps and I began to cut the logs for the last trap. It was hard work but, surprisingly, my knee did not seem to object. It was the climbing up and down the hill that hurt. I also asked Moos Blood to check the path for signs of the enemy. I told him to be careful but I hoped that he might spot things we had not. When they returned at night I had the logs cut but not the trap and so we worked, in the dark, for an hour, while we made a wooden wall for the logs. The simple expedient of striking a single wedge would create the timber avalanche that I hoped would sweep the enemy from the path.

After we had eaten that night, I said, "Tomorrow will be the last day that you can cook, Laughing Deer." She nodded, "As of tomorrow we all arm for war. I shall wear my bearskin and helmet. I will carry my sword and hatchet. Moos Blood, you can use the timber axe. I want you all to have full quivers of arrows. We will walk towards the iron hills until noon and watch for the enemy. If they are not in sight by the middle of the afternoon then we will return here."

"And if they come at night?"

"Then we rely on our traps but tonight will be the last night we do not mount a watch with sentries along the path. Tomorrow I will arrange that duty."

The longhouse was more crowded now but, as people spoke long into the night one could not make out the words. The words were private. I cuddled close to Laughing Deer, "We have enjoyed a good life, have we not?"

"Without you, husband, I would still be a prisoner of the Penobscot. I would have died years ago. Whatever life I have had is due to you."

"And had you not fished me from that river then I would not have had a life. The Norns spun. All those within this longhouse owe their lives in one way or another to us."

"Even Long Nose?"

"Had I not returned to the village then he would have tried to kill Eagle Claws and he would be dead. No, my love, our lives have had a purpose and that is all that we can ask. Whatever happens in the next few days, I am content."

"As am I."

I went to sleep with a buzz from the others. The words would be different but the promises and the meaning would be the same.

I woke early and it was not to make water. I was nervous. I dressed for war. I wondered if I would regret melting down my byrnie for arrowheads. I donned my head protector but left the helmet to one side. I took some cochineal and smeared it across my eyes. When my helmet was placed on my head it would have an effect. I had heard that the Ulfheonar did the same and I would use anything I could to gain an advantage.

I smelled food being cooked. I smiled for my wife had ignored my orders that we were not to have hot food this day. She knew that we would be better warriors with warm food and a full belly. There was a false atmosphere of jollity as we ate. The men were trying to appear as though it was an ordinary day. I just smiled and ate. For the youngest three warriors, Bjorn Tooth, Golden Bear and Long Nose it would be a propitious day. Long Nose and Golden Bear had used slingshots when the Moneton had attacked but they had been at a safe distance. This day could see them face to face with warriors who would not care that they were young. They would smash their skulls in regardless.

"It is time." I held my bow and spear. Laughing Deer donned my helmet for me and kissed me. Then she placed the bearskin over the helmet. Bjorr Tooth and his family had never seen me in the skin and they recoiled. My sons saw the effect and so they smeared the cochineal across their eyes and cheeks. With their paler skin, it stood out more and would make an enemy pause.

I led them down the hill. They followed in a line and Moos Blood brought up the rear. When we reached the deep trap, I led them carefully through the woods. I had marked the safe passage from Eagle's Shadow side so that we could find the way. "Mark our way. When we return you will not see the marks on the trees."

It took us some time to reach the place where the traps began. I had already divided them into three groups. Moos Blood led Humming Bird and Bjorr Tooth to the right. Brave Cub led Golden Bear and Fears Water to the left and I stayed on the path with Long Nose. I waved them forward. We would not speak. Their orders were to walk until noon and then wait. Three whistles would be the signal for danger. If none had come in two hours then they were to return to the main trap and wait with me there. I knew that Long Nose and I were the ones most likely to meet any enemy for, as I knew well, this was the main path from the iron ridge. As we walked along it, doubts began to assail me. What if they had come by water? Almost as soon as the idea entered my head, I dismissed it. They would lose men coming by water. What if they chose to delay their attack? While that, too was a possibility, I doubted that Eagle Claws, once he discovered where I lived, would wait even an hour. They would come but the question remained, when?

I had learned to estimate the time when standing a watch on the drekar. Then I used an hourglass to mark time. It lay in my chest in the longhouse. I had not used it since we had landed at Brave Eagle's village but the many hours, days and weeks on watch had given me an hourglass in my head. An hour had passed when I heard the noise. We were squatting on either side of the trail, disguised by undergrowth. I felt, first, the vibrations from the feet coming down the path. Long Nose had not heard it. He was picking at the scab of some old scar on his arm. I attracted his attention and made the sign for vigilance. I drew my sword and slowly rose so that, whilst still hidden, I was upright. Even Long Nose detected the pounding of feet as someone ran down the trail. I wondered at that. No one, except us, had used the trail and I had expected Eagle Claws to send scouts. If he sent just one then he was a fool and this was a single warrior who ran down the trail. That too confused me. A scout does not run. He looks for danger, ambush, and traps. He does not run as though he is taking an urgent message. The undergrowth and the twisting nature of the trail meant that I only had glimpses of the warrior as he ran. I saw his skin, his hair, his feathers. I even saw the tip of his spear but I did not see the whole warrior. I was confident that I could take, without killing, a single warrior. I knew the effect my appearance would have when I stepped on the trail. The warrior would be shocked and stunned. My sword would be at his throat before he knew it.

 I timed my move to perfection and the young warrior's eyes widened as the bear with the shining metal in his hand stepped from the undergrowth and the tip pricked his throat.

 "Black Feather!" Long Nose recognised White Fox's son.

 The young warrior's face broke into a grin, "Shaman, I have found you. You do not have much time." He turned and pointed towards the distant hills, "Eagle Claws camped at a cave where he found a fire. He knows where your village lies."

 I nodded. It was good information and I wanted more but we had to gather my clan. I whistled three times. "Follow me, Black Feather, and do not deviate from my steps. Long Nose, bring up the rear. As we run tell me your tale." With my knee complaining, I began to run, albeit slowly.

 "When I reached Eagle Claws, he would not let me return to my father. He said that I could lead his warband. There are forty of them. I played along with him, Shaman of the Bear, and said that I would happily lead so long as he ceased his tax on Brave Eagle."

 I smiled, "You are clever, Black Feather, for Eagle Claws would expect such treachery."

 "My father had described where you lived and I headed for the ridge of blue leading them there. For the first two days, they were suspicious and I was tethered but long before we neared the ridge, they took the tether off me. Perhaps they thought I would not escape. We reached the pass and found a fire. From the broken stone around the fire, Eagle Claws deduced that it was you who had camped there. That seemed to make them less suspicious of me. Then one of his men spied smoke in the distance. Even I could work out that it was your village. I rose during the night and laid a trail as though I had returned home and then found this trail. He is coming and he comes to kill you all and take your magical flying boats."

"You have done well, Black Feather, and my clan is in your debt. Know that there is a world of difference between Eagle Claws' intent and the reality of what he will do."

We had reached the main trap and I led the two boys to the place we had selected for our ambush. I handed my ale skin to Black Feather and he drank. We heard, coming through the undergrowth, the others and they had surprise on their faces when they saw Black Feather.

"The Allfather has sent us another warrior. Black Feather stay with Moos Blood. He will command." White Fox's son nodded. "We intend to ambush them here and, when I blow this horn," I tapped the old horn I had brought from Orkneyjar, "then you will fall back to the longhouse. Moos Blood will instruct you." I smiled, "Black Feather has brought us news that there are forty warriors in the warband and they know where we live. Forty is fewer than I thought. We only need to kill five or so each and they will lose. Now spread out and remember, not a stone or an arrow must be used until they have fallen into this trap. I will send a red fletched arrow and that is the signal for you to unleash a wall of death upon them. Listen for the horn. I want no heroes."

Brave Cub said, "Except one, Erik the Navigator, who will sacrifice himself for his clan."

Black Feather looked aghast and I smiled, "My son exaggerates. I have no intention of dying but I do intend to terrify."

We had prepared the ground well and we had barriers we had constructed. They were there to slow an enemy down. Small branches were bound with vines and brambles to make somewhere that would disguise our position and give us some shelter. I stood next to a large tree. I would be largely alone and ahead of the others. Closest to the enemy I was the one unprotected by the barrier. Once I sounded the horn and they began to fall back I had to disappear and become Ulfheonar.

They were slower to arrive than I had expected. It was the middle of the afternoon when we heard the first cry that told us they had found our first trap. The shallow trap we had made was intended to make them leave the trail and enter the maze of vines and pits that littered the forest. There were more cries as they found other traps that were intended to maim and wound. We had no idea how many men were hurt but we heard at least eight cries as they tripped over vines or stepped onto stakes. A voice echoed in the forest and then there was silence. Eagle Claws had not been one of those hurt in the traps for the voice was one of command. My plan, however, was still working. I had hoped that the early trap would send them into the forest and slow them down but I hoped that, eventually, they would seek the trail. Then they would find the false traps. I wanted their eager warriors, the braver ones, to be the ones who found the trap. The battle was yet to come. My young untried clan would have to face Eagle Claws' killers. The battle would not be easy and, as we prepared to face them my knee suddenly buckled. Would my old wound come back to haunt me?

Chapter 19

When I heard pounding feet, I knew that the enemy had returned to the trail. After sheathing my sword I took my bow and I nocked the red fletched arrow. The others would be doing the same. I was gambling that my clan, young though they were, had more heart than this warband. We were protecting our families and they were seeking simply to hurt us. As we had found when we had rescued Brave Eagle's family, the former was a more powerful force than the latter.

The three warriors at the fore all crashed into the trap. Spikes impaled them but also broke bones. The screams from the three filled the forest. I heard Eagle Claws as he shouted to his men, "More traps! Take to the forest."

Callously leaving the three men to their fate the warband spread out and I saw them in the trees. There was one more line of traps and I waited until they had fallen and they were just thirty paces from us before I sent my arrow at Eagle Claws' lieutenant. I recognised Night Stalker from the charcoal smeared down his face and the black feathers in his hair. He was a large warrior who thought himself the best Powhatan warrior. The arrow that slammed into his chest, burying the shaft up to the fletch, showed him that he was wrong. His spear and shield fell from lifeless hands and as the others turned to look whence came the danger, more arrows and stones flew into bodies unprotected by shields. Enough men fell to make me proud of my clan. I sent a second arrow at the warrior who ran towards Humming Bird in his hidden nest. My arrow struck his upper arm and drove through his body.

"Hold. This is an ambush. Put your shields before you."

Eagle Claws was being clever. He was not at the front. In my view that made him a bad leader but it allowed his men to make a shield wall. I had not seen a shield wall for many years. They were effective but, as I drew an iron tipped arrow, I knew that we had the beating of them. As the wall of hide shields approached, I sent an arrow to smack into a shield. The iron head tore through the hide as though it was parchment and entered the chest of a warrior who thought he was safe.

"Charge!"

I sent another arrow at them and then, as my clan, now just a few paces from the enemy furiously fought I sounded the horn and then, trusting that they would heed my command, crouched down beneath the bush at the bottom of the bole of the tree. I drew my sword and remained still.

As I had expected, the sight of my clan fleeing encouraged Eagle Claws. "We have them! On! We will feast this night on their food and enjoy their women." While it might have been the right encouragement for his men, I knew that it would simply harden the resolve of my clan.

I heard the warriors coming from behind me. I prayed that their eyes would be ahead and not down. I smelled the two warriors as they passed me. They stank of sweat and grease. I risked raising my head and saw their backs as they hurried towards the barrier behind which my clan had sheltered. I saw their frustration as they could not get at my retreating clan and they hacked and chopped at the barrier. Even as they did so I heard the thwack as a stone smacked into the forehead of one of them. My clan was doing what I had asked and were retreating in pairs. Now that we had Black Feather, Moos Blood had the luxury of three warriors. They were making Eagle Claws' killers pay for every step that they took on our land. After sheathing my sword I nocked an arrow and sent it into the back of the second warrior who had passed me. I then ducked down and moved one hundred paces to my left. I had not been seen but I was taking no chances.

One event I had not counted on was the timing of their attack. I realised that it would be dark by the time my clan made the safety of the longhouse. We had carved four arrow slits in the walls but they would only be useful if there was light to see by. I slipped my bow over my shoulder and drew my sword and hatchet. As I moved along, I saw a warrior crawling. He had a broken bone sticking out from his leg and he was in pain. It was not mercy that made me end his life with my hatchet but expediency. Wounded, he could still give the alarm to his warband. I then turned to head after the others. I had to stay at least twenty paces behind them as a stray arrow or stone that missed them could still strike me. Darkness was not far away. Already the last rays of the sunlight were making a red glow in the west. My clan needed to be within the longhouse before darkness fell. Eagle Claws' warriors hurried as he urged them on and that meant I had to hurry.

Perhaps I made too much noise, even though I was trying to be silent. Whatever the reason the warrior turned as I was about to stab him in the back. He remained silent for when he turned, he saw a bear and I watched fear fill his face as his mouth opened to scream. My sword stopped any scream when I rammed it in his throat. I passed another six bodies of dead or dying men as I moved through the forest, avoiding the trail. By my estimate we had to have killed or wounded many warriors but until daylight came and we could count I would not know.

It was then that my son released the timber avalanche. I was well away from the path but the majority of the warriors were not. The sound of the logs rumbling and crashing down the path was punctuated by the screams of men as the logs smashed into limbs breaking bones as though they were twigs.

The darkness, when it came, was sudden as though someone had snuffed out a candle and darkness fell. In the dark, I heard the moans of dying and wounded men. Some asked for help and others called for relief from the pain. Then I heard Eagle Claws as he called, "My warriors to me. We have them trapped. Now we can burn them out."

Although there was the possibility of using fire, we had soaked the turf roof and walls with water. It would take a mighty conflagration to set the longhouse on fire. I crept closer to the warriors. I had the advantage that I knew the land better than they did and I knew where to hide. I moved around the trees knowing that there were no traps until I had the warriors between me and the longhouse. I could see them but, hidden by the undergrowth and my bearskin I was invisible. I counted fifteen warriors left standing. I saw shadows moving on the path and knew that they were the ones wounded by the timber avalanche.

One of the warriors said, "Chief Eagle Claws, perhaps we should send for more men. We are a handful compared with the men we started with. The logs that they used have taken another six men. We have not enough to fight them."

Eagle Claws turned angrily and raised his tomahawk, "I will kill any who speak of retreating. They are boys led by an old man. We are the best warriors in the clan. We cannot afford to lose. If we lose to this Clan of the Bear then it may encourage others to rebel against my rule. There will be no retreat, do you understand? Fetch wood. There is kindling over there near that outside fire. Collect that. They may be inside their walls but they cannot fight a fire."

"Could we not attack the door?"

I heard his sardonic laugh, "They would like that for I am sure that they will have arrows aimed at the door. This Erik is no Shaman but he is clever. He is a trickster. Fetch wood."

I noticed that he did not move. Perhaps I could have nocked an arrow and killed him while he was alone but I did not. It proved wise for a figure ghosted from the forest not far from me. He had not seen me but if I had drawn my bow he would have.

"Chief Eagle Claw, the rest of our warriors lie dead and there is something else. Long Bow was killed by an arrow in the back."

Erik's Clan

The chief whirled, "You mean they are not all within the longhouse?" He stared around wildly. He might suspect I was abroad but he did not know and that doubt would make him jump at shadows. "You, Stone Knife, will watch my back. If there is one left outside I would have him taken. We can use him as a hostage to make them surrender."

"Do you think that they would?"

"The Clan of the Bear is like their leader, sentimental. It may be one of his sons. He would not wish them to be tortured. This Erik is the clever one and he will be in the longhouse. Hurry with the kindling."

As men hurried to his side, I took the opportunity to slip around them so that I was almost behind the longhouse and any arrows I sent would hit them in the front. Stone Knife's words had been a warning. I crouched so that the wood store was in front of me and I nocked an arrow. I saw the spark as one of the warband lit a brand and then the warriors ran towards the door. I aimed at the man with the brand. The others were before him. Arrows flew from inside the longhouse but the arrow slits meant that the arrow flights were not as accurate as they might have been. Two warriors were hit but only one dropped his load. I had no such constraints and my arrow slammed into the chest of the fire carrier. He fell and his falling body doused the fire. The others had, however, managed to make the longhouse. They had dropped their wood and kindling. As they hurried back, I heard one say, "Eagle Claws, they have a ditch."

"Make fire arrows."

I watched them as they began to make fire arrows. It was not easy and I knew that it would not work. They also discovered that they were too close to the longhouse when an arrow flew from one of the arrow slits and hit a warrior in the back. They moved out of range. It was as I counted them that I realised one was unaccounted for, Stone Knife. I laid my bow down and drew my sword and my hatchet. I rose then turned so that my back was to the wood store. I knew that I was being stalked and I stayed as still as I could. Movement would be the only way that Stone Knife would find me. I spied his movement. He was good and had realised that the arrow which had slain the fire carrier had not come from the longhouse. He knew roughly where I was but the movement of his head from side to side told me that he could not see me. If I remained still then he might not find me.

It was the fire arrows that were my undoing. Although I did not look up as they soared over my head to sizzle and die in the wet turf, Stone Knife followed them and it was as one descended that he caught sight of me. He raced at me with a wild scream that rent the air. He had a shield and a spear. I stayed still hoping that with the fur to disguise me he might miss. His spear came for my head and although he struck it the bear and my helmet stopped it. I saw the surprise on his face as I drove the sword up under his ribs and into his heart. Pushing his body from me I ran into the trees. I would lead them down to the river and the landing stage. If they were chasing me then they could not attack the longhouse.

My movement was seen and Eagle Claws screamed, "After him! I want him alive, whoever he is!"

I zig-zagged through the trees. My knee was complaining more than ever but I gritted my teeth through the pain. I knew exactly where I was and when I spied the large tree we had left I stopped and stepped behind it. I heard the warriors following me. They had seen just a shadow and they did not know where I had headed. As the first warrior came past the tree I lunged with my sword and stabbed him in the side. The warrior following him must have seen his companion fall and arrested his descent. As I stepped out, I had the same effect I had the first time and the shock froze the warrior. It cost him his life for my hatchet split his skull. However, it meant I was seen and I saw the warriors in the dark as they obeyed their chief. There were fewer of them now but I was tiring and in pain. I headed for the river. Water would be my salvation. This time I ran straight and when I reached the river I turned right and ran towards the landing. Without pausing I slipped into the water. It was icy cold for I was hot but its blackness would hide me. I lay on my back with my head hidden by the overhanging grass and the wood of the landing.

I heard the panting breath of the warriors as they appeared above me. They stood on the wooden dock and I knew they were searching the water for me. "He has disappeared!"

"Aye, but did you not see? It was a bear. That was Erik, Shaman of the Bear and he has turned himself into a bear."

"We should go now. How can we fight such magic?"

"Eagle Claws will kill you if you say such things. Now that his best friend has been killed, he will stop at nothing."

"Then let us head home. He will not know we are gone and will think that we are dead."

"He will punish us when he does get home."

I heard laughing, "The only warriors who will survive this are those who flee. We cannot fight magic. Eagle Claws and any who stay here are doomed to die."

"You are right. If we follow this river, it will bring us to the Patawomke and we can always say we were lost in the forest."

Erik's Clan

I waited until their footsteps had receded and silence filled the air before I emerged, tentatively, from the river. Peering over the bank I saw that I was alone. Their numbers might now be less than our own but it was still too dangerous to tell those within the longhouse. We had done as well as we had because we had fought Eagle Claws on our terms. If my clan came out to fight then warriors would die and I wanted no deaths.

It took some time to emerge from the water. The bearskin was soddened and weighed heavily upon me but I could not rid myself of it. It was my protection. I sheathed my sword. I still had my ale skin and I took a long drink. It revived me although I felt myself shaking. I did not retrace my steps but headed across the trail that led to the house and followed the river. I risked running into the two fleeing warriors but they would be moving faster than I was. Once I reached the trees again, I stopped to catch my breath. I saw fire arrows were still being used. They soared into the sky and then landed on the roof of my home. I also saw that dawn was just a couple of hours away. The nights were shorter at this time of the year. Had I been younger I might have taken the fight to Eagle Claws. By my reckoning, he had less than eight men left unwounded but I was cold and I was tired and there might be others who, although wounded, could still fight. More, I knew that his arrows would not set fire to the longhouse. I crouched in the dark and watched.

It was when I heard the debate, just thirty paces from me that the idea came to me. Eagle Claws' men were also tired and they wanted to rest and attack again at dawn. I could tell that Eagle Claws was tired too for he did not command them but tried to persuade them to continue the attack. Their attention was on each other and I took a chance. I crawled back to the path. The shape of the slope would hide me as I made my way up to the longhouse and the enemy. I moved slowly, to be truthful that was the only way that I could move for my knee had almost seized up. The danger would come once I reached the flat top where the buildings and the fire lay. I was saved by our fire. Although unlit the tripod and cooking pot hung there and they masked my movements. Eagle Claws and his men were on the other side. I had miscalculated for there were ten men in addition to Eagle Claws. They had lit a small fire to ignite their arrows and I guessed they were fifty paces from the longhouse, which stood behind me now, and thirty from where I waited. I would use the same strategy I had when we had rescued Brave Eagle's people. The sun would rise from behind Eagle Claws and it was not far away. My sudden appearance might just tip the wavering warriors over the edge. The conversation of the two men who had fled had told me that they believed I had magical powers. I did not but I could use that fear to help me.

Eagle Claws unwittingly helped me, "We will eat and make water and when the sun rises then we attack the longhouse but do so on all sides. Birch Branch, keep watch and we will relieve you."

I need do nothing but wait. The problem would come when I tried to stand. I was not sure if my knee would support my weight. I prayed to the Allfather and the spirits that had guided me thus far that they would give me the strength for one last act of defiance. If I could make the warriors, or most of them, flee then my clan had a chance. They would be inside the longhouse wondering if I lived or died. Even if they peered through the arrow slits I doubt that they would have seen me for I would just have been a shadow on the ground. I smiled to myself. I had become Ulfheonar. Here I was hiding in plain sight. Even my warrior brother had never managed that feat.

The food and the drink brought heart to Eagle Claws' warriors. I heard the weariness leave their voices as they returned to their small fire, which they fed and spoke of what they would do to my clan when they captured the longhouse. I peered through the tripod supporting the pot and saw the sky begin to change.

Eagle Claws saw it too, "Build up the fire and make fire arrows."

"We have only twenty arrows left to us, Eagle Claws."

"War Club, take your brother and go into the woods. Bring the arrows from our dead and their belts. We waste nothing."

I was bought time and I watched the sun slowly begin to make the sky lighter. I had to judge this perfectly. I had already slid my sword from my scabbard and I began to draw my good knee up beneath my body. My good leg would need to bear the weight of my body. The two warriors returned and their attention was on the damaged arrows. I saw the sun suddenly flare and, using my sword to push me to my feet I stood. They were not looking at me and when I drew my sword and raised it, it was my shout that made them turn, "I am Erik Shaman of the Bear and you are not welcome in the land of the Clan of the Bear, begone!"

All the newly gained confidence left them as the warriors, Eagle Claws excepted, stepped back fearfully. "This is a trick, get him!"

I remembered the conversation between the two men who had fled and knew that the heart had gone from these warriors who had seen most of their comrades perish already. I stepped from behind the cooking area and faced Eagle Claws, "Let you and I settle this, Eagle Claws. Enough of your men have died and you cannot fear an old man, can you?"

Erik's Clan

His eyes betrayed him. He did fear me but my words had seemed reasonable to his men. He looked at them and they nodded encouragingly. If their chief wished to fight me then so be it. They would watch. I heard a noise from behind me. I did not take my eyes from Eagle Claws for I knew he was a cunning man and would attack if I turned. I heard a creak and knew that the bridge over the ditch had been lowered.

"And to make sure that there are no tricks then the Clan of the Bear will watch." Moos Blood's words were the confirmation that Eagle Claws' warriors would do nothing.

The glory hunting chief took out his dagger and held it in his shield arm and swung the war club easily in his right. "You are an old man. My father held you in high regard and held me back. I have hated you since that time and when I have ended your life then the blood of the bear will be spilt and your line will end."

He launched himself at me with a flurry of blows. He almost caught me out for as I tried to step forward to meet him I forgot my weak knee and it would not support my weight. My sword barely held his powerfully struck war club. With his shield protecting his stone knife he slashed at my head. The stone rasped off the skin and helmet beneath making my head ring. Any thoughts I might have had about melting down the helmet ended as the helmet saved my life again. It was a powerful blow and without the helmet, I would be dead. Even as he raised his club again, I hacked at his knee with my hatchet. I bit through to the bone and his scream echoed through the forest.

I stood, "Now we are evenly matched."

The hatred in his face and, I dare say his heart drove any thought of defence from him and he rushed at me. He was using the last of his strength to overcome me before the wound in his knee incapacitated him. I fell and he crashed on top of me. The wind was knocked from me and his mouth was close to my head. The words he hissed chilled me, "You made me kill my own father for he would have given the tribe to Brave Eagle because of you. I sacrificed all and now you will pay."

His weight was on my left hand and he raised his war club to end my life. Even as I brought my sword around, I did the only thing I could do, I headbutted him. The bearskin and the helmet combined to make his head reel and the club struck not my head but my shoulder. My hatchet fell from my hand. I stabbed blindly with my sword. It was not the cleanest of strikes but the sharpened edge tore a long line across his lower back and he fell from me. We both struggled to our feet, panting and faced each other. He saw that I had no weapon in my left hand and he punched his shield and dagger at my head. Even as he did it, I knew that he would strike with his war club at my right arm. There was an edge to his war club and if he disabled my right arm then I was a dead man. I lunged and the Allfather guided my aim. Eagle Claws drove himself onto the blade and I pushed and twisted until I felt his stomach. He tried to curse me but all that poured from his mouth was not words but blood. He slid from my sword.

There was a cheer from behind me and I felt myself beginning to fall. I began to feel dizzy. Suddenly Moos Blood and Brave Cub were supporting me. I had to speak before darkness took me. "Eagle Claws' warriors if you swear never to raise a weapon against my family again then I will give you your lives. If you do not swear then all will die in this Land of the Bear."

They all dropped to their knees, "We swear."

That was the last I heard before blackness enveloped me and I spied Gytha waiting for me.

As ever she was faint and looked like smoke but it was her. She held out her hand to me but it was palm uppermost. Behind her, I saw my father, brother and cousins. They too held up their hands.
"Now is not your time Erik. You are sorely hurt but your work is not yet done. You are the Navigator and carry in your veins, our blood." She spread an arm behind her. The others began to fade. "Your days of fighting are gone. Now is the time of your sons. You must trust in them and their arms. They will fight your battles. One more blow will send you to us and we are not ready. Your wife is a good woman and has something of the volva in her. Trust to her and trust to her counsel. Between you, you will make a clan that will endure beyond ten men's lifetimes."
I saw her begin to fade and I tried to speak but no words came. As she faded the darkness came and then I smelled honey and all my pain disappeared like an early morning mist.

Epilogue

When I awoke, I was in my longhouse and Laughing Deer was holding my hand. I was naked beneath the bjorr skin fur. I had a bandage on my arm and when I put my hand to my head, I found another bandage. She smiled when my eyes opened. "Your sons thought the worst for you were barely breathing when you were carried in."

"But it was just a wound to my shoulder."

She reached down and brought up my helmet. Turning it she showed me the huge dent and crack on one side. "The blow to the helmet slowed the war club but it did not stop it. Your skull was cracked and there was blood. You have lain here for seven days, barely moving. We fed you liquid while you slept and used the last of our honey on the wound. You began to breathe easier last night."

I closed my eyes, "And Eagle Claws' men?"

"They left as they promised, taking with them those wounded by the falling logs. Brave Eagle and White Fox arrived two days ago. After you left them they went to Eagle Claws' village. The people there asked for him to be the chief of the tribe. He came here with his warriors to end the reign of Eagle Claws, you did that for them and they are happy." She smiled a thin smile, "That is all that I will tell you for the problems of Brave Eagle are unimportant compared with the health of my husband. Now I will fetch food and then you will rest. None shall see you until I am ready."

"They are still here?"

"Brave Eagle and his son sent his warriors back but they have remained. They would not go until they see you walking and that will not be until tomorrow at the earliest. You may be chief of this clan but I am the one who will decide when you are well."

I smiled, "Of course." Gytha had advised me and she was right. That day as I drifted in and out of sleep, I saw only my wife. She forbade all others from entering the longhouse. I could hear their voices without. I was woken now and then by one of the bairns wailing but it was as if I was still in the Otherworld.

I woke the next day and felt the need to rise. Laughing Deer was still asleep and I tried to slip out of bed without waking her. My knee betrayed me and I could not rise. She opened her eyes and shook her head, "If you wish to rise then wake me."

I gave her a weak smile, "I need to make water."

Erik's Clan

"Good that is a sign that you are getting better." She stood and held her hand out for me to hold. She was a strong woman and she pulled me to my feet. She slipped a kyrtle over my shoulders and was careful not to touch either of the bandages. She led me from the sleeping chamber. The rest of the longhouse was asleep and as she opened the door, I saw that the sun had yet to rise. I saw the yehakin of Brave Eagle and his son as she led me to the trees. It was a relief to empty my bladder and I could not help laughing.

"What is it, husband?"

"I am like a baby again. I am learning how to do things."

Leading me back to the longhouse she said, "And Moos Blood and the others have decided that you do too much. From now on they want you to be as Long Spear and spend your days watching others work."

Entering the longhouse I said, "Gytha came to me and told me my days of fighting are over. Moos Blood shall have my sword and Brave Cub my hatchet." It was only when I said those words that I felt relief. I was no longer carrying the clan on my back and my recovery began that day.

When I was dressed and sat before my clan as well as Brave Eagle, his son and a couple of warriors who had remained with him, I learned more about the events that had led to his arrival.

"Our clan was unhappy that Black Feather had not returned and that it was your clan that had to shoulder the responsibility of challenging Eagle Claws. We armed for war and went to the village of Eagle Claws. He had taken with him all the belligerent warriors and the ones who remained were of the same mind as us and did not like the new warlike chief. When we learned that Eagle Claws had marched to war, we followed for we wished to end this time of discord. We found some of the warriors you had defeated and they swore allegiance to us. I am now the chief of the Powhatan tribe. While you have lain here, close to death, emissaries have come from all the clans to also swear allegiance. Once more, Erik the Navigator, you have saved me and my family. This shall be your home but know that if you ever need the tribe then I will bring every warrior to defend you and Erik's clan, the Clan of the Bear."

I nodded, "It shows that we all need to be vigilant. I thought that a man like Sweyn Forkbeard, a man greedy for power, was a thing of my world. I have now seen that even here men's hearts can be changed by the abuse of power."

"And I swear that I shall never change, Erik. The Brave Eagle that you rescued is a man of peace and I will do all that I can to ensure that the tribe remains a peaceful one."

I smiled, "Then I am content and I have now found the home I sought when I left Orkneyjar. Erik the Navigator will stay in one place."

My whole family cheered and I was at peace. The spirits of the past would always be there and in my heart but this haven on the Shenandoah would be my final resting place.

The End

Glossary

Alesstkatek-River Androscoggin, Maine
Aroughcun -Raccoon (Powhatan)
Beck- a stream
Blót – a blood sacrifice made by a jarl.
Bjorr – Beaver
Byrnie- a mail or leather shirt reaching down to the knees.
Chesepiooc- Chesapeake
Cohongarooton- The Potomac River above Great Falls
Fret - a sea mist
Galdramenn- wizard
Gingoteague - Chincoteague Virginia
Lenni Lenape- Delaware- the tribe and the land
Mamanatowick - High chief of the Powhatans
Mockasin- Algonquin for moccasin
Muhheakantuck - The Hudson River
Natocke – Nantucket
Njörðr- God of the sea
Noepe -Martha's Vineyard
Odin- The 'All Father' God of war, also associated with wisdom, poetry, and magic (The Ruler of the gods).
Onguiaahra- Niagara (It means the straits)
Østersøen – The Baltic
Pamunkey River -York River, Virginia
Patawomke – The Potomac River below Great Falls.
Pânsâwân- Cree for dried meat
Pimîhkân – Pemmican
Ran- Goddess of the sea
Skræling -Barbarian
Smoky Bay- Reykjavik
Snekke- a small warship
Tarn - small lake (Norse)
Wapapyaki -Wampum
Wyrd- Fate
Yehakin – Powhatan lodge

Erik's Clan

Historical references

I use my vivid imagination to tell my stories. I am a writer of fiction, a storyteller, and this book is very much a 'what if' sort of book. We now know that the Vikings reached further south in mainland America than we thought. Just how far is debatable. The evidence we have is from the sagas. Vinland was named after a fruit that was discovered by the first Norse settlers. It does not necessarily mean grapes. King Harald Finehair did drive many Vikings west, but I cannot believe that they would choose to live on a volcanic island if they thought there might be better lands to the south and west of them. My books in this series are my speculation of what might have happened had Vikings spent a longer time in America than we assume.

Pinus echinate or shortleaf pine is native to Virginia and grows both in swamp plains and mountains. For the purposes of this story, I have the Powhatans call it the shortleaf pine.

The name Shenandoah was not, as history might tell us created by George Washington. The name of the river existed before George Washington undertook his expeditions. I am assuming that in the one thousand years since the time of Erik, the river will have changed its course but I have tried, wherever possible to use the river as it is now. I have canoed down the river and can attest to the shallowness in places. The snekke would, indeed, have had to be carried over them.

I am unsure yet if this is the last in the series. I thought that Erik the Navigator would be the last but I found that I wished to write another book. As Sean Connery said, 'Never say never again.' So who knows?

I used the following books for research:

- Vikings- Life and Legends -British Museum
- Saxon, Norman and Viking by Terence Wise (Osprey)
- The Vikings (Osprey) -Ian Heath
- Byzantine Armies 668-1118 (Osprey)-Ian Heath
- Romano-Byzantine Armies 4th-9th Century (Osprey) - David Nicholle
- The Walls of Constantinople AD 324-1453 (Osprey) - Stephen Turnbull
- Viking Longship (Osprey) - Keith Durham
- The Vikings in England Anglo-Danish Project
- Anglo Saxon Thegn AD 449-1066- Mark Harrison (Osprey)

Erik's Clan

- Viking Hersir- 793-1066 AD - Mark Harrison (Osprey)
- Hadrian's Wall- David Breeze (English Heritage)
- National Geographic- March 2017
- Time Life Seafarers-The Vikings Robert Wernick

Griff Hosker
May 2022

Erik's Clan

Other books by Griff Hosker

If you enjoyed reading this book, then why not read another one by the author?

Ancient History

The Sword of Cartimandua Series
(Germania and Britannia 50 A.D. – 128 A.D.)
Ulpius Felix- Roman Warrior (prequel)
The Sword of Cartimandua
The Horse Warriors
Invasion Caledonia
Roman Retreat
Revolt of the Red Witch
Druid's Gold
Trajan's Hunters
The Last Frontier
Hero of Rome
Roman Hawk
Roman Treachery
Roman Wall
Roman Courage

The Wolf Warrior series
(Britain in the late 6th Century)
Saxon Dawn
Saxon Revenge
Saxon England
Saxon Blood
Saxon Slayer
Saxon Slaughter
Saxon Bane
Saxon Fall: Rise of the Warlord
Saxon Throne
Saxon Sword

Medieval History

The Dragon Heart Series

Erik's Clan
Viking Slave
Viking Warrior
Viking Jarl
Viking Kingdom
Viking Wolf
Viking War
Viking Sword
Viking Wrath
Viking Raid
Viking Legend
Viking Vengeance
Viking Dragon
Viking Treasure
Viking Enemy
Viking Witch
Viking Blood
Viking Weregeld
Viking Storm
Viking Warband
Viking Shadow
Viking Legacy
Viking Clan
Viking Bravery

The Norman Genesis Series
Hrolf the Viking
Horseman
The Battle for a Home
Revenge of the Franks
The Land of the Northmen
Ragnvald Hrolfsson
Brothers in Blood
Lord of Rouen
Drekar in the Seine
Duke of Normandy
The Duke and the King

Danelaw
(England and Denmark in the 11th Century)
Dragon Sword
Oathsword

Erik's Clan

New World Series
Blood on the Blade
Across the Seas
The Savage Wilderness
The Bear and the Wolf
Erik The Navigator
Erik's Clan

The Vengeance Trail

The Reconquista Chronicles
Castilian Knight
El Campeador
The Lord of Valencia

The Aelfraed Series
(Britain and Byzantium 1050 A.D. - 1085 A.D.)
Housecarl
Outlaw
Varangian

The Anarchy Series England 1120-1180
English Knight
Knight of the Empress
Northern Knight
Baron of the North
Earl
King Henry's Champion
The King is Dead
Warlord of the North
Enemy at the Gate
The Fallen Crown
Warlord's War
Kingmaker
Henry II
Crusader
The Welsh Marches
Irish War
Poisonous Plots
The Princes' Revolt
Earl Marshal

Erik's Clan
The Perfect Knight

Border Knight
1182-1300
Sword for Hire
Return of the Knight
Baron's War
Magna Carta
Welsh Wars
Henry III
The Bloody Border
Baron's Crusade
Sentinel of the North
War in the West
Debt of Honour
The Blood of the Warlord

Sir John Hawkwood Series
France and Italy 1339- 1387
Crécy: The Age of the Archer
Man At Arms
The White Company
Leader of Men

Lord Edward's Archer
Lord Edward's Archer
King in Waiting
An Archer's Crusade
Targets of Treachery
The Great Cause

Struggle for a Crown
1360- 1485
Blood on the Crown
To Murder a King
The Throne
King Henry IV
The Road to Agincourt
St Crispin's Day
The Battle for France
The Last Knight
Queen's Knight

Erik's Clan

Tales from the Sword I
(Short stories from the Medieval period)

Tudor Warrior series
England and Scotland in the late 14th and early 15th century
Tudor Warrior

Conquistador
England and America in the 16th Century
Conquistador

Modern History

The Napoleonic Horseman Series
Chasseur à Cheval
Napoleon's Guard
British Light Dragoon
Soldier Spy
1808: The Road to Coruña
Talavera
The Lines of Torres Vedras
Bloody Badajoz
The Road to France
Waterloo

The Lucky Jack American Civil War series
Rebel Raiders
Confederate Rangers
The Road to Gettysburg

Soldier of the Queen series
Soldier of the Queen

The British Ace Series
1914
1915 Fokker Scourge
1916 Angels over the Somme
1917 Eagles Fall
1918 We will remember them
From Arctic Snow to Desert Sand

Erik's Clan

Wings over Persia

**Combined Operations series
1940-1945**
Commando
Raider
Behind Enemy Lines
Dieppe
Toehold in Europe
Sword Beach
Breakout
The Battle for Antwerp
King Tiger
Beyond the Rhine
Korea
Korean Winter

Tales from the Sword II
(Short stories from the Modern period)

Other Books
Great Granny's Ghost (Aimed at 9-14-year-old young people)

For more information on all of the books then please visit the author's website at www.griffhosker.com where there is a link to contact him or visit his Facebook page: GriffHosker at Sword Books

Printed in Great Britain
by Amazon